MURDER IN A TWO-SISTER FAMILY

AUGUST C BOLINO

KENSINGTON HISTORICAL PRESS

Murder in a Two-Sister Family

Copyright © 2019 August C. Bolino

Kensington Historical Press

PO Box 221

Fenton, MI 48430

All Rights Reserved

ISBN-13: 978-1732301016

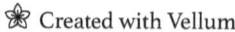 Created with Vellum

PART I LUCIA

HOW A CHILD IS LOST

Nicola Gallo kissed his wife, Anna, goodbye as she got into the carriage to go to *Bari* to shop for her Sunday dinner. As they approached the city, the right wheel hit a boulder in the road and veered to the right. The carriage flipped over, throwing Anna out. She landed on her head and was killed instantly.

When someone knocked on the door, Nicola said, "*Entrare.*" (Enter). It was his neighbor Pietro (Peter).

Seeing the sad look on his face, he said, "*Che incontrate?*"

Pietro hesitated, then answered, "*Anna e morte.*" (Anna is dead).

Nicola yelled loudly, "*Come?*" (How?)

Pietro answered softly, "*La carrozza e schianto, e Anna caduto en su capo. Essa e morte.* (The carriage crashed and Anna landed on her head. She is dead).

Nicola said nothing, but his eyes watered. He did not speak for the rest of the day, but on a day in the next month, he went into the dining area, reached for a glass jar that was on top of a piece of furniture, and he emptied all of the money it contained.

Lucia and Maria, his young daughters, watched in amazement. Nicola smiled as he told them, "*Domane, noi va a La'Merica.* (Tomorrow we go to America).

Lucia asked, "La moneta e bastante?" (Is the money enough?)

Nicola responded boldly. "*Io Lavora ogni giorno per questo viaggio.*" (I work every day for this journey).

For the next three days, they were separating things to take and not take. When ready, they said good bye to Italy and they headed for Bari and a taxi to Naples, where their passenger ship was docked.

The dock was packed with people, so when Nicola Gallo stood on the dock in Naples, Italy in June 1913 with his two daughters Maria and Lucia, he only brought one photograph of himself and his two daughters. He held Maria's hand, because she was the youngest at age ten. He had three tickets to board the *Duca degli Abruzzi*, which went non-stop to New York City. He had labored for years to save the $105 he needed for passage to the United States. He doubled his efforts when his wife died in that carriage last April.

When the sailors put the gangway up, Nicola gave Lucia a ticket while he held on to Maria. When the gangway was opened, the crowd pushed and there was chaos. He saw Lucia behind him, so he told her, "*Sta atento, non perduto*" (Careful, don't get lost). She told him, "*Io sono bene.*"(I am well.)

Soon, the boarding got out of hand. With all the adults pushing, Lucia got separated from her father and sister. In total confusion, she kept yelling "*Lasciare fouri*" (Let me out). She returned to the dock and watched the ship leave the port. She found a guard who spoke Italian, and he told her she would have to re-board tomorrow.

Nicola and Maria reached New York City in thirteen days, and they made their way to Brooklyn, where they had *paisini* (people from their own village). Nicola had written down the address: 10 President Street. They told him to go back to the dock and ask about Lucia. He did, and no one had any record of her, so they returned to Brooklyn. It was there that the immigrants created a new word. There was no indoor plumbing, so they all used the outhouse, which they called the back house. Soon they called it *la bacausa*.

After two days, Nicola and Maria boarded the train to Boston where Nicola met his sister, Rosina and her husband, John Magnifico at their home. Nicola told her how he had earned enough to pay for the trip to Ellis Island with his two daughters. But only he and one daughter made it to New York City.

The apartment in East Boston was big enough for the four persons. Maria learned English very slowly, so she signed up for the Americanization program. She did not last long there because, as she explained, "*Americani non scrivere I parola come se parlare*" (Americans do not write words as they speak them).

When her father's ship pulled out of port, Lucia was helpless. She was only twelve years old, spoke no English, and had no food or money. She felt totally abandoned because she did not know that her father had tried every avenue to locate her. She did not hear Maria, who was only ten years old, say on the pier, "*Noi potare trovare essa in il propio stanza*" (We can find her in the right room). But it was not to be.

As Lucia looked lost on the pier, a couple walked by her. The woman said, "David. That little girl looks lost. Let's talk to her."

He was not as keen as she, but he took her arm and walked towards Lucia. "Are you lost?" he asked her.

She did not respond, so he asked her another question, "Are you going on the next ship?"

Still, no answer. David and Ellen Bayard took her hand and went inside the large building. Approaching an inspector, David said, "This girl is lost, and we don't know what language she speaks. Can you help us?"

"Joe," he yelled, "see what language this girl speaks."

He approached her and tried German, Polish, Hungarian, and finally, Italian. "*Come si chiama*" (What is your name?), he asked her.

Her small face lit up. "*Mi chiama Lucia*" (My name is Lucia), she told him.

"*E dove e su genitore?*" (Where are your parents?)

"*Mio padre e mia sorella far vela iere*" (My father and sister sailed yesterday).

Ellen Bayard spoke eagerly, "David, you know we have tried so many times to have a child without success, and now God has given us one here."

"Ellen, you just can't take someone else's child."

"Well," she answered, "with all those hundreds of persons who sailed yesterday, how will we ever know who she belongs to?"

"Okay. Here is what we will do. We'll ask all the officials in this building if there is a missing child from yesterday's manifest. If there is not, we will keep her.

Ellen was bubbly. "Oh I am so happy. She is beautiful and she is healthy, and we know she speaks Italian."

As they were settling this issue, Lucia pulled her ticket from her pocket and handed it to David. "Can you believe this, Ellen? She has her own passage. This must be God's gift to us."

The new family stayed in the hotel on the dock for that one evening, and they all went to dinner together. They chose not to change their clothing because they had no luggage for Lucia, who they now started calling Lucy.

When they got to the dining room table, there was another problem: what to order for her. They called the waiter to the table and asked him if he spoke Italian. When he answered that he could get by with the language, they told him to ask whether she wanted meat or fish.

She responded quickly. "*Filetto di salmone*" (A filet of salmon).

They watched in amazement as she quickly consumed everything on her plate. Ellen, acting as a new mother, said, "The poor thing. She must be starving."

The next day, they boarded the *HMS Caserta* for the trip to New York City. They were stopped at the gangway because they had second class tickets but she was in steerage. They settled the problem when David offered to pay the $10 difference for Lucy's ticket.

The voyage was pleasant because they did not have to see the horrible conditions in steerage, where people were vomiting in all areas and on all decks. And they did not have to put up with all the odors, which only the salt breezes could overcome.

When the ship pulled into New York Harbor, almost all the passengers crowded on the starboard side to view the Statue of Liberty and the skyscrapers, which most passengers had never seen before. A sailor on board started to give a brief history of the Statue: "It all began in 1865 when Eduord de Laboulaye proposed that France give the United States a statue on its centennial. The government of France reacted positively to this idea, and it appointed Frederick Bartholdi as the sculptor for the project. The statue was completed in 1884, and during the next year Publisher Joseph Pulitzer raised $100,000 to bring the statue to New York City. The pedestal and the statue were put in place on October 28, 1886. Over one million persons lined the street of New York City during the first ticker tape parade."

The second class passengers did not have to pass inspection, so the new Bayard family went directly to the railroad ticket office. Many immigrants were cheated there when they exchanged foreign money for dollars. David had to shell out nine dollars for the three tickets to Wilmington, Delaware.

It was only about a two-hour ride, then a quick taxi to their home on North Bancroft Parkway. It was a beautiful four-bedroom brick house with six upstairs windows and two pushout windows downstairs. As they walked up the front path, Lucy could not believe what she was seeing, because her home in Italy was really a shack. The newly-wed Bayards had expected to have children, so they bought a home much larger than their current needs. Now, it won't be too large. But they had many immediate problems to deal with. What kind of clothes to buy Lucy, and where will she attend school?

1

LUCY GOES TO SCHOOL

As a twelve-year old, Lucy should have been in the middle school. But she could not read English, so she needed some kind of special class to learn English quickly. The Bayards decided to obtain an appointment with the principal of the nearest public school. Her name is Phyllis Howard.

They went at the appointed hour, and they were ushered into her office. She greeted them warmly. "Well, Mr. and Mrs. Bayard. I congratulate you on your new daughter. Did you adopt her?"

"Yes," they lied.

"Where is she from?" asked Miss Howard.

"Italy," they both answered.

"And she speaks no English?"

"No. What do you suggest?"

"Well," Howard hesitated. "There is no place we can put her because of her age, so I think the only recourse you have is to home-school her."

Ellen was confused. "What does that entail?"

"We'll give her some tests and based on the results, we will put her in a class she is qualified for. Then we will give her assignments, and you will make sure she does them at home."

"How long will that take?" asked Ellen.

Howard waited a few seconds, then she told them, "It all depends on how quickly she learns. If she is a good learner, she can jump several grades and then she can attend classes with girls and boys of her own age."

Before the parents could comment, Miss Howard added, 'You realize she is right on the edge of puberty. That is a complicating factor. As her mother, you will have to explain all the coming events. In a year she will be a teenager, which you know is another headache for parents."

Ellen and David thanked her for her time and her suggestions. Then they asked, "Does she start right away?"

Howard smiled. "It is summertime, you know. Let's get together when classes start in four or five weeks."

2

LUCY BECOMES AN AMERICAN

Lucy Bayard easily made the adjustment as an American. She got more attractive as the months passed. She had that Italian look with her olive skin, and all the boys in her classroom noticed her sensuous appearance. They must have imagined what her growing breasts would look like under her Lana Turner sweater, and they must have noted her hair was cut like Betty Grable's.

Lucy glided into puberty, and all the fifteen year old boys seemed to be preparing to feel her delicious body. But she preferred boys who drove automobiles, because they could take her to places that were hard to find. She knew that she had to join the cult of coming of age.

It involved doing and dressing what would please boys or men. Women are more easily manipulated, but the main danger is that some men are always ready to use violence. Any attractive teenager can be convinced that this good looking male means no harm, but there are no dark warnings playing across her brain.

The high schools had dress codes that prevented young, budding girls from revealing a line between their breasts. But even a button-down blouse can reveal a different view when the teenager sits at a desk and leans over. There is no rule or standard that guarantees modest decorum, especially if the young girl pays it no attention.

Lucy, the budding new teenager, was enamored of James Grey, the quarterback of the football team at Padua Academy. But she probably didn't know of the increasing sexual assaults in high school and colleges. It was more prevalent on college campuses, but there were some rapes in high school, particularly by college athletes. It seems that football players, who are rewarded for being aggressive on the field, are more likely to use physical pressure to engage in sexual activities. Of course, Lucy knew nothing of this, because in Italy football was soccer.

Lucy was especially fond of the new-craze in dancing called swinging or jitterbugging. She loved its beat and the wildness of the steps, especially when the boys threw their partners outward all over the dance hall. She loved the jazz and swing of Benny Goodman, Artie Shaw, and Count Basie.

Ellen Bayard did not know that her daughter was going on dates at night clubs where she could easily pass as a twenty-one year old. To accomplish this, all she had to do was to enter with an older man. Ellen was more interested in having her daughter get a head start in school. She went to the neighborhood stationery store, and she bought the Italian-English cards for learning a language more quickly. Each day, she and Lucy would recite the Italian and the English words. Lucy seemed to learn words very quickly, and Ellen was most happy when Lucy would respond to all questions with "Yes, Mother," and then they would embrace.

The school year and the time flew by. Lucy learned quickly, and soon she was placed in grade six, where she also excelled. As she made friends among the girls, they all told her she should enroll next year at Padua Academy. Lucy was all excited about going to a place with an Italian name. She went home and told her mother all about what she learned about the school. It was known as the Pandas. It had over 600 girls, and the emphasis was on college preparation. The school's Latin motto was *suaviter sed fortiter* (soft but strong). The Pandas took six state championships that year.

What she did not tell her mother was that there was a very good boys' school within walking distance of Padua. It was named *Salesianum,* and there was an exchange program that allowed boys and girls to attend classes at either school.

The Bayards were not Catholics, so they needed to discuss this option. Their first comment was that there were very good public schools near their home, and they paid taxes to support them. But they had to consider the fact that they took this young girl away from family and her Catholic environment. When they looked up the record of Padua Academy, they were impressed. Almost all of the graduates went to top colleges—a fact that swung them over to a yes vote.

They told her at dinner that night about their agreement, and she was as happy as any teenage girl. She kissed them and told them they would not be sorry. She even pledged to repay them the tuition money as soon as she began her work career.

Ellen wanted to talk to Lucy about girl things. The first was what color uniform. Lucy told her that the requirement was for a light blue-grey skirt, a white blouse, and a dark blue jacket for winter. The next issue was more profound: Sex. "Lucy you are now fifteen, and you have begun to use Kotex. You will have these monthlies until you are over fifty.

"These years are the ones when you will be most active sexually. You will need much control. Boys will want things you should not provide. It will take a lot of self-control, but you should save yourself for the man you love, and that should be the man you marry."

Lucy had a very simple response, "I know, Mother."

Ellen stopped to think. She was trying to decide whether to bring up a very personal topic. She decided to tell Lucy something very personal.

"You know," she began, 'Even if a man really loves you, he can falter. David did only once. It was many years ago, and he was very weak. He was temporarily assigned to another branch where he met a beautiful actress with great eyes and brilliant white teeth. Her name was Marjorie. She was the first woman who tempted him shortly after we were married. She did what any woman can do. She broke down his resistance, as he committed adultery. When he came home, I sensed that he had done something very wrong. He said he was a villain, and he had betrayed me. He told me all the details and promised me he would never make that mistake again. I thought he would keep his word."

Lucy noticed the tears that were gathering around her mother's eyelids. She consoled her. "Even the best of men can fail if a woman is very determined. Men really are weaklings when it comes to women."

Ellen embraced her, kissed her, and thanked her.

3

LUCY WINS A PRIZE

The years at Padua went well and quickly. Lucy was a top student, and she blossomed into a beautiful woman. The Bayards were amazed at how many boys came calling. But Lucy cared more for her studies than for dates. She was driven, because she realized what her world would have been in that village in Puglia. She would have gone to school for three years only, and she would probably have married a farmer who could not feed a large Italian family. She knew she was part of the American Dream, and she could not waste time with dates.

When graduation time arrived at Padua, she realized her ambition. Her parents were there and they were proud of her, but she was nervously awaiting the announcements for the various prizes when the featured speaker was finished.

The principal announced the first award was for the best student in mathematics, then followed the best student in religion, best student in science, best student in history. Then he stopped for a second or two and said, "The last prize is something special because it goes to a foreign-born student. The prize for the best student in English Literature goes to Italian-born Lucy Bayard." The entire audience erupted in applause.

Lucy had achieved her goal. A crowd gathered about her. They squeezed and kissed her. Ellen and David finally got to her, and they too were overjoyed as they kissed her.

"Have you chosen a college yet?" her mother asked.

"I am still waiting for a couple of replies," Lucy told her.

"Well, with that writing prize, you can name your own school. Your father and I are overwhelmed with this prize. We knew you were doing well, but this is beyond our biggest dreams."

The response that Lucy was waiting for finally arrived one afternoon in the mail. It was from Harvard University. She read the letter slowly. "We are happy to inform you that your application for enrollment has been approved. Please report a week before classes begin for Orientation."

She stopped reading and ran downstairs. "Mother," she screamed. "I made it into Harvard!"

"Well," said Ellen. "We are going to lose you," she said sadly.

"But Mother," Lucy said, "it's only three hundred miles to Boston. And it's less than three hours flying time."

Ellen knew of Harvard University, but she knew little of it, so she researched its history. It was started in 1636 by John Harvard, its first benefactor. Its motto is *Veritas* (Truth). She was happy to learn that it has the largest library in the world. She was happier to read that most students get scholarship aid. The University is on Irving Street—a very famous address. Professor William James lived there, and poet e.e. Cummings, historian Arthur Schlesinger, and economist John Kenneth Galbraith were also neighbors. After reading of all the famous persons who went to or taught at Harvard, she was more excited than ever.

4

CURRENT EVENTS

Lucy decided that she ought to know more about current events if she is going to be a student at Harvard. She headed to the library where she learned that her high school years were full of major events.

The major headline in the newspaper shocked her. In June of 1942, Guadalcanal was controlled by the British, but the Japs captured the island and they built a landing strip that allowed them to blow up many American ships that were heading into Guadalcanal Bay to take the island. By the end of the summer, 11,000 U. S. Marines were shot in this endeavor. For those who survived, there was little edible food or drinking water, causing much starvation. Later, the Americans got the food and whiskey that was left by the fleeing Japs.

The USS Quincy was the first ship sunk by the Japs, and they later sank four out of five cruisers in just 40 minutes. As the war developed into a personnel vendetta, it became a war of savagery, which was made worse by malaria, mosquitos, and dysentery.

As the war progressed, Lucy was concerned, because the early 1940s were the cadence of doom. When Poland surrendered, she feared they would go from depression to war. The bombing of London and the resulting fire was the largest conflagration in world history. Before she got too gloomy, her mind shifted to the wonderful sounds of Benny Goodman, Artie Shaw, and Glenn Miller. She felt that the American songs had a beginning and an end, and they were therefore a story.

Lucy was very disappointed when she learned that Glenn Miller had stolen one of her favorite songs, "Tuxedo Junction." The song was written by Erskine Hawkins, whose orchestra was a college dance band formerly known as the Bama State Collegians. The song is about a jazz and blues club in the Birmingham, Alabama, a suburb of Ensley. The area is referred to as "Tuxedo Junction," and it was the location of a streetcar crossing at Tuxedo Park, hence "Tuxedo Junction."

In the 1930s, Hawkins and his Orchestra often used "Tuxedo Junction" as their sign-off song before the next band would take the stage, so that the dancing would continue. By 1939, when Glenn Miller copied "Tuxedo Junction," it rose to number seven on the national hit parade.

Hawkins problem was that he was not literate, so he could not apply to copyright the song. This allowed Glenn Miller to copy Hawkins' version of the song, note by note. But Miller slowed down the tempo and added trumpet fanfares. His Bluebird recording sold 115,000 copies in the first week alone. Its sales skyrocketed, so that when he bought a home in California, he named it "Tuxedo Junction." Lucy thought Miller could have given Hawkins a part of the proceeds.

Despite this one episode, Lucy believed that if you learned the words of a song in the United States, as most persons her age did, you could sing along. This was more difficult in Italy. But as she considered these events, she thought the United States is indeed a great country and she was very fortunate and happy to be raised there.

There was another event that only touched Alabama. It was a hurricane that crossed the coast near Beaufort, SC on August 11, 1940 just north of Savannah, GA. As a Category 2, tides were very high north of Beaufort, with Charleston, SC reporting 10.7 feet above mean low tide. Property damage was estimated at several million dollars, with an estimated $3 million in damage just along the coast. An estimated 50 deaths were due to the hurricane.

That summer, Lucy was appalled when she heard a song about a lynching of a black man in the American South on a jazz radio program. It was called "Strange Fruit," sung by Billie Holiday (also known as Lady Day). The lyrics were heart wrenching. Coming from Italy where there was no fundamental hatred for colored persons, Lucy was unable to grasp the truth of the lyrics she had just heard.

Lucy was surprised to read that the unemployment rate for that year was 20 percent, but it helped her to understand the passage of the Works Progress Administration, which provided the prevailing hourly rate of pay for the unemployed who did mostly manual labor.

But Lucy was much more impressed with the creation of the Civilian Conservation Corps, which offered employment to new high school graduates who could not find work. It built highways and roads, constructed bridges and public buildings, built public facilities, and widened and lengthened airport landing fields. She was also surprised to learn that the United States had just passed a Social Security Act, because many European countries already had such a system much earlier.

As Lucy kept reading about the 1940s, she was amazed to learn of the desperate conditions facing average American families, most of which she thought were rich. She felt it was a romantic dream. She read of the Hoboken bread lines, where mothers waited all day without shoes to get a small bucket of watery soup.

The rest of the summer flew by quickly, so Ellen and Lucy made a list of things to buy for living in Cambridge, Massachusetts. Lucy was well prepared. Her long list included brown and white shoes, a Cashmere sweater, jeans, and a number of personal things.

PART II MARIA

MARIA FACES THE CRUEL WORLD

Maria did graduate from East Boston High School in 1931, and she got a job at Gillette's in South Boston. She loved to dance, so she went regularly to the Wonderland Ballroom in Revere, where she met Jo Ann Kelly, who worked in the Boston Public Library. Maria loved the jitterbug and swing, especially when the boys threw the girls out and under their legs.

The only thing about these two young ladies that was the same was that they were both Roman Catholics. They became such good friends that Jo Ann suggested they rent an apartment together. They were a good match, but they could not have been more different in their choices of occupations and of boyfriends.

They went to Morgan Memorial to buy second-hand furniture. They chose a four-drawer dresser, a French style mahogany bed, and two inlaid end tables, both had a small piece of veneer missing. They completed their purchases by selecting a cabin table with matching white pine chairs.

When they were settled in their new place, Jo Ann suggested they buy a record player. They agreed on the player, but they could not agree on what records to buy. Maria favored Benny Goodman, but Jo

Ann preferred ballads. They agreed to buy one each on paydays, which totaled 70 cents.

Jo Ann asked Maria about her family. Maria did not even know how to begin her complicated history. "Italy is a difficult country to understand, because it is so new. It became a country in 1861, so the people are known more by their provinces than by their nation. The United States has 48 states, but Italy has only 20 provinces. My father came from the province of Avellino, which is about 49 kilometers from Naples, so he is really a Neapolitan. They are happy people who drink wine and sing a lot. Most of the leading tenors, like Caruso came from this region. But my mother came from the eastern part of Italy, from Puglia, with Bari as its capital city. These people are more industrious, more serious in their behavior, probably due to the fact that they were settled by the Greeks in the 6th and 7th centuries.

In modern times, Italy was strictly an agricultural Nation until Mussolini became prime minister and head of the Fascist Party in 1929. He chose to have Italy fight in World War II on the side of the Axis powers, but the country surrendered in 1943 when combined English, American, and French forces captured Sicily and pushed northward. By 1945 an anti-Fascist government was established in the liberated regions, and Mussolini was caught and executed. He and his mistress were hung upside down in the square. The post-war economic boon changed Italy from an agricultural to an industrial nation."

Jo Ann Kelly was soon ready to reply about her family. She said she was born in South Boston to Irish immigrants, Lawrence and Jennifer. Jo Ann attended the James O'Donnell High School, where she met Robert Ryan. Her parents made it into the United States before Ellis Island opened and before the National Origins Act was passed, which established quotas by nations, but it favored the northern countries.

The story is familiar to all Bostonians. During the famine of the 1840s, thousands of Irish left Ireland. Some were called "Black Irish" because the Spanish invaded Ireland and left some olive-skinned babies behind who had red hair and blue eyes. They were starving, and the British refused to allow the United States to donate food, so starvation was everywhere. Many left for Boston. Almost all settled in South Boston. When these impoverished immigrants filled South Boston, wealthy Bostonians settled elsewhere.

JoAnn's father, Lawrence Kelly, got a job repairing sidewalks and streets as soon as they landed, but Jo Ann's mother just sat all day in the nearby pub drinking beer. Little Jo Ann did not understand what was transpiring, but she knew it was not right.

Jo Ann was a good pupil. Her grades were high in all subjects, but she liked writing most. In that, her mother could not help her, so she spent much of her growing years reading in the public library built by Andrew Carnegie—who was Scot not Irish. By the time she was a senior in high school, she was told by her teacher that she was the best writer in the class. As an immigrant's child, she was elated over that statement.

When Jo Ann was a senior at O' Donnell High, Jennifer was concerned about how her young daughter would deal with the dating problem. She knew that she would be judged by how successful Jo Ann would be in selecting a mate. Jennifer learned about dating parties, and how young girls could be involved in sex parties. But love and romance need not include intimacy.

In the early 20th century, prospective spouses met under family supervision, but as women went to work in factories, their independence allowed young girls to meet men in conditions by which parents were offended. Many saw no difference between this situation and prostitution. Women learned to sell themselves in a form of flirtation. For years, women waited at home while men who worked came to call, but when women began earning money all rules changed. By doing so, women achieved an independence they never had before, which tended to kill the romance. As more families obtained automobiles, young girls had to choose between being a virgin and a slut. But all things changed again. A woman must have a plan, and she must not let the man change her ideas. After marriage, wives were expected to suddenly crave more sex.

When she graduated from high school in 1940, Jo Ann had to find employment. She had querulous eyes that were thickly lashed with her perfectly formed lips. She went first to the public library where she offered to work at any job. The director of the library asked for her report card as a senior, and when she saw the high marks in English, she said she could offer a clean-up kind of job that meant she would work until closing time when many books and periodicals needed to be put back on the appropriate shelves. Jo Ann was delighted to receive this job offer when there were still seventeen million persons unemployed in the United States.

Bob Ryan, Jo Ann's boyfriend, had a much more difficult time finding employment. He was a wholesome man, about five feet eleven with a thick crop of hair and wide, strong shoulders. He came dressed with a conservative suit that made him look like a banker. He could have applied for a place in a CCC camp, but he did not want to leave Jo Ann. He soon found out what the cold world around him was really like. His high school counselor told him he could get a scholarship to a local college. He laughed to himself. *"Boy that would be something. Me in college. Wouldn't the gang on the street have a big laugh."*

When he visited Jo Ann at the library one day, she handed him a printed document and said, "Read this." The title read "The Origins of the WPA." But as he read on, he was discouraged by one sentence that stated the WPA is for family men who need work. When he was most discouraged, Jo Ann came to his aid.

"Why don't you go to work at the Maverick Mills in East Boston?" she said. "You can get there by subway."

"How much does it pay?" he asked her.

"It's a dollar a day."

"How do you know all this?" he asked.

"I read a lot, as you know, but I also know one of the foremen on the night shift. You will start at the bottom, but you are smart enough to rise to a better position."

"Does he live around here?" he asked.

"Yes, he is just around the corner on Jackson Street."

5

RYAN MEETS DOROTHY O'TOOLE

Robert Ryan did talk to the foreman, and he did get a job. It paid a little more than Jo Ann had told him – 15 cents per hour. Everyone at the Mill treated him well, especially all the young babes. One thing surprised him: the foreman and most of the employees were Italian. This was new to him, because there were few if any Italians in South Boston. There was often blood between the two groups—from rumbles and even at the football games between "Southie" and "Eastie."

The foreman, Charlie Pastore, asked him if he was married.

"Are you kidding?" answered Bob.

"Well then, I'll put you next to the blond babe on the second row. Can you handled her?"

"Shit, man. I like those tits. Is she married?"

"No, she just likes to get laid."

"Well, I like this job already."

Charlie took him over and introduced him, and when Bob took her hand, it was warm too. Charlie told her his name was Bob Ryan, and he was single. The next day he found out that her name was Dorothy O'Toole, and she lived in Winthrop. He did not want to make his move too quickly, so he just made small talk with her.

Bob Ryan was surprised at the crudeness of the banter around the plant. Even the women were shouting f--k and s--k concerning various other parts of the human body. He decided it was time to make a move. He smiled as he approached Dorothy. "Are you busy Friday night?" he asked.

She was disappointed at his choice of evenings. "Yes, I am, but I am free on Saturday night."

"How about Chinatown?" he offered.

"That would be fine," she replied.

"I'll pick you up at seven," he told her.

"Do you have car?" she asked.

"No. Why do you ask?"

"How are you going to get from Southie to Winthrop?" she enquired.

"I never thought of that," he said.

"I'll tell you what," she answered. "Why don't we meet at the Devonshire station? Then we can walk to Chinatown."

"Hey, you're pretty intelligent. So we'll meet there."

Bob Ryan showed up early at the subway stop, so he went outside. He walked to the Old State House. It was Georgian brick (he asked Jo Ann to research it for him but did not tell her why). There used to be a Merchant's Exchange in the basement, and in the 19th century it served as the Boston City Hall. As late as 1881, there was talk of demolition, but the Boston Heritage Society saved the structure.

As he was perusing the building, Dorothy showed up.

"We are going to visit Mr. Li.," he told her. "He is an old friend. He's the owner of Sung Low Li." We used to call this place "One hung low."

She did not grasp the full meaning, so she just said, "Come on. Let's walk."

They reached the restaurant in less than ten minutes, and after being seated, they ordered. Bob chose the Shrimp Chow Mein, and Dorothy chose the Egg Fu Yung. The food was quite satisfactory, and they took a long time to finish eating it.

Dorothy wanted to talk. She said her people came in the mid-nineteenth century when the famine was at its peak. She used foul language to discuss the role of the English in this starvation. She told Bob—which he did not know--that the English had blocked American ships from bringing food to the starving Irish. She was also very irritated by the passage of the Johnson-Reed Act of 1924 that established existing quotas: 66,000 for the British and only 18,000 for the Irish. Not only that, but the single Irish women had to be guarded on board ship, and they were sent to a heavily guarded building on Castle Garden where most immigrants were processed before Ellis Island was built.

What irritated Dorothy the most was that the British quota favored the large number of English who had settled in the United States before the quota was established, and it restricted persons from Southern and Eastern Europe.

Bob wanted to change the subject. "Your parents came here early, so they did have an advantage."

She cut in, "Well, I wouldn't call it an advantage when the only jobs Irish women could get were as maids, and all newspaper ads stated "Irish need not apply."

Bob wanted to pacify her. "I agree the Irish had a tough time, but it's partly their own attitude. Many are hostile bitches with sullen eyes. They did not seem to want a job."

As they walked back to the subway station, Bob began to assess the evening. Did he want to repeat this evening or go back to the woods with Jo Ann? Dorothy was a luscious piece, but where could he bed her down? There were no woods in Winthrop, and he had no car. His only hope was that her parents were going out of town.

Amazingly, it did happen. The O'Toole's had relatives in New York, and they would be visiting in August—just two months away. Bob was ecstatic. All he had to do was explain to Jo Ann why he could not see her for seven days. He fumbled his answer, which made her very suspicious.

6

A SEVEN DAY HOLIDAY

When August came, Dorothy was as prepared as Bob was for this seven-day holiday. Jo Ann was more than furious, but Bob's chief task was to explain to his parents why he would be coming home so late at night.

After putting her mother and father on the train at South Station, Dorothy headed directly to her home on Coastal Avenue in Winthrop. Bob took the bus to Winthrop, and when he saw her mansion, he was very impressed. It was nothing like the many three-story buildings in East Boston.

Dorothy, who had waited for him, led him into the living room. It was all New England. The water colored paintings had the blue of the ocean and the mountains of Western Massachusetts. It was appropriate for Coastal Avenue. There was a large window facing the water, a fireplace, and there was a medium-sized motor boat along the walkway.

"Do you like boats?" she asked him.

"I don't know. I have never been in one."

She was incredulous, but she remained silent.

"I have to leave at a decent hour because I don't want my parents to know we are here alone," he told her.

"Well, maybe we should get going if that is how it is," she responded and pointed. "The bedroom is right over there."

She took his hand and led him into the room. It was very grand also, with its Mediterranean furniture, King Charles desk, and bathroom nearby.

As he perused the situation, he saw that she was slowly undressing. He put his hand on her shoulder and gently began to travel down to her loins, while also taking in the curves of her breasts and buttocks.

"Don't you think you should undress too?" she asked softly.

He was naked in minutes, and in that time she shed her remaining garments and they were together under the blanket. She just lay there with her eyes closed not moving. He touched her breasts gently, and it was as if a 200-volt live wire had touched her. She moved in all directions at once, then she was motionless. His left hand caressed her face softly as he groped for her body. Then he kissed her cheek gently. With his other hand, he carefully slid down her soft body. With delicious pleasure he kissed her navel, and then he was ready to penetrate her. When he entered her body, it was peaceful for him, but soon she moved intensely as he poured his seed inside her. He was taken by surprise by her actions.

She told him, "I thought I was twirling on air. I enjoyed it so much, but as I flew, I asked myself why would God give us such a strong sex drive and then tell us it was wrong to use it?"

Bob responded, "He did not tell us it was wrong; he only said that there are limits on when we can enjoy it," When he finished talking, he said to himself: *This settles the issue of Dorothy versus Jo Ann. Dorothy is a better lay.* Soon they were sleeping soundly. When he did awaken, he looked for a clock but none was available.

"Dorothy, what time is it?"

"Let me get my Timex," she told him. Grabbing her wrist watch, she informed him "It's two o'clock."

Jumping out of bed, he yelled, "I must get home, but there are no more buses."

"I'll have to drive you," she said. "Let's hurry."

They quickly dressed and boarded her parent's 1937 Packard. He did not have time to admire the grand vehicle, because he was trying to figure out how he would make his parents understand why he was so late.

She dropped him off quickly without even a good night kiss. As he entered the living room, his mother, Rebecca, said simply, "We'll discuss this in the morning."

When Patrick left early in the morning to go to work, Rebecca had to make enquiries. "Well, Robert Ryan, can you explain your late arrival?"

He had to lie. "We listened to the Benny Goodman radio program at 10 o'clock and we danced a bit, then we must have fallen asleep on the couch."

"Do you expect me to believe that?" she answered.

"It's the truth," he countered.

She seemed to soften with his strong response.

When he left for work the next morning, Rebecca and Patrick Ryan discussed last evening's episode. Patrick told her, "All parents want their daughters to be virgins. But that is not how the world spins. I am sure she is a nice girl, or Robert would not be with her. All teens play with themselves when they reach puberty. Don't tell me you didn't."

"Wait a minute," she broke in. "How can you be so ugly about your son and his sweet girlfriend?"

He continued, "It seems that today the only virgins are nuns, and even they have played with themselves. According to Freud, some use coke bottles."

Rebecca did not know how to respond. "Well, they can deal with it in the confessional."

"Sure, he said, "and the priests can use pretty little boys and girls for their enjoyment."

While they discussed this topic, Bob Ryan decided that he was not going to give up this luscious piece of woman. He visited her as often as he could, and they enjoyed the intimacies of their bodies. His next task was going to be much more difficult: how would he explain his absence to Jo Ann. It was going to take a lot more lying.

He began with a small lie: that the plant was working overtime to finish a new order. "I really haven't done anything all week," he lied again.

She interrupted him, "Then we should do something this week. Are you free any nights this week?"

"I am not sure," he told her. "I can let you know later this week."

When he met her again, he gave her two choices. "We can go for a ride on the swan boats, or we can walk the Freedom Trail."

"Let's go walking. I was on the swan boats when I was much younger. It's really for the very young."

They began walking, and Bob Ryan acted as the guide. "This is a two and one-half hour walk," he told her, "and it has 16 historic sites along the way."

"Let's just go on to the most important places," she answered quickly.

"Everybody starts at the Boston Common. From the Common at Tremont Street we can head down to Faneuil Hall." He stopped at the old Granary Burying Ground.

"Look at the dates on those burial stones," she exclaimed.

"Well, these are the people who fought in the American Revolution," he added. "Do you know that at one time there was an asylum and a poorhouse on each side of the graveyard?"

She was very impressed with his knowledge of Boston's most famous historical sites.

As they walked for more than two hours, they passed the historic Faneuil Hall, where they lingered. They ended at the Boston Common, which got its name because it was the common area for cows to roam. It also was where the British troops were quartered in 1775. They skipped the old North Church, which was famous for telling the soldiers "one if by land and two if by sea." They also skipped Paul Revere's house.

By this time, Jo Ann was ready to quit. "That was fun,' she told him as she kissed him on the cheek.

7

RYAN AND DOROTHY AT WOOD ISLAND

When he got home, Bob Ryan sat in his soft chair trying to find a way to enjoy Dorothy again. It came to him after much analysis that she has a car, so we can go to Wood Island, which has plenty of woods. As he explained conditions to her, she was more positive. They chose next Wednesday, when she could get away with a decent excuse. When she drove up, he jumped into the Packard, and he directed her to Neptune Road and the opening to the woods. The heavens were in their favor because it was a beautiful summer evening.

After they parked the vehicle, Bob surveyed her outfit. He learned that she wore an Italian skirt and a Chinese silk blouse. When Dorothy opened the trunk and pulled out a large piece of plastic that would protect their bottoms in the grass, he praised her preparedness. "Boy, you know how to plan things," he told her.

She did not respond; she just walked around and found a good place after perusing the neighborhoods.

"Look out there toward Boston Harbor." He pointed. "Do you know that Perini Construction Company has a contract to expand our small landing place into a major international airport? They say that the company will cut Breed's Hill in half, and it will pour all the rocks and dirt into the harbor to expand the runways."

It was all small talk, and Dorothy stopped him. "It's dark now."

He did not need another hint. He leaned toward her and pulled her closer with one hand and felt her body with the other. He could feel her breath as he caressed the warm parts of her, but she edged away from him.

This time, which puzzled Bob Ryan, they did not copulate. There was total silence all the way home. He wondered if this was the end of their affair.

8

THE KELLY'S DISCUSS SEX

Despite Jennifer Kelly's efforts of trying to talk to Jo Ann about the issues of sex, there were things happening outside of class that Jennifer did not understand completely. They were all associated with the time of puberty. Jo Ann was suddenly aware of a growing urge within her body. She felt it in her limbs and in her womb. She wanted to be on one of those beaches where she could just jump into the water to cool her bottom parts. But she was nowhere near water, so she ran into the nearby woods where she could lie on the grass and touch her interior body. This went on for several days until Bob Ryan offered to relieve her burden. He took her to her favorite part in the woods, where they sat down. He began gently by just barely touching her young breasts.

"Why are you so breathless?" he asked her.

She did not answer, but she knew that she wanted more.

"May I just hold your hand?" he asked her.

But her mind was not on her hands; she was thinking of the womb. She was transformed as he got closer to her. He opened her legs with his hands and kissed her thighs.

"Aren't you going to do it?" she screamed.

At that tender moment, he was a gentle lover, but she was uncontrollable as she gave herself completely to him. When they were done, he kissed her hands, her stomach and her feet.

"I suppose you hate me now," he said.

"No, no," she said plaintively. "It did not hurt very much. In fact I enjoyed it. God knows that you have been good to me."

"Then would you object if we did it again someday?" he asked quietly.

"Oh no," she responded. "Sex is an intimacy that goes beyond friendship. It is not an accident. It is a deep organic process that requires a tender skill to arrive at total satisfaction."

In fact, this part of the woods became their favorite love-making locale, and they each learned much about the art of love.

When Jo Ann returned home, Maria Gallo was not happy with how Jo Ann was comporting herself. She thought that perhaps it was time for her to make a break. She remembered what her counselor had said when she left East Boston High School. "You should apply for a college scholarship. Your grades are very high."

9

BOB RYAN VISITS JO ANN

Jo Ann was surprised when Bob Ryan telephoned her. She thought he was wild about Dorothy.

"How is your love life? Do you think she satisfies me as much as you do? You know what she is lacking I can provide."

"You are right on that matter," she told him. "You are the only person who has provided satisfactory sex for me."

"Well then, why don't we meet for old time's sake?" he suggested.

"Why don't you go with that pig from Maverick Mills," she answered.

"Come on, Jo Ann, you know that you were my only girlfriend. We can make a pretty good Irish couple."

"Are you proposing?" she asked.

"I had not thought of it that way," he began, "But we did make a fine couple. I was just asking you out on a date, nothing that serious."

"What do you have in mind? Wood Island or a real date?" she countered.

His answer revolved in his mind. "I meant a real date. How about going to the Wonderland Ballroom?"

This really caught her by surprise. "I would love to, but how are we going to get there. Neither one of us owns a car."

He had an answer. "The second last subway stop on the blue line goes very near the Ballroom."

"It's a date," she said. "What night?"

"It has to be Friday or Saturday," he told her.

"I'll take Friday," she said firmly. "Let's meet at the Revere stop at eight o'clock."

He was elated. Perhaps he was thinking of things other than dancing.

They were each on time, and each perused each other's clothes.

"I did not think you would wear your zoot suit," she exclaimed.

"Why?" he asked.

"Well," she began, "it's not ideal for dancing with those big box shoulders and the baggy pants which choke at the ankles."

"Don't worry," he told her. "I have been dancing with this suit for a long time. Now let me say that you look gorgeous. Your neckline is just perfect, and the dress will allow you to swing out in the jitterbug."

The orchestra confounded their plans by playing a waltz, so they had a few minutes to talk about their lives. When the band started playing "No Name Jive," Bob took her out into the middle of the dance hall where he tossed her out and pulled her back in several times. He told her, "This song was very unique in many ways. It was the first song that was recorded on both sides of a vinyl record, lasting 6 minutes and 27 seconds. For those jitterbugging it was a real workout."

Then the Master of Ceremony told the dancers to separate—boys in front and girls in back. Then he yelled, "Walk straight across the dance hall until you reach the opposite end, where the boys and girls meet their next partners. This is repeated several times so that each dancer can dance with different partners. Couples dance until the music stops, then all couples say goodbye to each other and grab the next best partner who happens to be close by."

Jo Ann, who was totally confused, asks Bob, "What do you call this?"

He responded, "It goes by several names. It is called mixing music, but its real name is Paul Jones. In most cases, the caller orders, 'Guys inside, gals outside'. Then he calls, 'Now gals inside, guys outside. Honestly, don't you really miss all those nights we were together?"

"Our intimacy was adequate," she said forcefully.

"Is that all you want in life is adequacy?" he queried.

"This conversation will never satisfy us," she said. "So let's dance."

As they walked toward the ballroom, Ryan told her firmly, "Neither will your sexual arrangement satisfy you."

Jo Ann was furious. "I am sorry I agreed to this date. I am going home."

10

BENTLEY COLLEGE

As Maria learned all the machines at Chelsea Clock, she realized there was no future for her there. She discussed her problem with her best friend—Jo Ann.

"Just what is troubling you?" Jo Ann asked.

Maria took a while to answer. "I just don't want to work at Chelsea Clock all my life," she answered.

Jo Ann pursued the problem. "What do you have in mind?" she asked.

"Well I have a lot of relatives in Italy who are teachers. Even when I was a child, I thought about being a teacher."

"But Maria, you have to go to a teachers college to be certified."

"I know. I have been looking into several small low-tuition schools, and I think I have found one."

"What is it," asked Jo Ann loudly.

"It is Bentley University," Maria told her.

Jo Ann seemed puzzled. "Tell me about it."

Maria was well-prepared to respond. It is an old University that was founded in 1917 as the Bentley School of Accounting and Finance by Harry C. Bentley who served as the school's president. It is on Boylston Street, and it offers two or four-year programs.

Jo Ann was skeptical. "How are you going to pay the tuition, and how are you going to pay one-half of the rent?"

Maria had investigated the answers to her questions. "They have some programs without tuitions, and they do have work programs."

Jo Ann was startled at her responses. "Are you going to leave me?"

"No. I will take the subway, and I will pay for one-half of the rent."

Jo Ann was still puzzled about this whole affair. "How did you find out about this program?"

"I went back to East Boston High School to the room where they kept all the documents about applying for a scholarship. As I flipped the pages, I came upon this college which was founded in 1917 and which offered many programs without tuition. I thought I would have a better chance of getting into a program like Bentley, so I filled in all the forms and mailed them to the downtown campus.

As I flipped the pages, I decided to apply at Bentley College that was located in Waltham. I was surprised that I applied at Bentley College, because it had no classes in education. It has a very good program for the MBA, and it was only nine miles from Boston. It is just north of the Massachusetts Turnpike. I awaited the results. As the days passed I became a little more morose, and I began to accept the notion that I was not successful. When the reply did come, my hands shook as I opened the reply. I read the last paragraph slowly. It said 'For this reason, we can only offer you a scholarship of two years."

Maria had about a month to prepare. She was glad that it was just two years, so she could wear what she had been wearing in the factory. No one she knew had a car. When she told Jo Ann Kelly she was leaving, they embraced, and Jo Ann asked her, "How are going to move all your things?"

Maria's answer came close to crying, "I don't know what I will do."

"Let me ask Bob Ryan. I know that he has several girl friends who have autos, so maybe he can help. I know how to please him."

With that offer, Maria hugged and kissed her. "I am going to miss you a lot."

Jo Ann disagreed. "You are going to be happy to get rid of me because you don't approve of my sexual activities." It was one state-ment Maria did not contest.

Bob Ryan did come through. He finagled a car from one of his many girlfriends, and they left on the last week of August, so she could be present for the Orientation. As a Junior College, it was nothing like Harvard. The college had not yet built any dormitories, so the students were put up in hotels and boarding houses.

Maria kissed Bob Ryan goodbye, and she went to register. She decided to take general studies because she did not prefer any of the majors being offered. Her first year curriculum was English, general science, history, and political science. She was near the top in all of them.

That first year went by quickly. And when she began her second year, she realized she had to choose a vocation. As she walked around the town, she learned that there was a great need for teachers, which made her ask herself, do I want to be a teacher? The more she thought about it, the more she could not think of an alternative. At that time there was no program of Education at Bentley, so it might be difficult for her to be certified.

Maria sought help from the Counselor's Office. The director agreed it might be difficult for her to obtain employment with just two years of college, but she told Maria that the elementary grades needed teachers, so if she chose that option she probably could get a job offer.

Maria thanked the director, and as she often did, she plunged into her subject to become educated before she decided what to do. She headed to the library and started her research on elementary educa-tion. It was then that she found a very interesting publication by Martin Luther dating to 1530 on "A Sermon on Keeping Children in School."

His ideas were revolutionary. He wrote that schools had to be public and available to all. And he wanted to include girls. He believed that all young students should learn history, science and literature. Because he thought the world would end soon, he wanted everyone to be better prepared to meet God.

After finishing Luther's Sermon, Maria decided. She had to become a teacher. She thought her best chance of obtaining employment was in the black community. She obtained the name of the best school where most of children were black. Going there, she spoke to the supervisor, who asked her why she wanted to teach at this school. Maria anticipated this question, so she answered quickly, "I was informed that the black children are not keeping up with the standards established by the local politicians."

The Supervisor said, "You have no experience."

Maria responded, "No, but I was a child once, and I know children need to succeed in this discriminatory world."

She got the job, but she did not know what grade she wanted to teach. After a few thoughts, Maria told her, "These children need to catch up to the white children."

Maria had passed all of her subjects at East Boston High School, and the only A she received was in political science. She knew that many families needed help, so she worked her way up the Democratic Party. When she was elected Chairperson, she was very elated.

11

A NEW TEACHER ON THE LOOSE

When Maria met her new class, she was surprised that there was not a single white person present. When they were all seated, she said to them, "Hello, I am Miss Gallo, so call me Miss Gallo if you want to speak to me."

She had studied the manual for second grade teachers. In second grade, most children apply what they learned earlier about the meanings of letters and numbers to more complicated material. By that time, most students can read and write at a basic level. The emphasis is on fluent reading (reading without stopping). In this grade, children also become better at telling and writing stories, and their handwriting often becomes smaller and neater.

Mathematics is more difficult for second graders. By this time, they must learn to add and subtract two-digit numbers, and to understand the meaning of multiplication and division. Maria thought that Science was too advanced for that grade, but they were able to comprehend some patterns in the natural world. They were able to learn about the Earth and its natural resources, and how people use these resources to get energy. They looked at how the Earth changes over time and how we learn about the history of the Earth through fossils. They may do a deeper study of the life cycles of plants and animals.

In the second grade, children also increase their knowledge of the world around them. For the black children, they would have to compare themselves with the white world. They were expected to understand the importance of rules that are the key in helping people to get along.

Putting aside all these regulations, Maria selected one person in each row to stand up and give their name, their age, and tell the class something that they did during the summer.

In the first row she chose number five to stand up. The girl was tall; she had long black hair. She said, "My name is Darlene Harris. I am eight years old, and last summer my parents went fairly often to Jones Beach."

"That was fine, Miss Harris. Now would the third person in the second row please stand."

The girl who stood up had much lighter skin, and her hair was a series of rings. "My name is Carrie Jones. I am eight years old, but we didn't do anything special this summer."

"That was fine Miss Jones. Now would the fourth person in the third row please stand."

The boy who stood was bigger and had powerful muscles, and he had an Afro haircut. He clearly was an athlete.

"My name is Luther Thomas, and I am nine years old. I spent the whole summer getting ready for the basketball team."

A girl in the second row in front of her raised her hand.

"Yes Miss. What is your question?"

"Can you tell us something about yourself," she asked.

Maria was not prepared for this question, and she did not know how much of her private life she should divulge. "Well," she began, "I came from Massachusetts, and I attended Bentley College, from which I just graduated. I will tell you more later. Class is dismissed. I will see you tomorrow at the same time."

Before the class could leave the room, Maria had the students line up so she could address each one as they left. In time she hugged each one, and they hugged her back. As she got to know her students, she learned which ones did not have hats or scarves or pencils or notebooks, so she provided them.

She walked the quarter mile to the private house where she is living, she hoped temporarily. She continued to read the fat manual that they gave her when she was hired.

12

MARIA MEETS MARION MAY

When it was time, she prepared herself for dinner and headed to the dining room where she was seated next to a rather handsome man.

"Hello," he said, "my name is Marion May. What is yours?"

"Good evening," she answered. "My name is Maria Gallo."

"That is a beautiful name," he told her. "Is it Spanish, or what?"

Because she did not want to disclose her complicated family history, she told him, "I am from Massachusetts."

"Are you connected with Bentley College?" he asked.

"Yes, I graduated from there, and now I am a school teacher," she told him.

"That's interesting," he said. "What grade do you teach?"

"I have a beautiful class of second graders."

"At what school?" he continued his probe.

"Whittier Elementary," she said softly.

He finally stopped the interrogation. "I'm sorry. I should let you eat. Perhaps some other time we can complete our discussion."

Maria did not respond as she ate quietly.

The following night, they met again. "So," he said, "are we going to be sociable tonight?"

"I am always sociable," she told him. Then she added, "You know what I do for a living, so it is your turn now."

"I am a stock broker," he said.

"Do you work on Wall Street?"

"No. My clients are all in this neighborhood."

"You must be making a lot more than I do as a teacher."

"Well," he responded, "You don't have the worries I put up with every day."

"Okay, tell me where you went to college."

He was happy to respond. "I got a BA from Princeton and an MBA from Harvard."

"Wow," she exclaimed. "You really are in the big time. And here I am with a certificate from Bentley."

He broke in, "But you are doing more for society than I am."

She almost knocked a chair over as she leaned over the table to kiss him on his cheek. "You are sweet, and I thank you for picking me up. But I must prepare for tomorrow's classes. Good evening. I hope your stocks do well. *Arrivederci.*"

The next day she repeated herself. She took care of some personal things, and then she proceeded to the dining room where Marion was waiting for her. "How about if I take you to a good Italian restaurant? We have the famous North End, which is still all Italian because those who live there will only sell to Italians. There are three good restaurants on Hanover Street: The Strega, Giacomos and Luccas. There are 44,000 Italian Americans in Boston, so you'll be at home there."

"I hesitate, but let's give it a try," she said tersely.

He led her downstairs to his Cadillac, which a lot of stock brokers drove. When they arrived at the restaurant, a young man offered valet parking. Entering, they are seated in the back of the restaurant in a secluded corner.

"This is the Strega Restaurant, one of the best on Hanover Street." Switching subjects, he asked her, "How did you get to the United States?"

She smiled. "Obviously we did not walk. We came by boat from

Naples. We were processed at Ellis Island, and we took the train to East Boston, where my father's sister lives."

He seemed puzzled. "How did you know that you should go to East Boston?"

She hesitated, not knowing where to begin. "My father's sister lives in East Boston, so he gave us all the directions we needed. I worked at the Chelsea Clock Company, but I got a scholarship from Bentley, so now I am a teacher."

He was surprised at her answer, because in Boston she would have many more opportunities. "You will be surprised," he told her, "at all the things there are to see because Massachusetts is such an interesting state. It has the Boston Public Library, The Museum of Fine Arts, and the Boston Symphony, and there is the Boston Common and the public gardens. I loved my stay in Boston when I was at Harvard." Then he changed the subject. "Do you swim?"

Again, she did not answer quickly. "I swim a little now, but when I was growing up there were just farms all around us, and all we did was raise vegetables to eat."

He was ready to make a move. 'How about just sitting on the beach under a nice, big umbrella?"

"You are moving rather quickly," she cautioned him.

He was prepared for her response. "I don't think so. You are an attractive woman, and I am a single man."

"Well," she told him, "you are moving too fast for this country girl. Perhaps I should know more about you before we move ahead. Maybe we are not compatible."

"Okay," he replied. "What do you want to know?"

"Tell me about your early history. Were you raised a Christian or what?"

"Actually, I was raised as a Jew, but I do not follow any of the Jewish principles. I even eat pork when it is served to me."

Maria stopped him. "What do your parents think of this switch? Are they Orthodox or what? You will be a big disappointment to them if you abandon your heritage."

He seemed to be disappointed at her prying into his family

affairs, so he told her, "We have fought that battle already, and we each accept the conditions as they now are."

She was not through. "Do you practice the Sabbath or Rosh Hashanah or Purim or Passover?"

He was very upset at her questioning, so he threw it back at her, "Are you a Catholic? Do you follow your faith? Do you go to Confession?"

"My answer is yes and no. I have given up on such things as Confession. I don't understand how a person now living can forgive my sins of the past."

"So," he said, "we are both derelicts of our own religion."

As they sipped their *Chianti Classico Reserva* wine, he asked her, "What are you going to order?"

She was ready. "I think I am going to have the *osso buco*."

"What is that?" he asked with a kind of grimace.

"It means hole in the bone, and it's delicious. Try it."

He did, and he agreed it was very tasty. For dessert, she had her favorite, *Tiramisu*.

"Do you know what that word means?" she asked him.

"No. Tell me," he begged.

"It is from the verb *tirare*, which means to pull. For example, in Italy most doors say *Tirare* to open. So *Tiramisu* means pull you toward me."

"I'll second that motion," he said softly.

This was the first of several evenings away from where they lived. They did go often to the South Boston Beach, because it was a very close drive.

The next day she went to the principal's office, and when she entered the principal asked, "Yes, what is it?"

"This is Maria. May I talk to you?"

"Yes. Please tell me what is troubling you?"

Maria hesitated, then she began speaking slowly. "I know I am a new teacher, but I think I know something about the mothers of my students."

"Tell me," said the principal.

"Well," began Maria, "I know that most of these mothers are either single or their husbands have abandoned them. So when they go home after work, they have to shop, cook, clean the kitchen, and plan for the next day. I know this because I gave my students assignments and not one completed them. No one has the time, so we should cease giving homework assignments to these second graders."

"Thank you Miss Gallo. I will raise this question at the next meeting of the higher ups."

13

MARIA AND MARION DISCUSS MARRIAGE

Marion asked Maria the next week, "Do you read the newspapers?"

She was bothered by his question. "Of course I read the newspapers. Why do you ask?"

"The Nuremberg Trials are going on now. The first trial is the trial of the leaders of Nazi Germany. It was organized by the International Military Tribunal. The judges and prosecutors are from the four wartime Allies: France, the USSR, the United Kingdom and the United States. The indictments are for working with other people to commit a crime against peace, war crimes, crimes against humanity, planning, initiating, and waging wars of aggression and other crimes against peace.

"The trials are to be held in the Supreme Court Building in Berlin. The prosecution is bringing charges against 24 major war criminals and six criminal organizations – the leadership of the Nazi Party, the *Schutzstaffel* and *Sicherheitsdienst* , the *Gestapo*, the *Sturmabteilung* and the High Command of the German armed forces."

Maria was amazed at his knowledge of these trials, but then she remembered he was a Jew. "Were any of your family killed by the Nazis?" she asked him.

The easy-going character of his face changed. "Yes, several of my family were sent to the gas chambers," he answered as his eyes watered.

Maria rose from her chair, walked around the table, hugged him and kissed his cheek. "I am so sorry," she told him.

"We are not married yet," she said.

"Okay," he replied. "Let's set a date."

She stopped his haste. "If we are to have both a priest and a rabbi at the ceremony it will take a lot of time. You will need to talk to the priest on several occasions. I think it will take months, so talk to your parents."

Marion did talk to a rabbi who told him that according to the Torah and Jewish Law it is prohibited for a Jew to marry a non-Jew. You can find this in Deuteronomy 7:3, "You shall not intermarry with them; you shall not give your daughter to his son, and you shall not take his daughter for your son."

The rabbi continued, "There is no way for a Jew to marry a non-Jew in accordance with Jewish Law except for the non-Jewish person to undergo a conversion. This means an Orthodox Conversion. But Conservative Judaism and Reform Judaism both offer their own conversion programs which have various degrees of requirement. Conversion is a very serious step and a very difficult process. Conversion for women has an impact on her own life and on the lives of future generations, because only a truly Jewish mother can produce a truly Jewish child. Of course, any couple can be married where the local law permits."

While Marion was talking to a rabbi, Maria visited her priest. "It is possible to get married in the Catholic Church with one person being Jewish," the priest answered slowly. "If the woman leaves the church, the church loses money and support because there is a small chance of any children being raised as Catholics. Usually in these circumstances a Rabbi is present, but I am not sure if the church allows him to go up to the altar. It might be simpler if it is done in a hall instead of a church."

Maria agreed with his answer. Usually when Marion and Maria went to dinner in their guest house, they talked about what had transpired on that day. On this occasion, the subject was chosen for them. How to take care of this marriage problem. Neither one had an idea that could resolve the issue. It seemed insoluble.

Maria spoke first, "Do we want our children to be raised as Christians or Jews?"

Marion threw her another curve ball. "You are assuming that we can produce children. So we could marry and take what comes."

"But," interrupted Maria, "what do we do if we did have children? As your lawyers might say, "What is the case before us?" She continued, "I have no parents, but you do, so why do you not consult with them. Then we can finish discussing this topic later."

Marion agreed.

Maria expanded the controversy. She asked him, "Do you believe that there is a God and that he created the universe?"

His answer was scientific, "Can there be a universe without a God?" He continued, "According to scientists, our universe is 13.7 billion years old. It was created in the big bang. But they cannot observe it, so they must rely on science."

Maria joined the argument. "If there is no God, how was something created out of nothing? Each of the scientific models is extrapolated backward in time. God has created many miracles. We have hundreds of cases in which persons who had heart attacks were given all kinds of medicines and procedures that failed to revive, and suddenly these persons awoke."

Marion offered a new problem. "Do you know," he began "that the universe is expanding? The Big Bang is not an explosion because it has no beginning or end. It means that space is expanding. This is an odd universe, but it is the only one we have."

He wasn't finished. "The term 'primordial' was coined nearly 100 years ago. It describes a chemical broth that was how Earth could create organisms. Since then scientists have been trying to replicate this soup in a lab. They are searching for chemical combinations that produce life. The chief problem is that this thick, sludgy solution moves very slowly, so that it is difficult to see how it manages to reproduce itself. Today, when cells reproduce organisms, specialized proteins called enzymes produce a DNA double helix. We don't know how this happens."

Maria was anxious to change the subject. She looked straight at Marion and asked, "Is it true that there is a custom that requires a Jewish family to eat eggs after a funeral to symbolize the continuity of life?"

Marion was not prepared to respond. "If that is true," he began, "it probably refers to Orthodox Jews." He wanted to drop that subject. "I read an interesting article in the *Boston Herald* about class in the United States. According to the writer, we always assume that we have no classes in the States, but that is untrue. The bulk of the working class is assumed to be white, but that ignores the blacks and Hispanics. Thomas Jefferson said that we are a classless society, but it is more difficult for American families at the bottom to rise, much more difficult than in Germany. There is a new thing taking place right now that may change American society."

"What is it?" asked Maria.

"It's called the G.I. Bill. It allows all veterans to go to college with all expenses paid. This will completely re-define our middle class, but we will still have the racial problem. The black middle class is nowhere nearly as well off as the white middle class. This will take a long time to correct because many in the American South still believe that blacks are not human. We saw this problem during the New Deal in the Great Depression when the Southern contingent of the Congress refused to grant any benefits to our black population."

Maria, who was a small child during that time period, could not believe Marion, although it was all true.

As the days flew by, Maria was still waiting for Marion to visit his parents. She knew he hadn't taken a single step because he was with her every night at dinner. When he sat next to her, she asked, "What is the topic of discussion for tonight?"

When he made no offer, she told him again that she reads during every break in her schedule.

"So, what's the question for tonight?" he asked as he ate his Swiss steak.

"There was a meeting somewhere. I don't remember where," she told him. "But the discussion was about the future of marriage. I thought this would interest you."

"Sure," he responded. "What was the result of the question?"

"It all began with a sentence spoken in 1847 by Susan B. Anthony, who said that someday women would be liberated and there would be no reason to marry, which would introduce an era of more single women than married ones."

While Maria and Marion were waiting to resolve their wedding plans, she injected another problem. "When we marry, where are we going to live?" she asked.

Apparently, he had not dealt with this important topic. "We have two choices," he told her. "We can move into my apartment, or we can buy a house."

Maria asked happily, "Can we afford to buy?"

Marion seemed offended by her question. "Do you thing I would mention it if I could not afford it?"

She ran to him and kissed him intensely. "I have always dreamed of having my own house, and now it is coming closer." She continued, "If we bought, where would we choose?"

"Well," he began, "the most expensive houses are along the Charles River, and the next one down would be on Beacon Hill."

Maria realized she was not prepared for this question, so she told him, "You will have to decide, and you will have to pay."

14

THEY MARRY AT A RENTAL HALL

They decided not to marry in a synagogue or a church, because of the problems raised by both parents. The rabbi and the priest did show up at the rental hall. Marion's father and mother, who were orthodox Jews, sat throughout the ceremony as if they were in agony.

Maria thought, "*Here we are, Marion and I, supremely happy. He had known other girls and I had some share of other men's attention, but for me this was an impassioned jump of two people soaring skyward over clouds of a first love.*"

Marion's mother told him, "Child, remember that the racial and religious differences between you and your children will be pulled in two different directions." His mother continued, "You know we attend an orthodox synagogue; we observe the dietary rules and all the ritual holy days. Like all intelligent young Jews, we look with tolerance on these parental habits but he denies them for himself."

At this time, I pointed out to my father that Marion does not want me to cook kosher, and remember that, although I love the teachings of Jesus, I do not belong to any church, so that the priest and a rabbi do not stand between us.

Mr. Gallo arose as he felt the need to speak. "We must not forget," he began "that Jews are an oriental race, so Jews and Christians cannot easily meet. Jews are sensual, aggressive, ostentatious, and cunning. It is their heritage. They accomplish things in business because they never hesitate to seize an unfair advantage. They accomplish things in science and art and Hollywood. We have the science of Einstein and Freud, the Jewish painters like Picasso and Modigliani and the clever works of the theatre and Hollywood. But these productions are full of sex and sensuality, and they do not cater to the religions of Jews and Christ."

Mrs. May's face projected sadness, but she told Marion something he told Maria later. She said that, "Marion is my favorite child," and facing him she added, "Well, then, if you love her and are sure that she is the one woman for you, you have my blessing. Above everything I want you to be happy."

Shortly after, Nicholas Gallo met and embraced Mr. and Mrs. May, and they soon forgot their differences. Marion and Maria were married by a civil judge, and all the discussion turned to where they would go on their honeymoon.

15

A HONEYMOON SKY

Their honeymoon had to be practical, because neither one could get time off for over one week. They chose the beach at Millville, Delaware. It was just what they wanted: a short drive and a deserted place.

They unpacked their stuff, and Maria had brought her portable phonograph player. She chose to play one of her favorites, Beethoven's 3rd Symphony.

As they dressed for the beach, Marion had his first chance to see her coveted breasts that she was saving for him until they were married. He thought, "*Now is the hour.*"

On that same sunny day, Marion had suggested that he and Maria go to a beach. Maria wondered why he chose Delaware, but she agreed.

When they finished unpacking their umbrella and their chairs and they enjoyed the cool breeze, Maria kept staring at a couple not far away.

"Marion," she said, "That woman was at our wedding."

"Go talk to her," he said tersely.

Maria walked up and said quietly, "Were you born in Italy?"

"Yes," she answered, 'Why do you ask?"

Maria persisted, "Were you born in Puglia?"

"How do you know that?" the other woman replied. "I think I am your sister, Lucia, but I am known as Lucy now."

They embraced. "Is this your husband?"

"Yes, his name is Marion."

"And what is your last name now?"

"I am Mrs. Marion May."

"And does he know your history?" Lucy asked.

"He knows that I was born in Italy, but I have not told him of our family history."

"Do you have any children?"

Maria did not answer quickly. "Marion does not seem to want any children."

"So," interrupted Lucy, "Neither of us may ever have an offspring. Let's talk about something pleasant. What does Marion do?"

"He is a stock broker. He graduated from Princeton, and he has an MBA from Harvard." Turning to Lucy she asked, "Are you married?"

"I am married, and I married an Italian. I am now Mrs. Mario Milano. His people came from near Naples."

"What happened to you?" Maria asked.

Lucy wanted to give her a true answer. "I tried to get on the boat, but the crowd pushed me back. A wonderful couple took care of me, and they adopted me, so I became Lucy Bayard."

Maria interrupted, "So that is why we could not find you. Pa and I looked everywhere, but we finally gave up with a bad taste in our mouths."

Lucy continued her personal history. "When Mario graduated from the Harvard Law School, he was near the top of his class. He got a good-paying job as assistant prosecutor, so I could finish my degree at Harvard. We moved into a nice apartment on Beacon Hill."

Maria had a jealous tone to her voice, "So, you two |finished at the top."

Lucy wanted to know more about her sister. "Tell me about you and Marion."

"Well," began Maria, "you will be surprised to know that Marion was raised as a Jew, but you would probably call him a 'Fallen Away' Jew. As I said, he has a degree from Princeton and an MBA from Harvard. We have not bought a house yet because we cannot decide which one to buy."

After two hours on the sand, the two couples separated without kissing or saying goodbyes. It was clear Maria was jealous of her sister. She cleaned up and she made Marion a light, delicious dinner. They talked for hours about how they met and how they fell in love. When they appeared to tire, Maria pointed to the bedroom. She was trying to tell him that it was the time for Isaiah 66.

When it was bedtime, they each undressed slowly, and he saw her naked for the first time. He noted that she had a beautiful body, and her breasts were pointed outward and they seemed to be firm and not sagging.

When they were totally naked, they got into bed and they snuggled as their two bodies became one. She squeezed her breasts so he could more easily kiss her nipples. At that point her entire body seemed to be on fire. She screamed, "Thank Ye, Jerusalem!" and he answered, "Hallelujah True," and she felt for the first time that circumcised thing inside her. She thought that it does not matter whether we go to a church or a synagogue, this is our heaven.

They slept well and when he awoke he saw her frying eggs in the kitchen. He joked, "I did not know that you could cook."

She smiled and told him, "All Italian Women are first taught how to cook. Then they learn everything else."

As they ate, Maria said, "I had an interesting talk with your mother. I asked her if she had breast fed you. She said you gobbled up all of her milk. I wondered whether your appetite for female breasts has a connection to your earlier breast feeding. I did some research, but the only thing I could learn was that babies that were breast fed had much higher IQs and the more the baby drank the higher the IQ score. They were higher in mathematics, memory, and motor functions. There was one curious result of this research. When the child sucked on a teat, some women got the same feeling as if they were having sexual intercourse. None of the scientists could figure out why." Maria put down her fork. "Now is a good time for us to discuss babies. I think it is better for us to have children when we are young. I know you are using condoms, but that is not the best way to deal with this subject. We never really answered the question, 'Are we going to have children?' The question of 'Christian or Jew' can be decided later."

Marion hedged her thoughts. "Let's take this up later."

After six days of heavenly living, they headed back to Waltham. He still wasn't sure whether he wanted a baby from this shicksa.

On their way back, Maria noticed something she had never seen before. "What were all these poems?" she asked Marion. He remembered some:

"Drove too long
      Driving snoozing
What happened next
Is not amusing."
"I can still quote another one:"

"Around the curve
      Lickety split
It's a beautiful car
Wasn't it?"

"Why are they on the highway?" she asked.
      "Oh, they are put there by Burma Shave," Marion told her. "They are meant to slow down speeding cars."

"How clever,' she responded. "Only in America."

When they unpacked their things, they headed up to their new bedroom. It was more grand than anything she had ever had before.

"I am going to make you a special dinner tonight."

"What is it?" he asked her.

"Sorry. You will have to wait until it is done."

She had noticed a good piece of veal in the refrigerator, so she proceeded with the recipe that she already knew. When Marion joined her, she explained what she was doing. "Veal comes from a young cow, so it is a more tender texture, with a delicate flavor and it costs much more. I am making one of the most common veal dishes-- veal Marsala. It consists of thin pieces of veal topped in a Marsala wine and mushroom-based sauce.

"Marsala is a type of wine primarily produced in Sicily. It is made stronger by adding another type of alcohol. When making sauce for veal Marsala, sliced mushrooms are sautéed in butter or oil, with finely chopped garlic and onions. As the mixture cooks, the other ingredients absorb the wine and reduce the total amount of liquid for the sauce. Another liquid, such as veal or chicken broth or heavy cream, may be added to the marsala sauce to thin it out."

When the sauce was ready, she said, "Dinner is served." She served each plate individually, adding the sauce on top of the veal, and each time she said, "*Buon Appetito*." They all agreed it was delicious, and they looked forward to more of this Italian cuisine.

When they retired to their new, fancy bedroom, Maria told Marion that, "I have fears of being alone, and I desire to be loved and I have a craving for children. It is why women were created. A woman who never has children is not a complete person. She may be a good person, but she is incomplete."

She continued, "There is something inside me that reminds me of what is my primary role in life. Marion, I do love you, but my love will never be complete unless you give me a child. We can always remove any obstacles because we are intelligent persons, and we can produce intelligent children."

Marion walked over to her, kissed her on the lips, and siad, "My love, if that will fulfill your desires, then we will have children very soon."

Maria squeezed him, kissed him many times on the face and head, and she acted like a child who was just given her favorite toy.

"Do you want to begin right now?" he asked.

"Oh Marion, it is not a time for joking," she told him.

They listened to the radio for a few hours, then Maria said, "We should retire early. We have had a long day."

As they entered the bedroom, neither one knew who should undress first. Marion solved that problem. "I will undress out here and you can do what you must in the bathroom."

It took him only a minute to become naked, and he waited on the bed for his new bride. He was totally surprised when she exited the bathroom totally naked. She approached him with her arms spread widely.

He marveled at her body as it came toward him. He could see the breasts pointing outward, and as he admired them, she said, "Well, you have been wanting these for a long time so here they are."

She crawled into bed, and it took him only seconds to get next to her. He kissed her mouth and headed straight down to the breasts. When he kissed her there, she seemed to be hit by an electric charge. She guided him to where she wanted him to be. He was astounded at her sexual arousal. It did not take very long to complete what they both sought.

16

BACK TO SCHOOL

As she entered the school room all students stood.

"Good morning," Maria wished them well. "Please sit down. Now, children. Who can tell me who is the President of the United States?"

One child answered, "Mr. Truman."

"And why is he famous?" she asked.

No one responded, so she produced the answer. "He really ended the World War by authorizing the use of atomic bombs. What state is Mr. Truman from?"

Again only one child raised a hand. "Please answer."

"He is from Missouri," the child tells the class.

"How did he become President?"

Several hands went up. "I am pleased that so many know this answer." She points a girl in the front row. "Tell us."

"He became President when Mr. Roosevelt died."

'Thank you. I am pleased that this class is alive and well. I will see you at class tomorrow. We will deal with mathematics then."

17

A VISIT TO EAST BOSTON

J ust before Christmas, Maria took the New York Central train to Boston. It was a grand reunion with her Aunt, who baked every possible sweet Italian cookie she could for Maria, and every meal turned out to be six or seven courses.

Maria had to sleep with her Aunt Rosina, who was still single. Each night she would tell Maria whom she was dating and dancing with. Maria absorbed all of this information.

The next day she walked to Central Square and stumbled into the East Boston Library. She was impressed with its size and the large number of books. But she was more impressed with a book on the early history of East Boston. She could not believe that Samuel Maverick, who bought Noddle Island to graze his cattle, was the first slave owner in Massachusetts in 1633.

As she continued to read, she remembered that the first battle of the American Revolution was fought off Noddle Island. It was good for Maria to learn about her roots, but she had to leave to get back in time to prepare for her classes. When she returned, she walked toward Marion, who hugged her and gave her a very sensuous kiss on her lips. She was surprised, but she did not complain.

At the appointed hour, they headed for another Italian place: La

Stagione (the Summertime) She jumped into his Cadillac and as soon as they entered she realized that everyone was dressed very formally.

"Why didn't you tell me we were going to a high class place. I could have worn something a bit more dressy." She pouted.

"Oh, you look gorgeous,' he said, which brought him a small pat on the hand.

"I wanted to make this one all different." He smiled as he said it.

"I'm glad you can afford this," she said, 'because I'm still a poor school teacher."

The waiter interrupted this repartee, "What can I bring you to drink tonight?"

"I think we will have another bottle of *Sangiovese*."

When he brought the bottle, Maria asked the waiter, "Where is this from?"

"This is from Tuscany,' he answered.

"It must be good," she surmised.

As they drank more wine, their conversation got deeper. Marion started it by saying that women have all the advantages.

Maria pounced on that sentence. "When women are gathered in groups, they are still described with language that implies that they are really juvenile, even if they are working in a university. It's all considered 'girl' talk. We need some kind of safety net that will sustain us throughout our lives. We have real difficulty finding employment, and when on the job, we cannot climb the promotion ladder. As one young lady put it so succinctly: we do better on our backs."

18

MARIA IS PREGNANT

The next day was Sunday, so the May family just sat all day reading the Sunday paper, watching a football game, and eating Maria's special for the day.

As she served it, she explained how to make it. She said, "The Linguine and Clam Sauce was easy to make. Just bring a large pot of salted water to boil. Cook pasta according to package directions. Combine clams with juice, butter, oil, minced garlic, parsley, basil, and pepper in a large saucepan. Place over medium heat until boiling. Serve warm over pasta."

Then they watched the Jack Benny program. Marion learned earlier that Jack Benny was born Benjamin Kubelsky, and that he is an American comedian, vaudevillian, radio and film actor, and violinist. Benny is usually portrayed as a miser who played his violin badly. He was known for comic timing. He made his audience laugh with just a pregnant pause.

When Maria and Marion headed upstairs later, they knew what was on their minds. They needed no preliminaries or prompting. They each approached the bed nude, and Maria made sure that he was not using a condom. This time, it did not seem to have the fire of other evenings, but that was not what was on Maria's mind. All she thought of was semen. She was less satisfied, but much happier.

When she missed her period, she was happy, and when it continued into the third month she was happier still, despite the vomiting. It was time to call a pediatrician. He confirmed her pregnancy, and said all looked well. She hugged and kissed Marion each time he walked by. There was not a happier woman on this Earth.

As the months swept by, conditions turned to be unfavorable. The doctors noted that the placenta was separating from the uterine wall, which created a condition in which it could cut off the baby's oxygen. They decided that she had to have a C-section. This is not a problem for a strong woman, but Maria was getting weaker. They chose to make the incision between the abdomen and the uterus. If she had any blood clots, it could kill her. Women who select C-section deliveries are usually large, but Maria is small and shrinking.

When it was time to wheel Maria into the operating room, she felt a severe pain in the abdomen. The nurse called her pediatrician, who after examining her told the nurse to get her in the operating room immediately.

The three doctors agreed that they "must save the baby first." They cut her open to remove the fetus. Maria was suffering from very high blood pressure, which caused an infection and hemorrhaging. The medical doctors were very concerned because if the mother dies in child birth, those children are more likely to die within one to two years of their mothers' death.

When her time came, Lucy was in the hospital praying for her sister. When they made the incision, they found the baby girl to be in fair shape, but her mother was in a grave condition.

When Lucy spoke to the medical doctors, they seemed to be in a very mixed negative posture. They told her that the baby should survive, but the odds on the mother were extremely low. Lucy told the doctor that she was the mother's sister, and she would take care of the child if the mother did not survive.

When Marion saw the small baby girl, he yelled, "I do not want this baby. My mother told me I must produce a Jewish baby. She raised me. She did everything for me. I cannot ignore her wishes now. So I must say, 'Goodbye.'"

As he walked out the door, Maria felt a burden being removed. But what could she do next? How could she raise this Jewish-Christian child?

Lucy, who was in the waiting area, saw Marion hurry by. She went to the surgeon and told him, "I am Maria's sister. I will take the baby if she does not survive."

He paused as he tried to respond to her offer. "The baby is weak, but she will be okay. However, the mother is barely hanging on. If she survives two or three days, she has a good chance of survival."

But her good chance switched. One month after the birth, she began bleeding. Her physician found a large growth in her uterus, which he labeled choriocarcinoma. It was a very rare occurrence, which she survived.

19

MARY AND HER BABY SURVIVE

W hen Maria recovered, the legal question remained: who gets this beautiful baby girl? Obviously, Marion May had first choice, but he was not interested. When he saw the baby girl, he said loudly, "I do not want this baby." Interfaith marriage was always looked upon with very strong disfavor by Jewish leaders. In the Talmud, interfaith marriage is completely prohibited. In the Book of Malachi, the intermarriages that had occurred were a profanity, and several Jewish leaders eventually made a formal complaint to Ezra about these marriages. But excommunication of foreign women previously married to the Jews of Israel does occur in Ezra Chapter Ten.

She was the one who kept asking him for a baby. In the courts, the child custody cases were usually settled in favor of the grandparents, then the uncles and aunts.

Sister Lucy, who came to the hospital, was afraid that Grandma May would raise the girl as a Jew, which Maria would never accept, so she asked Mario if he would take the case.

He reminded her that his legal license was in Massachusetts. But then he remembered that one of his classmates at Harvard practiced in Trenton, New Jersey. Mario looked up his graduation booklet and found the name: James Neff. Mario found his phone number and telephoned him. They talked a little while about their class days and some of the funny episodes.

Mario broke into this discussion to explain why he was calling. Neff said he would take the case, but it would be difficult to win because the courts seem to favor the grandparents.

"But," said Mario, "isn't a sister a closer blood relative than a grandparent?"

"We will see in court," said Neff.

The trial was held in a small courtroom with few persons present. The grandparent spoke first. She told the judge, "This child is the blood of my blood, and she should be raised as a Jew."

Neff interrupted her. "Mrs. May, did not your son object to having a child and did not the mother have to beg him for the pregnancy? When his wife was in childbirth, did he not say, "I do not want this baby?"

Her answer was feeble. "I did not hear any of these conversations."

"Mrs. Milano, would you please take the stand?"

When Lucy was sworn in, the judge asked for her version of the case. Lucy was ready.

"Your Honor, when my sister and my father and I were boarding a ship from Italy to New York City, my sister and I got separated. As a result, we were raised in different parts of Massachusetts. For a long time, we saw little of each other, but lately we have been together more often. I can swear to this court that she begged her husband for a child, and when she was pregnant, there was not a single person who was happier."

She paused for the powerful words she was about to say. "Maria would be appalled to know that her husband refused their baby. For this reason alone, the May family should not be awarded this child."

The judge told those present he would need a recess so he can study the case and present a just opinion. Everyone watched the clock, and in 32 minutes he reentered the courtroom.

"After reading the documents that have been presented to the court, and after hearing those who testified, I rule that the child should be presented to the Milano family. This court is adjourned."

Mario hugged Maria as they wrapped the child in a blanket and headed home.

20

RAISING MARYANN MILANO

When the doctors decided that Maria might not survive her surgery, they gave her child to Mario and Lucy who took her to their East Boston home where they had some extra rooms.

She was born on April 11th, and they changed her name to Mary-Ann. She changed homes a month later. As she grew up, they learned that she was nothing like her new brother. She disliked studying, and she barely passed all of her courses in elementary grades and was no prize student at East Boston High School. She considered her brother too much competition.

MaryAnn chose all the easy courses she could, such as "How to Cook" and "Current History," where she could read in the daily newspapers. Even though Philip did not have the same parents as Mary-Ann, he considered her his sister, and he helped her whenever he could. He looked out for her especially after she reached puberty.

He was fearful she would be loose with her body, so he approached her and said, "MaryAnn, you are old enough now to get involved in sexual things. All the guys are going to try to get you to spread your legs. You must resist them for several reasons. First because it is a sin, second you might get pregnant, and third you might get a sexually transmitted disease.

"This is a complicated subject, because there are so many diseases which you may not know about. You have probably heard about gonorrhea, which is commonly called the Clap, and you must have heard of syphilis. But there are others you may not know. For example, there is chlamydia. Some couples use oral sex to avoid pregnancy, but in the process if continued they may get chlamydia."

MaryAnn interrupted him. 'What do you mean by oral sex?"

"It means using your mouth instead of your vagina."

Again she interrupted him. 'Do people really do that? It sounds awful."

"Unfortunately, it is a growing problem for young persons and homosexuals, because many find it pleasurable. The young exclaim that it prevents pregnancy. Most of the gonorrhea cases involve homosexual men, but the prospects can be grim for everyone."

"Like what?" she enquired.

"Like getting cancer of the mouth or tongue," he told her, and he added one of his favorite quotations from Karl Marx: "The road to hell is paved with good intentions."

"Let me change the subject," he said, "because you will be driving soon. Never drink before driving. The insurance rates for teen drivers are very high because they have most of the accidents, and many have been drinking. You must promise me that you will never drink and drive."

MaryAnn replied, "I don't like the taste of wine or beer."

"That is good news," he said as he ended his speech. He did not tell her that all the high school boys went to the Old Howard at least once, usually when they were seniors because they looked older then.

21

MARYANN STRUGGLED MOST

Because she was not a brilliant student, MaryAnn attended all public schools: P.J. Kennedy Elementary, Joseph H. Barnes Middle school and East Boston High School, where she did not graduate. She learned that "Eastie' was built in 1901 and was expanded in 1933.

One day Mrs. Eliot, MaryAnn's teacher, asked why she had chosen to write about Robert Frost. She said, "You live in a nice home, yet you selected Frost, and you wrote about woods. Tell me why."

MaryAnn had a ready answer, because her mother had told her about Italy many times. "Things are so different there," she began. "School was from eight to four, six days per week, and all the men constructed their own houses. They were really little shacks. Each family grew their own vegetables, such as basil and arugula, and on Saturday young girls helped their mothers make bread for the whole village. It was nothing like the United States. There was no toilet, so the men carried out the waste each week."

"How interesting,' said Mrs. Eliot. "So you are relating Frost in the woods with your parent's life in Italy?"

"Yes, I am," answered MaryAnn.

"Well, now I see the connection," said her teacher.

Lucy was discouraged by MaryAnn's school record. They began discussing various options. She offered a new proposal. "Why don't we send her to the Theodore Lyman School? It is close by on Gove Street. It is for disobedient, disrespectful young students who cannot do the work in regular public schools."

Mario did not want to hurt her, but he had to respond. "Your idea sounds good, but it is all wrong. The Lyman is a reform school for boys who are truants and disruptive. She has to make her way in the public schools."

While MaryAnn was not a brilliant student, she was active in the neighborhood. As a member of the Star of the Sea Parish, she was involved in many of the church's activities. She volunteered to teach Sunday School, which surprised her parents. She told her young pupils that they should not smoke or use dirty words, and they should obey their parents. She even scheduled a meeting with Congressman James Michael Curley, who had just been elected with the help of the large Irish component of Boston.

Curley was his usual garrulous self. He told his audience, mostly young girls, that he had driven the Protestant Brahmin out of the city. They all fled to the wealthy suburbs. But he wanted also to stress the wave of reform that he had brought to downtown Boston, including adding schools, playgrounds, and new beaches. But, more importantly, he expanded the transit system, which gave jobs to many, mostly Irish.

When Curley left, MaryAnn was forced to add a few comments. She told them that he knew Abraham Lincoln's slogan: "The ballot is stronger than the bullet," but he does gets things done, and he was known as the "Mayor of the Poor." While praising his efforts, she had to add that he had served a five-month period in jail for a conviction of fraud.

As she mingled with parents after Sunday School, it was clear that she cared about other people. Maybe she was not a good student, but she had good ideas. MaryAnn knew a lot more about entertainment than about education. She knew all the lyrics of Sinatra's songs and most of the Glenn Miller songs, and she loved the movies of Clark Gable, Errol Flynn, and Henry Fonda. The new decade offered so many promises of prosperity, but she seemed to ignore the news of Germany's capture of most of Western Europe.

22

MARYANN MEETS TOM COLLINS

On one of her working days, a tall handsome man approached MaryAnn.

"Hello, my name is Tom Collins. My folks live in South Boston, with all the other Irish, but I live in Beachmont. I am told you take the subway to work every day. But that is not necessary, because I could easily stop to pick you up. How about if I take you out to lunch today?"

"I'm sorry. I usually bring an Italian sandwich for lunch. Today, it's Genoese salami with Pecorino cheese made from sheep's milk, and basil leaves."

"If I pick you up, can you make me one of those sandwiches for tomorrow?"

"Sure," she answered quickly, and that was the beginning of a new romance.

When he suggested they date, she recommended that they dance, but he squelched that idea when he said, "I don't know how to dance."

Her answer surprised him. "I can teach you."

When they went to his apartment, she saw it was too small, so they rolled the carpet back to make more room.

MaryAnn and Tom got better at performing their dancing, and they danced closer physically and mentally. He tested her resistance as he kissed her on the mouth. When she did not resist, he was emboldened to go forward: first to the breast, then toward the female jewel. At first, she ignored this activity and she teased him. "You know I am a flirt. All good looking girls are flirts."

He decided to play her game. "I don't mind if you will flirt with me. But flirting is allowed only with un-married women. If we were to fall in love, it would become an entirely different thing. You know what the poet said, "Discretion is the better part of valor.""

MaryAnn did not know how to react. She wanted him to continue his romance, but she could not remove Philip's admonition from her escutcheon. It seemed to her that there was an angel or another figure floating above her telling her to cease.

"We had better stop, now," she ordered Tom.

As he continued his effort, she screamed loudly, "STOP NOW."

Disgusted, he zipped up his fly, tossed her coat to her, and led her out the door. For the next few weeks they did not converse. She was not ready to forgive him, until one day he walked up to her and said, "How about making me one of your famous Italian sandwiches?"

She did not respond immediately, so he repeated his request. "Pretty please. Make me a sandwich."

MaryAnn remained silent, and when he started to walk away, she told him," I'll make you a sandwich, but that's all."

"That's all I want," he lied.

When she delivered him the sandwich the next day, she said, "I will speak to you again if you will respect me."

"Agreed," he responded, and they were good friends again.

She expected his next suggestion. "Can we go back to our dancing lessons?" Then he threw her a real curve ball. "Do you read the bible?" he asked.

She floundered a bit and answered, "We read the Old Testament at Mass."

"Good," he said. "Have you ever read Isaias Part 66?"

She was stumped. "What does it say?"

"It's a peculiar image of Jerusalem as a woman." Then he said, "That you may be filled with the breasts of her consolation. He sees her as an overflowing torrent which you shall suck." He finished with "you shall be carried at the breasts.'"

MaryAnn did not know what to respond. "Why are you telling me this part of the bible?"

"Because God is telling us that there is something sacred about a woman's breast."

"Can we change the subject?" she asked meekly. She knew what he was getting at, and she would not approve.

Silence filled their air for a while.

"How do you keep awake?" he joked.

"Shall we talk politics or what?" MaryAnn responded. "There are some good movies playing now, including *Miracle on 34th Street* and *Life with Father*. And there are some weird ones that are also rate highly, including *Black Narcissus*.'"

Thomas was surprised that she was a movie buff. "So, should we go to a movie next?" he asked.

"The only time we can go is weekends," she answered.

When the waiter asked about their selections for the evening. Tom answered first. "I'll have the chicken *saltimbocca*."

"MaryAnn ordered something more uncommon. "Please bring me the shrimp *diavolo*."

When the waiter left, she asked Tom, "Do you know what all these words mean?"

He pleaded guilty. "No, I really don't."

MaryAnn was ready to show off her Italian. "The *saltimbocca* means to jump in your mouth. That means it's very spicy. I think you know that *diavolo* means devil."

They both enjoyed their dinners, and they started home because MaryAnn had some things to do. When they got to her house, Tom parked along the sidewalk. out of the way of walkers. It was very dark for what he wanted to do. He slid next to he, and he started kissing her.

"I know why you brought up Isaiah," she began. "You want to kiss my breast. But they will be available only for my husband," she said firmly.

"Well then, let's get married," he said. "I love you. Don't you love me?"

She was so overwhelmed by the offer that she could not speak. "I think I do," she answered softly as she hugged and kissed him all over his face.

"If that is a positive answer," he said quickly, "do I get your breasts then?"

"We are not married yet," she said.

She was late, so she gave Tom a quick kiss on the cheek and hurried inside.

23

THE CHELSEA CLOCK COMPANY

The next day, MaryAnn put on her Sunday finery and got on the bus to Chelsea. It stopped right at the factory gate. She easily found her way to the employment office, where they told her to wait. It was a slow process.

When they called her name, she was led into a private room where an officer, James Howard, was waiting for her.

"Well, Miss Milano. Why do you want a job at the Chelsea Clock Company?"

She was ready for that question. "I have always liked machines, and I would much rather be making something useful than trying to sell ladies underwear."

"But you have no experience," he told her.

"No, but I am a quick learner. I must have a job, because my aunt, who is raising me, cannot give me a bed in her small apartment, and she cannot afford to provide me with the money I would need to sustain myself. I promise you I will work hard, and I will not make many mistakes."

He was impressed with her response. "Okay. Report to work next Monday, and don't forget we start at 7:45."

"I thank you, and I promise you that you will not be sorry for hiring me."

"I'll see you then," he said as he walked away.

As MaryAnn got more acquainted with her co-workers, she learned more about the Clock Company. She had gone to the library to investigate the company. She was surprised at all the name changes—from Harvard to Boston to Eastman. When Charles Eastman bought the Company, he settled on "The Chelsea Clock Company."

When she met her boss, he said "You have no experience of any kind. Why did he hire you?"

She responded slowly, "I may not have experience, but I do have a brain and I learn quickly. Let me try for a week, and if you do not like what I am accomplishing, then you can fire me."

When she began her new job, she realized that it did not require a great skill. She was assigned to the kick press, which could punch a hole in a clock wheel with the right foot. It was monotonous, which was made more so by the time and motion experts who went around the factory illustrating how each employee could save several seconds by going through a routine. In MaryAnn's case, she was told to pick up the wheel with the left hand, put it in the kick press, kick a hole with her right foot, and put it in the box with her right hand. She learned later that this procedure was the product of Frank B. Gilbreth, who was an early advocate of scientific management and a pioneer of time and motion studies. He began his experiments in bricklaying, then he moved to other industries, including the Waltham Watch Company.

As she went through this monotony, she could hear all the men around her who spoke incessantly about getting laid. At seventeen she was fully grown, and she thought perhaps she was ready to join in the fun. But she could not appear to be eager. She had to be cool.

As the weeks flew by, Tom continued to court MaryAnn. One night, she reminded him that she reads during every break in her schedule.

"There was something in the papers about bonds. What is so peculiar about bonds?" she asked him.

"Bonds are different from stocks," he told her. "For a bond the principal is always safe, because you are loaning a company money for which they are paying you a principal. To be absolutely safe, you would need to purchase very high grade bonds. These are very safe, but they pay a much smaller principal. That would be about three percent today." He then added, "There is one risk with owning bonds. The value of your bonds will fall if the interest rate rises."

"Now I am totally confused," MaryAnn said.

"Let me explain," he told her. "Suppose you bought bonds that yield three percent, and the interested rate is raised to four percent by the Federal Reserve Banks. Your bonds will need to fall in price to yield four percent."

MaryAnn was more confused by his explanation, so she told him, "I will leave it to you to handle our investments."

24

TOM AND MARYANN MARRY

In time, they were kissing and in love. As MaryAnn thought about marriage, she could not see any impediments because they were both Catholics. Everything seemed perfect, but something happened on the job that affected MaryAnn. She was not aware that nearly all the employees were members of the CIO. She even had to ask, "What does CIO stand for?"

A female employee could not believe the question. "It stands for Congress of Industrial Organization. Were you not asked to join the union?"

MaryAnn responded quickly, "No. Nobody told me about it."

The questioner figured it out. "You work in the office now, don't you?"

"Yes, I do."

"Then that is why you are not a union member; you are considered part of management."

MaryAnn still did not understand. 'What does all this mean?" she enquired.

The questioner answered again. "It means that there will be a strike if we do not get a raise. John L. Lewis established our union when we could not join the AFL in the New Deal."

MaryAnn thanked her for the information and said, "I'll talk to my brother about this. He knows everything."

She had another problem. The four parents had not met yet. But when all the conditions were explained to the two couples, they agreed to meet in a South Boston restaurant, O'Reilly's. It was there that Danny and Mary Collins met MaryAnn Milano.

The Collins ordered beer, and the Milanos got red wine. As they bragged about their children, Mario and Lucy were pleased to learn that Tom Collins had graduated from Boston College with a degree in marketing. He was doing clerical work until the last of the Great Depression was history.

It all seemed compatible. The only question was in what part of Boston would they have the mass and the wedding. They decided on a coin toss, which the Milanos won, so the marriage took place in the Holy Name Church in East Boston.

Soon after they were married, Mary Ann told Tom he should find a job that suited his college degree. He agreed, and the first thing he did was to contact the U. S. Employment Service. The young lady he met told him that there was a job available in the Marketing Division of The Rexall Corporation.

He headed right to the branch on Washington Street, where he met Joseph O'Connor, who was in charge of Marketing. The first question he asked Tom was, "Why should we hire you at the Rexall Corporation?"

Thomas Collins was prepared for this question. He began, "As you know, President Coolidge told all of us that "The Business of America is Business." I agree, but I would modify that statement to mean "The end of all businesses is the three Ps: People, Products, and Profits." If a company respects its employees, utilizes their skills properly and pays them well, they will both benefit."

O'Connor was pleased with his response. "You seem to understand our work well. When can you report to the job?"

"I am ready any time."

"Well, how about if you began on Monday?"

"I will see you then," said Tom Collins gleefully.

He hurried home and told Mary Ann that the Rexall Company will enable them to buy a house in Jamaica Plain. It had a long history. First, it was part of Roxbury, then it became a suburb of Boston. It is near Northeastern University and Boston University. Most of the houses are triple-deckers, like in East Boston. There were two popular places nearby. One is the park designed by Frederick Olmstead, and there is the pond which is ideal for walking around or fishing or ice skating.

25

GATHERING KITCHENWARE

When MaryAnn learned that the movie houses were giving away plates and other kitchen necessities, she told Tom they should participate. All they had to do was to go to the movies on Friday evenings. When they walked into the movie house, they received a fairly large plate—one of many they would receive each Friday evening.

It was a very long night, because it began with people performing on the stage before the two movies began. The first performer was a young girl who sang "Blue Heaven." When she got to the line, "Just Molly and me and baby makes three," MaryAnn had to wonder if she would be pregnant soon.

When the show was half-way finished, an old man came on the stage with a concertina. Tom did not know what it was, so he was very impressed when MaryAnn explained how it worked. She told him that it is similar to an accordion, but it is played by stretching and squeezing the bellows and buttons between the hands.

The old man told the audience, "I play on a ferry every day, so tonight I am going to play the "Ferry Boat Serenade."

. . .

"I love to ride the ferry
Where music is so merry
There's a man who plays the concertina
On the moonlit upper deck arena
While boys and girls are dancing
While sweethearts are romancing
Life is like a mardi-gras
Funiculi, funicula."

The third performer played a Fender 100 guitar, and he played and sang a popular Hank Williams song:

"I tried so hard my dear to show that you're my every dream
Yet you're afraid each thing I do is just some evil scheme
A memory from your lonesome past keeps us so far apart
Why can't you free your doubtful mind, and melt your cold, cold heart."

The first movie was B Grade, and luckily each of the movies had to be only one and one-half hours long. Many persons left early, so Tom and MaryAnn joined them. When they got to their house, they wasted little time in falling into bed. They each had to work tomorrow.

PART III THE TRIAL BEGINS

THEY FIND A BODY

The police chief, Thomas O'Connell, looked tired when two of his men came toward him. He sensed that it meant trouble.

"What's up, Joe?"

"It ain't good news. Two visitors to Boston came across a body floating in the Charles River. The police took it to the Massachusetts General for an autopsy."

"Did he drown?" asked the police chief.

"He might have drowned, but he had two large bullet holes in the chest."

"Did you find any I.D.?"

"Yah, his name is Charles Eliot, and he is a professor from Harvard. He lives in Lexington. He was a member of the Eliot family that made history at Harvard as early as the nineteenth century."

"Do we have anything on him?"

"No. He is clean, but we have a scrap of paper with one name, Rodney Collins, and his address. It's an exercise place on Commerce Street in the West End. On the other side is a female name, Jo Ann Kelly."

"Send a couple of guys over there for now. We will find out much more later from the lab report."

During the autopsy, the doctors were looking for evidence of the cause of death. They weighed and measured the body, noting the characteristics such eye color, hair color, sex, and age.

When they removed his clothes, they searched for gunpowder. And they notes marks such as scars, tattoos, or injuries. They used X-rays to find the locations of the bullets or other objects. This cutting produces little blood because when the heart in not beating, there is no blood pressure.

The pathologist began the chest and abdomen autopsy by making a Y-shaped incision, the two arms of the Y running from each shoulder. The most common error is making this incision wrong. The gruesome part is to examine the organs in situ (in place), which mean removing the rib cage.

Once each organ has been examined, it is removed, weighed, and examined in further detail. In this case, they did not deal with the brain, because the shots were to the chest.

When they were finished, the body was then sewn shut, washed, and prepared for the funeral director.

26

THE EXERCISE ROOM

Sergeant Murphy and his assistant arrived at the Exercise Room on Commerce Street, and they thought it was well named because it was in the financial district, not far from the Federal Reserve Bank. The exercise place was on the third floor with no elevator.

The two officers knocked on the door, and they were led into a waiting room.

"Is there someone here named Jo Ann?"

"Yes, she is busy. Can you wait five minutes?"

"Sure. We'll just sit here.

It was longer than she quoted, and when she approached the men, they looked a little surprised. They told her about the piece of paper and the name. Then one of them explained the details of the murdered body.

"Do you know Rodney Collins?" he asked.

"I know him only as one of my clients," she answered hesitatingly.

"What do you do here?" he asked.

She paused momentarily, then she said, "We advise people who are having marital problems."

"So, you know nothing about his personal life?"

"No, I do not," she lied.

27

THE CASE BEGINS

The courthouse was on Tremont Street. It was full of light-brown marble. All the wood in the room was dark mahogany. As all the attorneys shuffled their papers, the clerk called the case number of the Eliot trial, and everyone in the room rose.

After everyone was seated, the room was still not crowded. The *Boston Globe* seemed not to be covering these events as they usually do with murder cases. The prosecutor, Harry Rubenstein, was busy reviewing his notes, and Rodney Collins, who was indicted, was taking instructions from his attorney, Stephen Stepinski.

Judge Thomas O'Connor was a man in his sixties, who had a full beard. He was the son of Irish immigrants, and he had been appointed by President Roosevelt. O'Connor had sold encyclopedias before receiving a scholarship to Harvard. He called immediately for a jury to be sworn in. It took just two hours, and it contained eight craftsmen and two women who were clerks.

The judge charged the jury and went over his various rulings. The prosecutor thought that he was a fair judge.

Rubenstein asked the clerk to please call Rodney Collins. This rich man, who lived in Lexington with many of the faculty from the

Harvard Business School, took his seat in the witness box. Rod had a golden upbringing. He attended Phillips Exeter Academy, and his father was an executive at the GE plant in Lynn. He got his son a good position at GE. Rodney was brilliant, but he was an unpolished diamond when he attended social functions. The ladies of his age laughed at his inability to socialize. Rod almost cried when he told his mother of this deficiency. In those close situations, she always hugged and kissed him. And she told him he would find a beautiful wife someday. Rod didn't comment, because he knew what he was becoming.

When Rod was seated, the prosecutor, Harry Rubenstein, read from a paper he was holding that was provided by Mario Milano. "'I really did better with men my age than with women.' So, you are a homosexual."

"Yes, I am."

"And you were close friends with Jo Ann Kelly."

"Yes, and I was appalled that the murdered man is a neighbor of mine and a Harvard Professor."

"Did you have sexual relations with that man?"

"Yes, several times."

"So you had no reason to kill him?"

"No, I loved him."

"That will be all for now, but I reserve the right to recall him."

"Will the clerk call Jo Ann Kelly?"

Many noted that the woman who stood up was curvaceous and carried a full breast. Her hair was cropped like a man's, and her attire seemed to want to emphasize a man's existence.

"Now, Miss Kelly, you wrote that you were appalled at all the men who came into your studio. Is that correct?"

"Yes. Some were very refined and educated. Others were revolting. Some had a very expensive smell. Others almost made me sick. It was too disgusting."

"In your deposition, you wrote that you are a lesbian. Is that true?"

"Yes."

"If men were so gross, why did you continue to allow them to touch your body parts and to penetrate you?"

"Well, as you must know, I have to pay the rent and to buy food."

"Yes, I know, but how did you become so intimate with Rose Bianco?"

"We both worked the same shifts, and we both agreed on the conditions of the men. It drew us closer. But this is a very complicated subject. I was raised in a very strict Christian family. Drinking and smoking were not allowed, and we had rules as to what we could say. But I think the biggest effect on me was the lack of intimacy and love between my parents. They seemed to just tolerate each other, so I was not surprised when they divorced. As a teenager, I really had to take over the kitchen and the house. My mother was in deep depression. What I learned from all of this chaos was that if you are treated unkindly by your parents, you will lack compassion."

Rubenstein told her he was sorry about her upbringing, and he added, "Why did you not change occupations?"

"That's easy. There is far more money in prostitution."

"But, Miss Kelly, how did that make you a lesbian?"

"The transition was very gradual. It all began when we rented an apartment together. It was so much cheaper, and the companionship prevented loneliness."

"But hundreds of women rent together, and they don't become lesbians," Rubenstein told her.

Kelly pondered for a minute, then she spoke more softly. "We discussed our problem constantly. We agreed on most things, especially that we did not want to become involved with any men who came to our studio."

Again the prosecutor was not happy with her answer. "You both could have gone to a church where you could meet straight, honest, Christian men."

"Well, we didn't have the time and we really liked each other."

Harry Rubenstein was getting more inflamed with these simple answers. "There has to be better answers for you to change your sexual preference."

"There is, but I do not want to bring it up."

"Please inform the court why."

"It involved my grandfather, who is now dead. I was only twelve years old, and I was just reaching puberty. He lived with us, and he slept in the upstairs bedroom near mine. One night he asked me to go up to his room. I did not suspect anything. He held my hand going up the stairs, and when we got into his room, he kissed me on the mouth, which he had never done before," Jo Ann told him.

Rubenstein told her, "Well, tell me exactly what happened."

Jo Ann hesitated. "At first, I did not expect him to do what he tried to do. He grabbed me by the shoulders and tried to push something hard against me. I did not understand what he was doing, but as I matured, he made several attempts to penetrate me. So when it happened the last time, I screamed, and he backed off. I punched him in the face, and he started bleeding from the nose."

Rubenstein wanted to know more. "How did he explain his nose-bleed to your parents?"

"He lied. He said he banged it against the wall going up the stairs in the dark."

"Let's change directions. Did this have a lasting effect on you?"

"At first I did not want any man to touch me or be near me. I preferred women, but later I found that I could make a good living with my body."

"So, you knew that you were a voluptuous person," Rubenstein told her.

"Yes I did, and that is how I became a prostitute. But the process was complicated. First, I quit high school, so I had no means of support, and I realized that men seemed to be glaring at me as I walked by. It was then that I knew I could make good money by selling my body. It was just business, because I never reached a climax with any clients. At first, I had problems, because I started having phantasies, which became masturbatory and often hysterical. My mother insisted that I see a psychiatrist, and she was sure that these anxieties and phantasies contributed to my becoming a lesbian."

"Did this choice of sexuality affect your relations with your mother and father?"

"Well, I did become closer to my father, and I argued more with my mother."

Now, the prosecutor was getting to where he wanted to go. "When your mother died, did you not say that you wanted to marry your father?"

"I cannot answer that question."

"Well, let me suggest an answer. Do not the conditions you just related lead you to want to kill some of your clients because you do not want them to do certain things that your grandfather did to you? The question is did you hate Mr. Eliot enough to shoot him two times and to bash his head in?"

Jo Ann was upset at these implications. "I did none of these things. I did not hate him, but I did abhor violence. I did not fear Charles when he came to my studio, because as a homosexual I felt safe."

Rubenstein stopped her. 'Why would a male homosexual come to a person who is a lesbian?"

"Well, we were good friends, and he did not come for sex."

Rubenstein cut in again. "So, two queers makes it all okay?"

Stephen Stepinsky protested. "Your Honor. I object to that characterization of my client."

O'Connor agreed. "The prosecutor will abstain from using this kind of language again."

Jo Ann was also riled over having these events become public knowledge. "These personal matters do not belong in a courthouse," she said.

"On the contrary," said Rubenstein. "If you are longing for physical love from your father and this leads to a crime, then it is very relevant here."

Stephen Stepinsky objected again, "The prosecutor is not a psychiatrist, therefore he is not competent to reach these conclusions."

"Well, Mr. Stepinsky, we did employ a psychiatrist. And all of these conclusions are his. Let me summarize what he said. First, hysteria leads to phantasies, and these lead to homosexuality. Both men and women can be victims of masturbatory phantasies which can result in serious crimes. Let's get to the case at hand." Facing Miss Kelly he said, "Did you not once slice off a man's penis and hit him with a baseball bat?"

"No, I did not."

Judge O'Connor sensing the fatigue of all the players announced, "We are adjourned until twn o'clock tomorrow morning."

Jo Ann was dead tired. She went home, and when Rose was not home, she decided to take a long bath in the tub. As the water revived her, she regained her strength so she began masturbating. It felt good for her to be released of that burden and to be clean again. She was always concerned about gonorrhea and other diseases.

When Jo Ann heard the door opening, she jumped out of the bath tub and dressed quickly. "How was your day today, sweetheart?"

28

ENTER ROSE BIANCO

Rose Bianco was born and raised on Brooks Street in East Boston. She was another child of immigrants who attended all public schools. She did graduate from East Boston High School, so her credentials were not very good for finding employment. But she was lucky to find a job at Jordan Marsh in downtown Boston as a clerk. She simply carried boxes and placed new items for sale in the proper places on the first floor.

Her first opportunity to meet someone happened at the water cooler as she waited for a drink during her ten-minute morning break. A tall, handsome blond, who was in line behind her, spoke first.

"How are you doing?" he asked her.

"I am okay," she replied.

"Where are you from?" he asked.

Playing coy, she replied with a question. "Why do you want to know?"

He was temporarily stumped. "Well," he said. "I see you getting on the streetcar each day. And I thought I might be driving by your house, and I could pick you up."

Now she was really interested. "I live near Bennington Street in East Boston," she told him.

His face showed joy. "I live in Beachmont, and I do go through the tunnel, so I could pick you up."

"That is very kind of you. But I need to give this some serious thought. My name is Rose Bianco. What's yours?"

"My name is Rudolpho Saviano, but everyone calls me Rudy."

She smiled as she spoke. "So you are another WOP."

"I guess so."

"Let me think about all this, and I need to talk to my parents about this arrangement."

Rose's mother agreed that she could accept a ride to work from Rudy. The next day he drove off the North Shore Drive to Brooks Street where he picked her up. At first they acted as just employees, then they became friends. As they got more friendly, he became more bold. He asked her if she could stay in downtown Boston after work so they could have dinner and dance later. She had a nickel, so she called her mother on one of the outside phones. She said, "Don't be out too late." Rose promised to obey her rule.

They ate at the Parker House which opened in 1855. When there was a moment of silence, Rose asked him, "Did your parents come through Ellis Island?"

He thought for a moment, then he answered, 'Yes they did, and they told me they were treated well on board ship, but as soon as they got on land they were derided and slandered. Some were promised places in the sun, and they wound up in swamps. Others who were fishermen were considered competition for American fisherman, so they were not allowed to go to cities by the ocean. There is a famous case of eleven fisherman who were lynched, and those who were guilty got away with the murders."

When the new love birds finished eating, they walked around the neighborhood until it was dark. Then Rudy got bold. "Let's go to the Tic Toc," he suggested.

Since she did not know the place, she agreed. When they entered, Rose knew she was not dressed for the place. Most of the men wore baggy suits and the girls had skirts high up their legs. They watched and listened for a few songs, and she told him, "Let's try it."

They tried but failed to duplicate what the crowd was doing. Rudy told her that they were doing acrobatics not dancing. She insisted that they keep trying until they reach the level of other dancers.

They kept at it until 10:00 p.m., when she remembered her pledge to her mother. They exited, and he drove her home in his 1942 Topolino FIAT 500. It was two-door, four-speed gearbox and had a top speed of only 53 miles per hour. He stopped in front of her house, and soon she recalled some things her mother had warned her about. But she was not concerned, because she knew he was a gentleman. At first, as they talked about their families and their about favorite things. But slowly his right hand moved across her shoulder heading downward.

She grabbed his hand and screamed, "That's a no no. You better go," as she opened the car door.

He said nothing as he drove off. The next day on the job was cumbersome for both. Neither spoke as they wended their way to their own places in the store. At lunch time he walked toward her slowly. She looked ahead avoiding his eyes.

"I apologize," he said softly. "I guess I had you pegged as someone else."

When Rose ignored him, he walked off. This episode occurred each day for more than a week. Then he found his mark: he kneeled before her saying, "I promise to be good."

"Do you mean every day?" she asked.

"I promise," he replied with a large smile.

"You may sit down near me," she told him, and their friendship was rejuvenated.

"Do you like baseball?" he enquired.

She did not answer, so he repeated the question.

Again she gave him no answer. "Okay," he said. "What do you like to do?"

What she told him really surprised him. "I like to knit."

Her answer completely baffled him. "What do you do away from home?"

"Well, I like roller skating," was her response, which frustrated him more.

"I like to cook, too," she replied strongly.

He was not going to give up. "What can we do together?"

"I swim in the summer."

"And what do you do in the winter?" he queried.

This time she answered quickly. "I knit."

He thought to himself: *This time I have linked up with a domesticated woman.*

As he was meditating, she told him, "We can always walk."

Again thinking to himself, he reflected. *She'll make somebody a good homebody.* To get away from the swing crowd, he decided to test her breadth of more civilized activities. "Would you like to go to the Bijou Theatre? They are doing Lillian Hellman's new play, "Watch on the Rhine." They used to do a lot of Vaudeville, but now they have "switched to classics."

Rose did not know much about plays, but she was willing to expand her recreational activities. "I would love to go," she said, which surprised him.

Meanwhile, she was thinking too. "What does your father do for a living?"

His response amazed her. "He is a brain surgeon."

She joked, "That's too bad. He won't be able to deliver our babies, will he?"

"No, he is a neurosurgeon. He deals with the central nervous system. He performs neurotomies."

"Wow," Rose exclaimed. "My father does outside work."

"Well," Rudy uttered. "Someone's got to do that kind of work."

Changing the subject, he asked, "How about a movie? Who is your favorite?"

"I'll take Clark Gable or Errol Flynn or Robert Taylor." Then she really shocked him when she said, "They can put their socks under my bed anytime."

When he had ditched his surprise, he took her to see Errol Flynn's *Robin Hood.*

In time their friendship grew, and their cuddling became more advanced, going from hugging and kissing to where he sought to go. As long as he kept his hands off her, their friendship turned to love, and they turned to when they should marry. They began to discuss serious things, such as children and church. Rose was surprised to learn that he was an Episcopalian.

When she asked him to point out the differences, Rudy answered as if he was a priest. He told her that it was Pope Leo XIII in the 19th century who challenged the validity of Anglican orders, and the Episcopalians responded that these errors were present in previous centuries. And Rudy stressed that many Anglican priests have converted to Rome, also many Lutherans.

"So," Rose said, "there really aren't that many differences. Are there? So we can raise our children in either church."

In the middle of this discussion, she hesitated to ask him, but she had to know. "Did you complete college?" she asked him.

"Yes," he said strongly. "I graduated with a B.A. in history."

Rose was surprised because he was working in a department store. "That is not going to get you very far in a depression," she informed him.

"That is true for now," he told her. "But it will be valuable when we leave this downturn."

She hoped he would not enquire about her awful educational experience.

When it was obvious that Rudy was pushing for marriage, Rose had to discourage him. She began by discussing his employment, and she saw how the many rejections were affecting him, so she offered an alternative. She told him how he could begin as a teacher's aide.

The following day, he confronted Rose about the possibility of teaching. He told her first, "Massachusetts is one of the strictest states to offer substitute teaching permits. It does offer something called an alternative teaching certificate, which involves curriculum and field work, which is an internship. But Boston has its own more difficult requirements: two years of substitute teaching."

Rose saw in his facial features that he was discouraged. "As you know," she began, "History majors have more difficulties finding employment, so you must find other avenues."

Rudy remembered the famous line from "Invictus." "I am the master of my fate and the captain of my soul."

Rose persisted, "Master and captain imply the sea, but what if you are on a sinking ship?"

When Rudy could not and did not respond, Rose was sympathetic but she felt that she had to give him a crippling blow.

"Rudy," she began, "you are a wonderful person, and I have enjoyed being with you all these weeks, but I do not believe that we are fully compatible, so I must say my goodbye."

Stunned, he walked away silently with his head down.

When he was gone, she reflected on one word of her last statement, "Compatible." She simply could not tell him that she was a lesbian.

29

ROSE MEETS JO ANN KELLY

Because Rudy had taken up all of her time, she was not able to seek better employment until she said her goodbye. She was fortunate to learn of the Exercise Room on Commerce Street in the West End. It was in the financial district, where all the Cadillacs were parked.

When she showed up for an interview with the Madam, she asked her to undress. She felt her all over to make sure that she had no imperfections. She felt her breasts and her legs, and she asked, "When do you want to start?"

Rose answered, "Immediately."

"All right. You can go to room five. Starting tomorrow."

The next day, she primped carefully waiting for her first customer. He was a very young man who seemed nervous and anxious to finish quickly. She helped him to hasten his desires, and she thought he could do better without paying for it.

When he left, she went next door to her neighbor's room. She shook her hand and told her that her name was Rose Bianco and she lived in East Boston. Her neighbor gave her a warm welcome. She said, "My name is JoAnn Kelly, and my family is Irish and lives in South Boston."

Since the traffic was light, they had a long time to get to know each other. Rose was very surprised when JoAnn said, "We should move in together. It will save us a lot of money."

She was overjoyed. "How kind of you. I accept, and I will start the moving project tomorrow."

Rose and JoAnn became more than roommates—they were lovers. JoAnn knew a lot more about being a lesbian, so she had to teach Rose all the aspects of love making.

As their love deepened, Rose needed answers. Her first question was, "Why can't we marry? We live together, and we love each other."

Jo Ann always had answers to her questions no matter how simple. "Lesbians and gay men are felons in most states, and newspapers did not help them when they published stories about queers and homosexuals."

Rose was appalled. "You mean I could be jailed for living with you?"

JoAnn was surprised. "So you haven't heard about the two men in Virginia who were in a loving position in bed when the police broke in and took them off to jail? There is a movement that is growing now to allow the gays to marry. The homosexuals make up a significant part of every groups of males and females, so there are several homosexual lawyers who are leading this cause."

Rose interrupted her, "What would it take to change things?"

JoAnn knew the answer. "It would take several liberal judges to support this kind of behavior."

Rose did not like this response. "If two people love themselves, it is the same as if they were man and woman."

JoAnn was flustered. "You are not grasping the problem. Most persons dislike homosexuals. That is why they are called queers. There is a radical feminist group that is urging these queers to be a revolutionary group to create new forms of marriage. There are other problems. Should the gays be allowed to serve in the military? Should they be allowed to teach our children? And there is another more serious problem. These gay people are often pedophiles who often indulge in bestiality."

Rose was apologetic. "I guess I just did not know enough about the question I asked."

"Oh SOS, same old shit," Rose answered.

"Nothing new, huh," Jo Ann asked.

"It was not all dull," said Rose. "There was an interesting discussion of why many more men become homosexual than females."

"What was the answer?" asked Jo Ann.

"It is not a simple question, so there is not a single answer. There is a project reported in the *Boston Herald* that covered the sexual motives of men. The problem with this study is that the ages of the men were from their teens to retirement. One major finding is that in one decade the number of male homosexuals doubled. Another finding is that despite this great gain, most men were ashamed for having bought sex. They seemed to believe that sex without intimacy is useless. They want to know the women they are bedding down with. Most of them wanted a real relationship with the women they are hiring. But another leading cause of hired sex is that men want to experiment on actions that their girlfriends or wives would not tolerate. This seemed to pertain to oral and anal sex. A final very interesting notion is that as a doctor related, 'When a man needs sex so badly to be relieved, he might be more willing to rape.'"

Jo Ann listened carefully, and then she said, "It all seems to boil down to what woman a man wants to lay. There are a lot of questions about prostitution. Are there more women than men? When do they begin? And do they ever quit?"

Jo Ann paused for a minute. Then she began again. "It seems that sex today is more about serving others than about dealing with their own desires. There is a sexual awakening in America. It seems that there is a lot more discussion about sex before adulthood. Even children's toys suggest desires. So many girls come of age sexually while they are still children. The result of all this is that there is a more rapid growth of rape, incest, and pedophilia. Much of the trauma of children being involved with sex becomes meat for psychologists. But many of them get only half of the story, because no one wants to divulge such occasions as a father raping his teenage daughter or a mother convincing her handsome son that he should sleep with her. All of these sexual awakenings are a family mess."

Rose got excited over those questions. "Why don't we go to the library to see if we can find answers to some of these questions?"

At that moment the doorbell rang, and two detectives came into the room. "We have a dead man in the morgue, and he has your name in his pocket."

Jo Ann was not flustered as she gave a speedy answer. "I see many men, so I need to see the body to tell you if I ever met him. Several of my clients come in for just a few minutes only."

The detective was flustered. "Come on," he said. "If he has your address, you must know him."

"He might have my address, but he never got to me."

The two men had no response, so they headed for their head-quarters on Maverick Street, East Boston.

Rose was happy that they had gone, because she wanted to bring up a question that Jo Ann had refused to approve.

"Tell me Jo Ann, why can't we have a dog? They are great companions. There was an article in the *Boston Globe* this week about a dog who mourned his master's death by going to the cemetery every day and sitting near the grave. There were so many people who saw the old dog that one man volunteered to adopt the twelve-year old animal. Doesn't this story really hit you inside?"

Jo Ann was tired of the subject. "Rose, you know that we are often gone all day. Who is going to watch the animal?"

"We can lock it up in the bathroom," replied Rose.

"But that's cruelty to animals," Jo Ann told Rose. "There is another aspect of this. Many women sleep with their dogs, and some use their animals for intimacy. These nuts actually fall in love with their dogs, and they become phantasy husbands."

"You are right. They must be nuts to do such a thing."

Jo Ann wanted to alter the subject. "You know, using animals for sexual pleasure is not a new idea. In the old Wild West many young boys used female sheep for pleasure. Apparently the sheep's vagina is similar to a female's."

30

THE CASE RESUMES

The case resumed on the following day, but before the prosecutor could question the witness, Attorney Stepinsky's assistant, Debra Boland, had a legal question for the judge.

"Your Honor, this whole line of questions is immaterial because Miss Kelly was arrested for prostitution, not murder."

O'Connor thought for a moment, then he told the attorney that some answers are germane to the case before the court. "So let us proceed."

The prosecutor called Pamela Graham. "Mrs. Graham. Tell us how you found the body on the Charles River."

"Well, my husband and I were visiting Boston, so we decided to walk along the river. He wandered off for just a minute, but I continued. When I stopped, I turned to gaze at the impressive sight, and it was then that this body came floating by. I could not tell if it was a man or a woman because it was face down, but because it was fairly large I guessed that it was a man. I saw a policeman not far off, so I hurried to tell him of the body. When he saw it he asked several questions: name, address, phone number, and he asked if I had a police record. I was offended."

Rubenstein apologized for his questions, but he told her it was all standard procedures. He next asked for Rose Bianco. When she was sworn, Rubenstein told her, "Do you know that the mafia intimidates people to have them give up their money?" Rubenstein continued, "When they commit a crime, they are sworn to total silence. Now, have you heard anything like this in the slaying of Professor Charles Eliot?"

She repeated her last answer. "No, I have no knowledge of it."

"So, you have no knowledge of Charlene hiring the mob to elimi-nate her brother?"

"No, I have no such information. But because her brother tried to rape her a second time, she might have harbored such thoughts."

"Now let's get to the main issue here. Let's assume that you are not aware of that."

"No, I am not."

"We have evidence that there were blood stains in your bathroom, and they are the same type as the victim we pulled from the Charles River."

Stephen Stepinsky objected. "How do you get the blood type from a person who has been underwater for many days?"

Rubenstein responded, "We will answer your question when our scientist is on the stand. On the subject of Miss Kelly, we have found certain conditions in her apartment that illustrate her modus operandi. One final question. Did Charles Eliot have a dog?"

Rose answered quickly. "Yes, he did have a dog."

"Well then," asked Rubenstein, 'why didn't the dog bark when he was being slaughtered?"

"The dog must have barked, but no one heard it because no one lives near his home."

"Thank you, Miss Bianco. Please call Dr. John Scott to the stand."

The man who stood up was about six foot three or four. When he sat down, Rubenstein began his questions.

"Now, Mr. Scott, you are a forensic scientist. Is that correct?"

"Yes, I am a graduate of MIT."

"Tell the court how you analyzed the blood sample."

"Well, the first rule is to make sure that you do not contaminate the sample."

Rubenstein stopped him. "If the body is underwater, how can that be done?"

Scott answered him quickly. "Those working on the sample must wear protective equipment, and they must dry and seal the specimen."

Rubenstein interrupted him again. "And how is that done?"

"We put liquid items in tubes, and we hang them in very dry rooms."

Rubenstein continued the interrogation. "And have you got any results yet?"

"It is too early for that."

"Thank you, Dr.Scott. I shall recall you later."

"Your Honor," said Stepinsky, "my client can explain a lot of the questions that the prosecutor is asking. Miss Kelly would you tell the court what you told me about the last time you saw Eliot?"

Jo Ann Kelly re-entered the witness box, straightened her short skirt over her knees, and began her story. "My lawyer wants me to describe Eliot's last day. It's a sordid story. He wanted me to talk for quite a while about his life. He seemed to be discouraged about his very existence. I tried to turn the conversation to something more pleasing, hoping to console him with words, but he seemed to be on another planet.

"I had been to his old grey house before. It is a mansion by the river with large gables, an oddity for a small town. The garden was also by the river. It was flanked by large fruit trees which were not cared for in many years. The property was bound by hedges and rocks. Because I knew the layout, I asked him about his animals and his plants. These questions seemed to have awakened him. He told me about his animal traps and the hissing of his ground snakes. I continued my queries. I asked him about his trees and plants, and he explained his birches and elms were not doing well. All the trees needed trimming, and the entire garden was out of order.

"The house has several windows that opened to the acres in back.

The fireplace in the living room burned wood, for which there was a good supply. The books and papers were littered all over the room, indicating that Eliot was a man of letters. As I entered his living room, he put down his pen. I judged that he was a man of about fifty-five years. He was slender with a firm mouth, and he was dressed elegantly. He had the air of aristocracy.

"He said, "Please forgive me, but I must provide copies of my work to several persons. I am sorry I must keep you waiting. I have been writing since I was in my twenties, and I have always loved literature."

"When he had finished talking, I caught a woman who dashed along the railing upstairs. He knew I had seen her, so he decided to explain her presence. "If a man is capable of loving, he will never cease to love. When a man has several loves, he will believe they all resemble each other. A woman can develop a passion for a man she has never married, but she will be willing to take care of him in the daytime and in the evening. This is true even if the man is three times her age."

"Our strange meeting got even more complex," said Jo Ann "He wanted to talk about sleep."

He asked me, "Do you know what happens when we sleep?"

"Of course, I was stumped. I thought he was going to connect it to sexual matters. I was wrong. He began, "Sleep involves secret ideas that affect your senses. While these senses are closed to the outside world, they do change your state of mind when you awake. There is a transmutation, so that you can alter any wrongs that you commit."

He continued, "Sleep is controlled by two systems: there is the circadian rhythm that is like a body clock, and there is the homeostat that builds up all day and when it is full it puts you to sleep. But there is an oddity here. It is connected in some way with an electrical charge. This gives scientists the ability to manipulate sleep."

"I was totally perplexed. And I was happy to leave. Not long after, he came to my studio, and for reasons I could not comprehend, he wanted to discuss his wife. As he spoke, his tears dripped on me. He said he had married her when she was twenty-two years old. He described her as having long, dark, brown hair with light green eyes.

Her cheeks were deeper in color, her lips were scarcely red. But he added she was a coquette, a tease, which is why he came to me regularly.

"I was stumped as to how to respond to this gloomy story of his past life. Before I could offer an answer, he shouted, "I want action." He asked me to undress quickly and get into bed. I was ready to comply with any of his wishes. He seemed to be very anxious, but I didn't hurry.

"When we finally were comfortable in the bed, he kept pulling my head towards his erection. I kept yelling, "No," but after a few more attempts, he punched me in the face very hard. I thought he was going to kill me.

"He roared something I could not understand, then he collapsed into unconsciousness, and I left the place as soon as I could finish dressing. This whole episode was surely one of self-defense."

The more Rubenstein learned of homosexuality in this murder case, the more he was convinced that the murderer was a homosexual.

31

IS HOMOSEXUALITY A CRIME?

When Rubenstein began to discuss this topic, Mario was the first to ask this question. Rubenstein had the answer quickly.

"The answer is yes, because in 1940 homosexuality was condemned in all states. For churches, it was sinful and immoral, and psychiatrists considered this behavior unusual and uncommon. In the military, conditions were worse. In some cases, some homosexuals were tied to trees and beaten. In other cases, they were scalded in their showers."

But Harry Rubenstein saw it in a different light. He was certain that there was a connection between homosexuality and the crime he was trying to solve. He got to this view when he listened to Jo Ann Kelly testify at the trial about being a lesbian, and when she decided to learn more about how beautiful women can reject men and choose women companions instead.

32

THE ELIOT CLAN

J o Ann hurried into her apartment to tell Rose what she just learned. Rushing in she said, "I just learned something amazing."

"What is it?" asked Rose?"

"The dead man was leading a double life. He's part of the Harvard clan. His grandfather was Charles William Eliot who was President of Harvard in 1869. I looked it up. *The Dictionary of American Biography* stated that he was the most important figure in the development of higher education. He was mainly interested in learning how education was related to economic growth. He thought that American education was too much controlled by clergymen and by not enough scientists. He wanted to connect the classroom to the trades, which would require some knowledge of scientific principles. He also wanted to improve the Lawrence Scientific School, but the big wigs at Harvard had no interest. So he headed to Germany, where he became enthralled with the German approach. When he returned to Cambridge, he was offered a position as Professor of Chemistry at the new MIT."

"Boy, he was a hot shit," exclaimed Rose.

"But that is not even the half of it," said Jo Ann.

"What do you mean?"

"Well, he fathered a child, and the rumor is that he raped his own sister."

"Boy, this is hot stuff," said Rose.

"Well, the worst of it is that he actually admitted his wrong, making the family very angry. The family from then until now is known for deception and secrets. They are trying to forget and redeem a family that has an honorable history but for one flawed man. There is one unusual aspect of this narrative. His sister would not testify against him despite the rape, because she is trying to protect the family history that goes back well over a hundred years. Because she cannot be compelled to testify, the prosecutor must find another more willing witness. But so far, no luck."

Rose was enthralled by this sordid information. "Do you think the two eras are connected?" she asked.

Jo Ann said, "Just connect the dots. The dead man passes as a gentle person, a family man, but he is a sordid, incestuous fraud, which is probably why he was killed. But the story is more degraded. The raped sister, who looks exactly like her mother, dies from an overdose of cocaine, who also died of an overdose of drugs. And you won't believe the next part: this rich, maternal bitch became a stripper and a top model. She married a billionaire from Louisiana who owned several oil refineries. She died on one of her islands off Georgia."

Rose listened to this deplorable history. "Do you have any episodes in the studio that are just as weird?" she asked Jo Ann.

"Well, the worst of it is the anal entry."

Rose was appalled. "Doesn't it hurt you to have all those things done to you?"

"No, I get paid well for it."

"How much do you charge?" Rose asked.

"If he just wants to use his fingers," it costs just $50. If he wants to penetrate, the fee rises to $100, and the most expensive is mouth and anus—these are $150."

"That's a lot of money for just a few minutes," said Rose. "But don't any of these upset you?"

"No. As I said before, I just believe that I am flying away from earth, and I think of you. You are my sweetheart and my only love."

Rose was not happy with the discussion. "Don't you ever think about the fact that you will never have a baby?"

Jo Ann was upset again at this repetitive statement. "You forget that many lesbians adopt a child."

Rose was still not satisfied. "But how can you feel that two women can comprise a complete family without a father?"

Jo Ann answered quickly. "Many lesbians are impregnated with frozen sperm, and in that case the second parent becomes a step parent. Many lesbians go to adoption agencies, but all state laws are very different. Some states now accept lesbian adoptions, and many are in the eastern United States: Connecticut, Delaware, District of Columbia, Maine and Vermont. The second parent has no rights, but some courts allow visiting rights."

"Well, as usual," said Rose. "You sure know your stuff."

On the following Sunday, Mario told his family that they should know more about Massachusetts, so they were going to visit Plymouth Rock. It was only about 50 miles from Boston. He drove through the Sumner Tunnel, and he headed southeasterly to Hingham and on to Plymouth. Mario gave his usual history of the place they were visiting.

Plymouth Rock was the site of disembarkation of William Bradford and the *Mayflower* Pilgrims who founded Plymouth Colony in 1620. It is an important symbol in American history. Strangely, there are no references to the Pilgrims' landing on a rock at Plymouth for 121 years, until 1741. At that time the rock weighed an estimated 20,000 pounds, but it is now only a fraction of that and is surrounded by an iron barrier.

The original Plymouth Rock was a large boulder about fifteen feet long and three feet wide, which was a convenient pier for small boats to land when the tide was right. But it is certain that no pilgrims stepped ashore on Plymouth Rock in 1620. No cautious captain would try to land a ship alongside a boulder during a heaving December sea. There were alternative, sheltered inlets nearby.

In 1774, the rock was split into two parts, with the bottom portion left behind at the wharf and the top portion being relocated to the town's meeting house. The upper portion of the rock was later relocated from Plymouth's meetinghouse to Pilgrim Hall in 1834, and in 1859, the Pilgrim Society began building a Victorian canopy at the wharf over the lower portion of the rock. In 1880, the two parts were rejoined, and the date "1620" was carved into the rock. In 1920, the rock was temporarily relocated so that the old wharves could be removed and the waterfront re-landscaped, and the care of the rock was turned over to the Commonwealth of Massachusetts.

During the times when the rock was moved throughout the town of Plymouth, several pieces were taken and were bought and sold. It is estimated that approximately one-third of the top portion remains. Today, there are pieces in the Pilgrim Hall Museum as well as in the Patent Building in the Smithsonian. It is clear that it is now an object of veneration in the United States. Pieces of the rock are also preserved in several towns in the Union. Is this stone part of the soul of the United States? Or is it just part of the treasure of a great Nation?

There are other days that are just as solemn. For example, we have 11-11-11. When his family looked puzzled, he explained.

"It stands for the eleventh minute of the eleventh hour of the eleventh day, which was how World War I ended. But today November 11th honors all military veterans who served in the U. S. Armed Service."

As they walked the beach, Mario asked a question, "Do any of you know what mooncussing is? It is very popular here."

When no one answered, he explained. "It is the local name for beach combing. You can find some excellent stuff here that washes up from one of the many wrecks at sea. The best place for searching is at Provincetown, which sticks way out in the water."

Lucy told him that they had to leave so she could prepare the Sunday dinner.

34

THE BAYARDS VISIT CAMBRIDGE

There was one issue they had to resolve: what would be Lucy's allowance. They thought by visiting Boston they would have an idea of what the living cost at Boston was compared to Wilmington. They had to talk to David, because he was surprised at the high cost of tuition. He had graduated from the University of Delaware at a fraction of the cost of Harvard. He chose not to work for Dupont or Proctor & Gamble, but began instead as an apprentice in the financial field, working for Edward Jones. He rose steadily to Vice President.

Ellen and David decided to resolve the question without Lucy. After making some computations, he told Ellen that it would be better if she could obtain some kind of help from the University or she could get a part-time job, maybe at the library. They discussed these notions with Lucy, and she was very receptive. She said she could get by with a small allowance, and she would definitely obtain part-time work somewhere in Boston.

Her father and mother decided to drive to Cambridge because they too wanted to see this famous place. They filled their 1937 LaSalle, series 50, two-door touring sedan. It was black with very large white-trimmed tires. It was made by Cadillac and served as a

companion marque. It was named after a famous French explorer.
David told the two women proudly that this auto was the Pace Car for
the Indianapolis 500 race, but the women did not seem to be
impressed.

The roads were not made for a LaSalle. They were winding and
bumpy. Fortunately, the weather was ideal so they could enjoy the
changing scenery. The New Jersey Coast was similar to the Delaware
Coast. The trip from New York City was over many hills, and it made
Lucy think of the hills of Italy.

When they arrived at Newton, they crossed over the Old Charles
River Bridge, which was built in 1891. It is the longest bridge to cross
the river to Cambridge, but it exited at MIT, not Harvard.

Lucy had already researched the history of Cambridge. She told
her parents that it was originally called Newtowne. The Longfellow
Bridge that crosses the Charles River was completed in 1763. For
almost fifty years Cambridge was a quiet farming village, but in 1846
it became a city. The potato famine of that time caused hundreds of
Irish to land in Boston and switch to Cambridge. Most of them
worked the clay pits and the brick yards. But when the twentieth
century began, Italians, Polish, and Portuguese settled in Cambridge.
There was also a small group of blacks in North Cambridge, most of
whom were runaway slaves. Lucy told her parents that Cambridge is
a cultural place with Harvard, MIT, and Radcliffe at its center.

They got a room at the Kendall Hotel, a moderately priced place
that was right downtown, and they prepared for the orientation,
which the parents were allowed to attend. It was the usual stuff about
all the rules and regulations, but most of those present paid more
attention when the provost discussed how the new students would
learn about where they will live and their new roommates. It was
simple. Go to the front office and ask for your assignment.

35

LUCY MEETS HER NEW ROOMMATE

David, Ellen, and Lucy got in line and slowly worked their way to the front. Lucy told the gentleman her name, and he handed her an envelope. She quickly opened it and showed it to her parents. They read it: Adams Hall and your roommate is Anne Schmitt.

Lucy stated, "I wonder if the hall is named for John Adams or Quincy. It seems that I have a German roommate."

Ellen was very curious. "Let's go see the place and meet your roomie."

They knew where Adams Hall was because they had studied the campus map earlier. When they got there, they agreed that it is an old building, but they expected this because of Harvard's age. They walked up to Room 314.

Ellen knocked, and a tall blond answered. "Hi. I'm your new roommate. My name is Lucy."

"Oh hello," she responded. "Please come in."

Ellen nudged David, and said "Why don't we let them get to know each other, and we can head back to Wilmington."

Lucy understood her mother. "We can talk later on the telephone, and you can come back any time."

The Bayards said their goodbye, and the two women hugged each other.

"Well," said Lucy, "tell me about yourself, then I will do likewise."

"That's a good deal," said Anne. "My parents are German, but they were born in the United States. Their parents were immigrants who came here in the mid nineteenth century. They settled in Philadelphia, and I am not sure why."

Lucy broke in. "And what does your father do?"

Anne continued. "He owns a clothing store."

Again Lucy interrupted. "That might be very handy," she said.

Anne turned to Lucy. "Now it's your turn."

Lucy was stuck as to how to begin. "Well," she began, "I don't know as much about my parents because I was adopted."

"How old were you when that happened?" Anne asked.

"I was twelve years old."

Anne was baffled by this response. "And where were you until then?" she asked.

Lucy had to lie. "They found me in Italy when they visited there."

"So, you came to the United States not speaking English?"

"Yes, but I learned quickly, and I became Americanized easily. It was actually easier because I was raised in a much smaller city, Wilmington, Delaware. The teachers were very friendly and very helpful. The Bayards go back to the beginning of the United States. Of the forty persons who signed the Declaration of Independence, five were from Delaware, and I was told that the Bayards knew most of them."

They switched their discussion to how to decorate their room. Anne told Lucy that she wanted a blue quilt because her hair was blond. When they chose a lamp with a red shade, Lucy asked how they would pay for it.

"Oh," she said, "my father will provide anything we want."

"But that isn't fair," Lucy told her.

"Don't worry about it," she told Lucy. "We need something to decorate the room." After a brief pause, she said, "I know what it should be."

"Tell me what," said Lucy excitedly.

"Well," she responded, "you are from Italy, so we must get an Italian copy of a famous sculptor. Maybe Michelangelo or a daVinci."

"Aren't you nice," Lucy told her, "but I insist that I pay for one half. We can get a piece of glass from Venice for a lot less money. There are a lot of glass statues of Venus."

"Okay. Let's do it."

The first month together was a full one. There were parties, dinners, and other functions to attend, and they became good roommates. But one thing separated them. Anne was drawn towards a member of the diving team.

After a while they became inseparable, so Lucy saw less of her. Lucy decided to learn more about this arrangement. "Tell me about your new boyfriend," she asked Anne.

Anne did not know what to tell Lucy. "Well, we are just friends," she began.

Lucy did not believe her. "I have seen little of you in the past few weeks. Are you letting him do things he should not do?"

"We just do a lot of kissing."

Lucy wanted a better answer, "Do you let him French kiss you?"

"I am not sure what that means," she told Lucy.

"Anne, if you let him use his tongue, he will want to move down to your pants," Lucy warned her.

"Oh," she said loudly, "I would never let him do that."

"Remember that when he is kissing you, his hands are free, so as the Italians say, "*sta atento*, (be careful)."

Anne waited before speaking again. "I do have one thing to watch. If I have a drink, I feel that the whole world is spinning around me, and I hear the little birds singing."

Lucy jumped into the conversation. "Anne, this means that you must not drink before he is kissing you. You must promise me. The Italians are smart about alcohol. They let young children drink small amounts of wine to teach them how to accept alcohol in moderation."

Anne seemed envious of that approach. "Germans certainly would never give a small child any amount of alcohol."

"What's his name?" asked Lucy.

"His name is Thomas Lonergan. He is Irish, and he is from Michigan."

"So," Lucy said, "we both have boyfriends. Mine is named James Grey, and he may be Irish also because he is from South Boston, where almost everyone is Irish. What a strange coincidence."

When Lucy went home for spring break, she found Ellen in a morose condition.

"What's wrong Mother?" she asked her.

"Oh, do you remember when I told you about David having another woman. I think he has gone back to her. I guess I didn't satisfy him."

"Has he gone?"

"Yes, he moved out," she said as tears fell from her cheeks. "What are we going to do?"

"Well," Lucy deliberated, "he will have to divide all of your savings and liquid assets. Do you have any idea how much it will be, because if it is a small amount, we will have to be much more frugal. I can always apply for a scholarship at Harvard, and if I can't get one, I can go to one of the local universities where tuition is much lower. I can also get a job. We will get by. The main problem is that we won't have a car. I never asked you before. Did you go to college?"

Ellen did not seem to want to answer. "I did go to one of the local schools that teach typing and dictation."

"That's great," said Lucy. "That means that you can get a job anywhere, because people who can take dictation are in scarce supply. But there is one left over problem. Who will pay the mortgage on the house? It will be a substantial amount because of its size. The only option seems to be to sell it and divide the equity."

Ellen wanted to be more talkative. "I think I am partly to blame."

"Why do you say that?" Lucy asked sternly.

"I am like many women," began Ellen. "They want a man, but most of them don't seem to want sex. They just lie there and assume that their husbands are satisfied. Most men accept this procedure, but they hate it, which is why so many seek satisfaction elsewhere. Too many women are dead inside themselves while their husbands are craving more passionate thrills. This may be why there are so many more lesbians now. And it may be why I lost David."

At this point, although she didn't love her life, Ellen had no other options. She had no family, no husband. She thinks back on when she had made plans to go to college, but it all collapsed when she married.

36

LUCY WORKS ON A SOLUTION

L ucy feels that there must be a solution. She tried first the Housing Office; it recommended the Scholarship Office, which was much more helpful. The director told her that if her mother cannot afford to hire a lawyer, then the University or the city could provide one. He gave her a telephone number to call.

Lucy hurried home and told her mother the good news. She telephoned immediately and got an appointment in three days. It was in an office of the city in Harvard Square, which is at the intersection of Brattle and Massachusetts Avenues. The Harvard Wall is the most obvious thing in the Square because it blocks the campus from the very busy community. The Square is full of museums, and it is a haven for chess players.

They entered the address they were given, and they were met by a very young man who must be a law school student. He greeted them warmly.

"Good afternoon, Mrs. Bayard," he said.

She reciprocated, "This is my daughter, Lucy."

"Let us all sit down, and you can tell me your problem."

Ellen looked at Lucy and said, "Do you want to tell him?"

Lucy knew she should not be involved. "I think you should tell him," she said, "because you know the whole story."

When Ellen finished, he said, "You have several rights here, and I will contact him or his attorneys concerning these rights. And I will contact you after we have a discussion with him."

Ellen thanked him and asked, "What is your name and telephone number?"

"I apologize. I should have told you earlier. So, as you probably guessed, I am a law school student doing *pro bono* work, and my name is Mario Milano and some of my friends call me M & M. You already have my telephone number."

Lucy's heart jumped when she found out he was Italian. "Mr. Milano, when we are finished here, I'd like to talk to you."

"Oh sure," he answered.

Ellen, sensing what Lucy had in mind, told her, "I'll just walk around the square, and I'll see you later."

Milano gazed at her approvingly and said, "Let's have a cup of coffee where we can talk."

They entered the Cambridge Coffee Shop where he ordered a *caffe macinato,* and she ordered a plain coffee.

"Well," he began, "what do you have in mind?"

"Were you born in Italy?" she asked him.

"No.' he answered, "but my parents were."

"Where?" she asked.

"Why do you want to know?"

"Tell me where?" she asked again.

"You wouldn't know the place," he told her. "It's a very small town east of Naples."

"*E come si chiamo questo piccolo villagio* (what is this small village called)?"

"Where did you learn to speak Italian?" he asked with great surprise.

"I was born there," she told him.

"And how did you get a name like Bayard?" he asked.

"It's a long story, and I don't have time now to relate it."

"Well then, let's get together some day or evening so you can tell me this fascinating story," he said firmly.

"Thursday is my shortest day, so you choose when we can meet."

"How about a nice Italian dinner?" he proposed.

She was delighted at the choice. "I haven't had a good Italian dinner for a very long time."

"Where can we meet?" he asked.

"Well, neither my mother nor I have car, so –"

He interrupted her. "I have a car. I'll pick you up. Tell me the address."

"I am at 314 Adams Hall," she told him.

"Okay. I'll pick you up at seven p.m. See you then."

37

IN THE BEGINNING

He came right on time. And when he saw her, he was pretty excited. When he saw her get out of the car, he thought "*Che bella figura.* (What a beautiful figure)." She was dressed for the nines (it seems to mean having a very large piece of fabric to make the dress), and he wore a suit and tie.

She was surprised to see that he was driving a FIAT. "Not many Americans would buy a FIAT," she told him.

"Why not?" he asked her.

"I guess you don't know what FIAT stands for," she said with a half-smile.

Puzzled, he asked, 'What?"

She tried to keep from laughing. "It means Fix It Again Tony."

He did not seem to enjoy her joke.

They pulled up to the Filomena Restaurant, and as they entered all of her past flowed before her: the red and green table cloths, the great Italian odor, and all the photos on the walls of Italian places. She was really overcome by so much of her forgotten history.

When they were seated, he ordered a bottle of *Chianti* – he was going Italian all the way – and he then said, "Now you tell me where in Italy you were born and how you got to the United States."

Lucy did not know how she should begin. After a long pause, she said, "I was born in Puglia in a small village, and I was named Lucia Gallo. I had a sister, Maria, and when my mother died, my father decided all three of us would go to the United States. We went to Naples to board the ship, and during the boarding process everyone was pushing me back toward the pier. Soon they pulled up the gangway, and I was left alone. I did not speak English, and I had no money. The Bayards asked me a bunch of questions which I could not answer, so they made enquiries inside. They learned that I was Italian and that's all. They tried everything to find out about a missing child, without success, so they took me home and named me Lucy Bayard. They were very kind to me. They sent me to a very expensive high school, and I was able get accepted to Harvard."

Mario was more confused now. "What happened to your father and sister?"

"I don't know. He went to visit his sister who lives in Massachusetts. I have no idea where."

"Wow," he said. "What a story. You should write a book about it."

She was taken by surprise at this suggestion because he did not know that she had won the prize in English Literature in high school.

"Now," she said, "it is your turn to tell me about your family."

"It's a typical immigrant story. My parents were just scraping by in a small village, Castellammare, near the coast of Amalfi."

"Do you have brothers and sisters?" she asked him.

"Believe it or not," he answered, "I do not. It's very rare for an Italian couple to have only one child, but because I was a few months early my mother had all kinds of problems in having me. She had low blood pressure and some heart defects. The doctors were afraid that any heart failure could cause other complications. They recommended that she not have another child for a while, which meant that she would go to the United States with only one child."

Lucy was very sympathetic. She told him, "There is both joy and sadness in not having a brother or sister. I know, because I am the Bayards only child."

As they continued talking, Lucy began calling him Mario, and he called her Lucia. He wanted more information. "What is your father's first name?"

She answered, "He was christened Nicola Gallo."

"Did you ask the Bayards to try to locate him in Massachusetts? The 1940 Census will be made public very soon."

"I think because they were childless, they were afraid of losing me," Lucy said very slowly. "Ellen did say once that I was their gift from God."

At this point, Mario became a lawyer. "Legally," he began, "they have really stolen a child because they made no effort to find the real parent or parents. Your father may have spent many hours trying to locate you, but he could not succeed because your new parents changed your name."

"But they were very nice to me," she told him.

"In law that counts for nothing" he advised her.

The waiter interrupted their conversation as he delivered her *melanzana parmigiana*.

"So, you like eggplant," he said.

"I love it, but I haven't had any since I left Italy. What did you order?" she asked him.

"I have always loved pasta with meatballs," he told her. "So, I ordered *cavatelli* and *pulpetti*."

She needed one question to be answered. "Are you going to call me Lucy or Lucia?"

Again, he acted as a lawyer. "Well," he began, "you are registered everywhere as Lucy Bayard. You can change it legally by going to court, but you may have to wait until you are twenty-one or until you are married."

They dropped the subject, and he drove her back to Adams Hall. As she got out of his FIAT, he asked, "Shall we do this again?"

"I'd love to," she responded as he kissed her on the cheek.

"I have your phone number, so I'll be calling."

They each waved goodbye.

After the two Italians met for the first time, they were inseparable. They met many days or nights when both were free. They were more like brother and sister than lovers, but lovers they became. Whatever their intimacies, they were performed in his FIAT. Her primary objective was to protect her virginity. She was determined to marry as a virgin. She was surprised that one day he even offered to get a motel so they could express their true love. She declined that, too.

By this time, Lucy was worried about the draft. She did not know if Mario had registered. What was she going to do if he got called to serve? 1942 was a terrible year for the U.S. Armed Forces, so more 18-year olds were being drafted. She heard about those physicals during which four or five very large needles were jabbed into the arms of the draftees, and several fainted. She did not want her Mario to go through that terrible experience.

He changed the subject one afternoon when he asked her, "Do you know how to dance?"

"I did a lot of dancing in high school. It was mostly fox trot and jitterbug. I never mastered the waltz with its 1-2-3 beat."

He wanted to tease her. "Are you one of the teens who fainted when Sinatra sang?"

"I never fainted, but I do believe he is the best singer around. Have you ever heard him sing "I'm a fool to want you?" Listen to these lyrics:

Time and again I'd say I'd leave you
        Time and again I went away
    But then would come the time
    When I would need you
    And once again these words
    I would have to say
    Take me back I love you."

"There are so many great singers in the United States. I like the Andrew Singers, the Mills Brothers, and the Ink Spots. And there are many great pop female singers like Kay Starr, Helen Forrest,

Peggy Lee, Helen O'Connell and Ella Fitzgerald."

Mario told Lucia that Frank Sinatra considered Kate Smith the best singer of her time and said, "When he and a million other guys first heard her sing "God Bless America" on the radio, they all pretended to have dust in their eyes as they wiped away a tear or two." He continued, "The first public showing of Kate's "God Bless America" was in 1940. America was still in a terrible economic depression. Hitler was taking over Europe and Americans were afraid we'd have to go to war. It was a time of hardship and worry for most Americans.

"This was the era when radio shows were huge, and American families sat around their radios in the evenings listening to their favorite entertainers, and no entertainer of that era was bigger than Kate Smith. Kate was also a large, plus size, as we now say, and the popular phrase still used today is in deference to her is, 'It ain't over till the fat lady sings.' Kate Smith, with her voice coming over the radio, was the biggest star of her time. Kate was also patriotic. It hurt her to see Americans so depressed and afraid of what the next day would bring. She had hope for America and faith in her fellow Americans. She wanted to do something to cheer them up, so she went to the famous American song-writer, Irving Berlin (who also wrote "White Christmas") and asked him to write a song that would make Americans feel good again about their country.

"When she described what she was looking for, he said he had just the song for her. He went to his files and found a song that he had written, but never published, 27 years before—way back in 1917. He gave it to her, and she worked on it with her studio orchestra. She and Irving Berlin were not sure how the song would be received by the public, but both agreed they would not take any profits from 'God Bless America.' Any profits would go to the Boy Scouts of America."

Changing the subject, she asked Mario, "Have you been reading about rape in high school and on campuses all over the United States?"

He gave her the usual male response. "The women probably drank too much, and they must have led them on."

Lucy was offended with this response. "Campus rape destroys the lives of many young women. For many men, they are damaged property. Of course, the schools want to hide these events."

Mario had to be a lawyer again. "Legally, there is a very particular definition of rape. It is defined as 'Unlawful sexual activity that is carried out forcibly.'"

"Most of the men claim that the victim gave a 'valid consent,' said Lucy indignantly. "And don't forget that most of these criminals are very drunk, so how can they act rationally? Rape is a method for males to control women," Lucy told him. "The possibility of rape dictates how women are to behave. They fear walking alone at night, something men need not worry about. This means that rape is mainly about gender, and all the advantages go to men. When I was in high school," Lucy told Mario, "we did a clean version of *The Rape of Lucretia*. It was performed by two choruses. At that time, Rome was in a position of depravity. The two choruses described the pagan story. While they were about to battle the Greeks, on the night before battle, a group of soldiers rode home and found most of their wives were betraying their husbands. Only Lucretia was the exception. But as she slept, Tarquinius crept into her bedroom and awakened her with a kiss. She begged him to go, but he raped her. She felt that she would never be clean again, so she stabbed herself and died. Now this has some relevance to today's news stories. Women who are raped must feel that they want to commit suicide also."

Mario, for the first time, was speechless. "I appreciate what you are saying, but all rape cases are different, so that in the court room we must treat each differently." He did admit that sexual assaults in high schools and college campuses were becoming a crisis, but he tried to change the subject.

Lucy was not through with this subject. 'The whole question seems to be on the meaning of the word 'no,'" she told him.

Mario agreed with her. "The legal problem," he said, "is that under current state laws saying 'no' is not sufficient to prevent rape. Our instructor quoted Shakespeare in dealing with this subject. As he said, 'The fault, dear Brutus, is not in our stars but in ourselves.' We need to change our behavior as well as our laws."

As their love deepened, the two Italians spoke more about marriage. Mario asked her, "Do you know the rule for the age that women should marry?"

Lucy was perplexed. "What do you mean?"

Mario smiled as he answered. "Well, a woman should be one-half of the man's age plus seven. I am twenty-nine so the answer is fourteen and one half plus seven, which equals twenty one and one-half."

Lucy smiled back at him. "Well, I am twenty two so I must qualify." She added, "What fraternity did you get that from?"

They switched to more serious issues. The one problem was she had no father to walk her down the aisle. David had no interest. It was decided that she could walk down alone carrying a bouquet.

They chose the St. Paul Church in Harvard Square at 29 Mount Auburn St. Ellen, who did not understand the Catholic ritual, depended on Mario to get everything right.

It was a small wedding because Lucy had only Ellen on her side. Lucy wore a subdued dark blue dress with a plain silver chain. Off to the side she wore a small gold brooch. Her face was deeply religious and beautiful at the same time. There were more Milanos, but there were few present. The priest went through the regular Mass, and then he got to his homily, where he seemed to be more alive. In describing marriage, he spoke of the sanctity of sex. He said, "God is a partner in the reproductive process. In the union of marriage, it is essential that children be born and that they are reared and cared for by both parents."

Continuing on the role of Jesus, Father Gallagher told his audience that "God wanted successive generations of persons to elevate their living together even if they have faults." And he added, "Christian parents must rear, educate, and train their offspring."

When the ceremony was over, the crowd shouted "Dance, Dance," so Mario took Lucy's arm and they glided around the floor, but then the crowd shouted "Tarantella" (Tarantula, the Italian dance), which they attempted but not too well.

As they left the church walking slowly, Lucy stopped and faced Mario as if she was going to make an announcement.

"Mario, I want a child. You heard what the priest said. "God is a partner in the reproductive process." It is far more important that we have a child than we worry about how to furnish a home. I would rather die than I not have a baby. Do you remember when we were children that all the women used playing cards face up to determine which of the women would be next to have a child. We always thought it was voodoo, but it was serious business. All the women, young and old, learned how to read the cards."

Mario hugged her and told her, "We will start tonight to give you that baby you want." Then he changed the subject. "Everyone thought it was a beautiful ceremony." But he still had to choose the place for their honeymoon and to pay for it, since David claimed most of the Bayard money.

Mario told Lucy one evening that they had to discuss several important things. They met at the coffee house again, and they got comfortable at one table in back. When they were settled, he said, "Lucy you must help me choose where we will spend our honeymoon. We have several choices: we can go to a beach, or we can go to Massachusetts to look for your father, or we can go to Italy to return to our birth places. Do you have any thoughts on these choices?"

She did not respond quickly. She started with a doubt. "I really don't know where I want to go. Massachusetts and Italy create problems. I do not even know if my father is alive. He would be fairly old, and we really don't have relatives in Italy." She tossed it back to him. "Do you really want to go back to Italy? I do not know about you, but my life in Italy was very dismal."

"Okay," he said. I have one more option."

She jumped in, 'What is it?"

"How about if we go to Venice and ride on the gondolas?" he asked her.

"That sure sounds nice," she said. "Have you ever been there?"

When he said no, she screamed, "Let's go."

It was all decided.

38

GOING TO VENICE

Mario had to make plans, get airplane tickets, hotel reservations, and brush up on his Italian. They probably could not leave for a couple of weeks.

During their first evening of marriage, they were full of love. It was a night of passion and sensuality. There was no holding her back now. She would let him have his way. There was no more fighting in the back seat of the FIAT with their clothes on. She now accepted his reckless approach that she had fought many times before. She really was a different woman.

She had struggled to keep him from her breasts and her lower parts. Now she badly wanted to offer them, but she had to wait until he could join her completely. Now was the hour as she lay in bed; she knew what would happen. He kissed her breasts and moved slowly down to her stomach. She felt she was burning inside.

As he was kissing her bottom part, she grabbed his head, pulled him up to her level, kissed him with a new fervor and guided him inside her. It was the culmination of what they each wanted for several weeks.

In two weeks, they took *Al Italia* to Rome. And they rented a car for the trip to Venice. They picked up their rented FIAT 126, drove up the coast to *Civitavecchia* (Old city), and they found a hotel. They walked the city and had dinner. They ate *Fritto misto* (fried mixed fish), *stracciatelli*, torte and coffee (black and very strong). Returning to the room, she went right to sleep on the *Matrimoniale* (double bed), Mario read and listened to Italian radio—a very strange mixture of American music and opera (for example, he heard *Traviata* and Chuck Mangione on the same program.

The next day they drove up the Tyrolean coast, and they stopped at *Grossetto* for the Saturday market. They bought some fruit and muffins for lunch. They continued on to *Livorno* (Leghorn). This is a Medici creation of the 15th and 16th centuries. They had *cacciuti* (a soup of squid, calamari and shrimp in a tomato sauce on two pieces of thick bread). Very tasty.

When it was Sunday, they headed for church. Because the Duomo was closed, they went to St. John Baptist Church. Breakfast was rum cakes. Then they left town heading eastward, stopping at *Piacenza* after some fantastic mountain scenery, and then driving on to *Cremona*.

Mario had an interesting episode there. He noted in the guide book that *Cremona* had the largest bell tower in Europe, so he drove straight there. They were disappointed to find it was closed, but he noticed an old man on the grounds. He spoke to him in Italian, telling him that all his people were born in Italy and they had come 3,000 miles to see the tower. The old man smiled, opened the gate, and offered to walk them to the top. Lucy, who had acrophobia, chose not to take part in this episode.

It was quite a find, because the clock was designed by Galileo in 1583 to prove the Copernican theory of the universe. The clock was four-sided and could predict earthquakes. The old man told Mario that earlier Galileo had predicted an earthquake on a certain date, and when it didn't occur he was mocked, but later it was discovered one had occurred in Australia at the very time he had calculated.

From *Cremona*, they motored around *Lago di Garda* (Lake Garda) to *Verona* and on to Venice. Venice is unbelievable even when you see it. You need a boat to cross the street or find a bridge.

They headed for the Visitor Building where they learned that there were no vacancies in the hotels. We were totally stumped until the woman in charge said, "There is a vacant room on the second floor of a museum that is not far from here."

Before she could say another word, Mario told her, "We will take it." When he converted the Lira to dollars, it turned out to be only $30 per night. The next day they saw the colorful blue lagoon, then they headed straight for a gondolier, who said in fairly good English. "I take you anywhere," and then he added, "*Io sa questa citta molte bene* (I know this city very well)."

"*E come si chiamo?*" Mario asked (what is your name).

"*Mi chiamo Enrico*" (my name is Henry).

Henry seemed to want to exhibit his manhood by rowing violently into the smaller canals whose walls were moldy green and the persons who lived there hung their laundry on ropes across from street to street.

As they approached *Villa Diamonte*, (diamond village) the gondolier asked, "Quanto *settamani sta qua?*" (how many weeks will you stay here?)

Mario answered in English, "Two."

Then the driver got down to business. "Do you want the gondola for the entire two weeks or by the day?"

Mario knew he was negotiating. "How much by the day?"

Henry told him $5 per day or $30 per week.

Mario looked at Lucy, and she settled the issue. "We won't need the gondola every day, so we will hire it when we need it."

The Villa was not too old, but it was a long way from the main city. There were many interesting trees and hundreds of flowers everywhere. Mario and Lucy were happy to learn that the owner was a Brit who settled there years ago. They would not have to grapple with the Italian language while they were there.

The next day they saw St. Mark's, and they learned that its gold altar was built in 976 and moved in 1100 from Constantinople. Each day they visited a different *momento* (an opportune time). Day Teo was the Doge's Palace, which had paintings by Tintoretto and

Veronese. Our *Academia della belle Arte* (Academy of Fine Arts) and the Saints John and Paul Church—built about the 13th century.

They usually ate the *Menu Turistico* (tourist menu) which was five or six courses for a fixed price. That night they ate veal *alla Milanese*, *baccala* (dried Cod) with polenta, penne, salad and espresso.

When they returned to their hotel, they met the owners, Robert and Elaine Manchester. They were typical Brits: reserved, soft spoken, and they mastered their kind of English. After talking with them for a while, Mario remembered an old expression: that the UK and the US are divided by a common language. But they were both kind and quite proper. They were both from East Anglia, where the Americans were just beginning to create bomber bases. Because they were in Italy, they did not experience the terrible fires in London, although they both had families who were there.

Mario told Lucy, "We are fortunate to be able to ask them about places to visit."

When they related where they had already been, they quickly said, "Oh, you must visit the three main islands of *Murano, Burano* and *Torcello.*" They explained that *Murano* is the closest island to Venice and is famous for its glassmaking industry, with pieces known for its particular colors and exquisite chandeliers.

They added, "Visit a typical glass factory and watch a '*maestro*' working on an artistic glass piece."

The most beautiful and interesting island, according to their assessment, was *Burano*, where one can find many of the fishermen's houses painted in pastel colors, and where you can examine their famous hand-made laces. Be sure, they added, "You have your camera ready because you would not want to miss this photo opportunity."

The Milanos learned that the third island, *Torcello,* is situated just behind *Burano*. It is famous for its cathedral, which has spectacular Byzantine gold and stone mosaics. They were advised to "not miss exploring this magical island, especially its ancient monuments and the *Ponticello del Diavolo* (Devil's Little Bridge), where the ancients believed that the ancient bridges were constructed with the help of the Devil."

When they headed toward their bedroom, Mario told Lucy he was surprised that they did not mention the Jews of these islands. Beginning in 1516, the Republic ordered the Jews to live only in areas of the city where their foundries were located, and they had to wear a sign of identification if they wanted to manage any of the pawnshops. The first Jews to comply with the decree were the Ashkenazim, who came from Eastern Europe. They gave us a new word. The Venetian word for school was Scole which can be compared with the Yiddish "shul," and the English "school."

In 1797, Napoleon ended the Jewish segregation as Venice was annexed to the Italian Kingdom. But in September 1938, the promulgation of the fascist racial laws deprived the Jews of civil rights, and the Jewish began another difficult period under Adolf Hitler. In September 1943, Italy changed from being an ally of Nazi Germany into an occupied country, and the Nazis started a systematic hunt for Jews in Venice as in other Italian cities.

Lucy was very impressed with her new husband's knowledge. "How do you know all of this?" she asked Mario.

"There are two answers: My father told me about all these Jews when I was a young boy, but I had to learn more about them when I started in law school."

The honeymooners did visit the Island of *Murano*, and it was as beautiful as the Brits had told them. Ellen bought a piece of *Murano* glass that was small but stunning. It looked like a number of ocean waves.

They undressed, and he suggested "Amore." But she told him she was too tired, so they both nodded off quickly. In the morning, they realized their marvelous honeymoon was ending. They took the entire day to pack and put all their things they had bought into the luggage. Mario thought it might take a Houdini, but Lucy managed it all.

When they got very friendly with one of the museum employees, he was very anxious to talk about the problems of Venice. He began by saying that Venice is very lovely, but it is being destroyed by all the hordes of sightseers. One writer called it a "tourist monoculture," which he blamed on the giant tourist cruise ships. Visitors take hundreds of photographs, but they will not replace the parts of the city that are barely able to survive. It was estimated that the city needed $5 billion to save all of the decaying structures. If they cannot be saved, Venice will become a story of photographs of things past.

They thanked him for this discouraging analysis, and they slipped him a few liras for his tapestry of sad memories.

The trip home was not spectacular, but they were very happy for what they had seen and done. They left Venice for Ravenna, which was past the Po River valley, and got back to *Firenze* (Florence).

On the way, they had another interesting episode. As Mario drove up and down the mountains (they are really hills), the car began to sputter. It stopped on a hill in sight of a small town—*Borgo San Orenzo*. He walked to the bottom of the hill where he found a garage and asked a mechanic if anyone spoke English, because he wasn't sure of the right words in Italian for auto parts.

He took Mario upstairs to a young girl, where he learned that she knew about ten words of English, including hello, Coca Cola, and goodbye. He went back and explained to the mechanic that the Fiat was just up the road. The Italian went up, pushed it down into the garage, opened the hood, and set the points (I think he called them *pontini*). He charged 2,000 lira (about $2.00).

They arrived in Florence at five p.m.—a bad time. It was a madhouse. He told Lucy to stay in the car, which he parked on the sidewalk. There were no vacancies anywhere. When he asked why, he was told that there were 27 American universities that had art programs there, and classes were still on. They finally got a *pensione* (a small place) near the *stazione termine* (train station).

When he rejoined Lucy, they visited the *Ufizzi Galleria* to see the Michelangelos, the Raffaellos, and da Vincis. What a stunning display of art. They walked over to the *Ponte Vecchio* (old bridge) to see some of the most amazing and exquisite gold shapes in the world.

Mario bought his new wife a gold ring with four emeralds. She was delighted.

They made it back to Rome and Boston without any problems. Lucy moved in with Mario, leaving Ellen alone. She also had to inform Anne Schmitt about her decision. Lucy had to quickly become a housewife, as well as a student. Because of this duality, each hour of the day was precious for both Lucy and Mario.

39

BLACKS NEAR FRANKLIN ZOO

It seemed fortuitous that the day after they returned from Europe that a local newspaper had a long story of the blacks who live near the Franklin Zoo. Mario read the article carefully, because when he attended Boston English High School, which was nearby, he was on the track team, which was almost one-half black. His best friend in high school was a black boy, William Berry, who beat him all the time.

Mario was concerned about the high unemployment rate, especially among sixteen to nineteen-year-old African American males. He wondered what was their future and the future of their children.

He asked himself *what can we do about it?* Then he remembered that in the Great Depression, when young men couldn't find jobs, they stayed in high school. But today these unemployed are not staying in high school longer. They could do well by taking training in vocational courses or by enrolling in community colleges.

The *Boston Globe* story began with William, who was living with his mother who was not well. The article said he had never seen his father. He talked often about his dysfunctional family. He was not proud of it, but he wanted to convey the plight of all the dudes in that neighborhood, as he called them. As he told me more than once, these people are the legacy of slavery. This terrible living can deliver poor diets and bad results in school. William always wanted to improve conditions, but his brother and many others were killed over minor squabbles.

Some of his friends had unreal ambitions. He told of one woman who looked about sixty but who was really in her middle thirties. She could barely read, but she wanted to become a medical doctor.

William decided that he had to break away from this environment. His first move was to stop selling drugs and getting a job at McDonald's. It was a grueling schedule. He missed several days of high school because he had to work the early shift, and he had to take care of his very sick mother.

But one of his teachers felt sorry for him. She knew what he was trying to do, so she volunteered to help. She was known as Miss Sowell. When she started with him, his grade point average was surely not high enough to get into any college. First, she got him medical coverage that included his mother, and she made sure he was saving a large part of his McDonald salary.

Gradually, his life changed. He began to care for his mother, and his grade point rose slowly to 2.5. Miss Sowell signed him up for a special project that could lead to a college scholarship.

She taunted him saying, "You were the person who said that black boys had no opportunities. Well, here is your chance." By the end of his senior year, his average was a high C, which was enough for him to be admitted to a community college.

During the graduation ceremony, William was asked to speak to the class. He thanked Miss Sowell, who had spent so many hours with him, and he preached that guns and drugs and violence would never be sufficient to meet life's challenge. He finished by saying he would need a better job to pay for all his expenses, and he was going to get one.

40

MARIO'S LAST CASES

One evening, when Lucy was finished speaking, Mario told her that he had nearly completed his law school program. Lucy asked him, "What are you doing in school now?"

He told her, "You are lucky, because today we debated a case that involved Harvard University. It is about what we call affirmative action for higher education. The case involves whether Harvard University discriminates against foreign applicants."

The University responded by saying that diversity is not just about race. It deals with geography and social class. It does not have any quotas. Unfortunately, the history goes back to 1636, which means that current policies reflect the prejudices of society. One of the Lowells refused to admit Jews. Today, about one-half of the enrollments is white.

Lucy found that interesting. "Did you deal with any other interesting cases?" she asked.

Mario hesitated, then he answered. "We had one other interesting discussion, but it was not a case."

Lucy was always interested in his studies. "I would love to hear about it."

"We were discussing how undemocratic policies were becoming

popular, and the professor quoted George Orwell, who wrote in 1940: 'Human beings don't only want comfort, safety, short working-hours, hygiene ... they also want struggle and self-sacrifice, not to mention drums, flags, and loyal-parades.'"

"What does all that mean?" she broke in.

"It means that our democratic system is deeply flawed," he told her. "But it also means that if the current system is not reformed, it could lead to violent solutions."

41

THE HARVARD CLUB

Mario was reading his mail one day when he came upon an invitation from the Harvard Club of Boston. There was plenty of time to consider it because the event was two weeks later.

He asked Lucy if she had any interest in attending. She said "yes" quickly, and she said, "We need to know more about these events."

Mario told her, "I'll take care of that."

Two days later, he gave her all the details. He told her, "The Harvard Club is old. It was formed in 1908 when 22 Alumni men met to organize the Club, with an annual fee of $5. It was located at 1 Federal Street. In 1909, a scholarship fund was established that granted $200 awards. During the Great Depression, the Club served as an employment agency. It allowed women to dine at the Club in 1940, but they cannot be members. The dress code is casual, and hats must be removed upon entering."

Lucy was very excited, as she said loudly, "Let's go."

Mario tried to reduce her excitement when he told her that the parking fee was $23.

"We can afford that," she told him.

On the designated day, she dressed in a plain white dress with a black necklace, and he wore plain slacks with a black T-shirt and a very light-colored sport coat. They parked at 415 Newberry Street as directed on the information card, and as they entered the large ballroom, they headed straight for a table by a window. Because they were on the 38th floor, their view was truly spectacular.

In a short time, their table was full of other alums. The conversation was chaotic because everyone was speaking at one time.

Soon an orchestra arrived, but no one was dancing. Mario asked his neighbor about it, and he smiled as he said, "It's allowed but no one ever dances."

There were red and white wine bottles at each table. The dinner was superb. It began with a fresh salad, then a lightly browned sirloin steak with a baked Idaho potato, and a scrumptious dessert covered with chocolate and whipped cream.

The man sitting next to Mario was a Massachusetts native, so after Lucy listened to their discussion, she asked Mario to find out how we can learn if her father is still alive.

Mario asked the question, and he answered, "Call the Massachusetts Population Division of the Census Bureau."

Mario thanked him for the useful information before they headed home. When they settled down in the living room, Lucy asked Mario, "Do you think my father will have a telephone?"

After a brief pause, Mario said, "If he does not have one, his sister might. Do we have any telephone books here?"

"Yes," answered Lucy. "The previous owners left several."

"Get the East Boston book, and we can check for Gallos."

She was gone for just minutes, and she told him, "You look up the names."

He went straight to the Gs, and he said, "There are a bunch of Gallos."

She was ready for that response. "See if there is one on Gove Street."

"I don't see one," he said.

She asked him next, "Is there a Nicholas or a Rosina?"

He quickly answered, "No."

Lucy sounded despondent. "They could have gone back to Italy. Or," she told him, "they could have moved to Lynn where my father said he had some *paisini* (persons from the same village) there."

42

GRADUATION

The Law School graduation was separated from the regular ceremony, perhaps because it was intended to show that these were more important individuals. Most of their speakers were members of the U. S. Government. On this day it was Secretary of State Cordell Hull. This man from Tennessee pursued President Roosevelt's "Good Neighbor Policy" with Latin American nations, which has been credited with preventing Nazis from obtaining influence in that region.

He also spoke of the United States foreign relations policies before and during the attack on Pearl Harbor. He was very suspicious of the document that the Japanese sent him, which was formally titled "Outline of proposed Basis for Agreement Between the United States and Japan." We learned soon that it was a deceptive lie. On December 7, 1941, Hull received the news that we were being attacked as the peace talks were taking place. As President Roosevelt described it the next day, "It is a date that will live in infamy." All the newspapers said that Hull's speech was one of the best graduation speeches ever given at Harvard University.

Lucy was sorry she did not attend, but she was very elated at the other news he told her. Because he was so high in his class, he received a job offer he could not refuse. It came from Harry Ruben-stein, the chief prosecutor in the murder case of Professor Eliot from the Harvard Business School.

The next day, Mario talked to his new boss. "How do you think I should start on this case?" he asked Harry, who said "We all use first names here."

Harry was prepared for the question. "I want you to go to that place downtown that they call "The Exercise Room." It's a whore house, and I think it is connected to this murder. Get all the info you can get on it."

43

MARIO'S FIRST ASSIGNMENT

When Mario climbed the stairs to the third floor he saw that it was an elegant place, where the clients could obtain manicures, a steam bath, or they could go to the private beauty parlor. The "Tea" room often served whisky. For those clients who preferred young girls, there were some who were as young as sixteen. Many of the older men asked for these sixteen-year old beauties.

One of these young beauties was named Edna. She was eighteen but looked sixteen. Her young face was clear as almonds, and her eyes were as blue as the deep ocean. But it was her luscious mouth that made her so popular with all the clients of all ages.

Each woman was assigned a room of her own. Jo Ann Kelly chose to make it her second home. In the middle of the room she placed a round oak table, in case the customer wished to talk before getting down to business. It was also a good place for the clients to make out checks or take out their cash. Against the opposite wall, she had an ornate couch delivered. But as some entered the room, the thing that caught their eyes was the very large four-poster bed with a frilly bed cover.

When Mario entered, he met Rose Bianco who talked a good deal about her roommate, Jo Ann. She said that Jo Ann was the most open in her selections of choice.

"Hello, Miss Kelly. I am the Assistant Prosecutor in the case of the Harvard Professor. It appears by your responses that you are a bi-sexual."

Jo Ann paused for a moment. "That may be true, but that is not the whole story. I admit that I enjoy sex of all kinds, but I prefer to choose the man who will provide it. I choose Bob Ryan because our love is quite different. It is deeper and has more meaning than the animal love I get from my clients."

When the madam told Jo Ann to go room six, Mario stopped her. "I have more questions to ask."

Jo Ann told the madam that this person has questions about that Harvard murder. "It won't be long," she promised.

Mario thanked her and got right into his questions. "I understand that Professor Eliot was a client of yours. Is that true?'

"Yes. But he did not come for sex. He paid to just have a conversation."

"Fine," said Mario, "and did he ever mention any other persons in these discussions?"

"Not that I remember."

"Well, I'll come back later," he responded, "when I know a lot more about this case.

When Mario left, Rose was still upset at all these choices, especially the anal entry. She said, "You claim that you are my sweetheart, my only love. When we are together in bed nothing else matters. But don't you think that a family without a father is not complete?" Rose had an answer. "It appears that you really are a bi-sexual."

Jo Ann paused for a moment. "That may be true, but our love is quite different. It is deeper and has more meaning than the animal love I get from Bob."

Rose was satisfied. "Okay. I still love you despite your convoluted approaches to sexual satisfaction."

When the madam told Jo Ann to go room six, she obeyed quickly. In that room she primped for the next customer. When he entered, her heart almost stopped. It was one of her old high school boyfriends. He was older, more mature but still handsome.

He looked as shocked as she. "I'll get another room," he said.

"Oh, you don't need to," she responded quickly.

He gazed at her longingly, then said, "Well, now I know where you ran off to."

"No, no," she said, "I haven't been in this business that long."

"Do you want to continue?' he asked.

"Why not?" she told him, adding, "We did have a lot of fun after high school. Do you remember it?"

"A man never forgets his first lay."

"Is that all you thought of it?" she moaned.

As he wrestled with her quick reply, she perused his stature. He was taller and more filled in. For a second she desired him, but then he jolted her. "I thought it was overrated."

"For your information," she said, "I am a lesbian."

The words coming out of her mouth really shocked him. "I don't understand how you can be so sexually dead now when you were so sexually alive when you were younger. Do you remember *Lady Chatterley's Lover,* which we read in English Lit, in which Lawrence wrote, "What is c---t but machine f---king—its all alike. Pay them money to cut off the world's cock."

"Do you think lesbians are worse than homosexual men?" she asked.

He responded quickly. "Yes, I do. When I uncover a lesbian woman, I want to have nothing to do with her because she is wasting her body. When I think of it, my blood rises. I cannot comprehend how she can complete the sex act. I want to leave her and hide."

Then she remembered who and what she was. "Let's get on with it," she told him. "I need the money."

"Can I have your phone number?"

"No. I'd get fired if I gave it to you. Even if I could, I wouldn't give it for free. I have to pay the rent and buy groceries."

As they prepared for the episode he had paid for, she remembered an English assignment on Bacchus, the carouser that they studied and which led eventually to the loss of her virginity. He led her from being a private to a sensuous woman. That episode became a part of a larger one that made her change from taking other guys to bed to Rose.

Returning to his office, Mario told Harry what he had learned. "Many of the older men ask for these sixteen-year old beauties. Each woman was assigned a room of her own." He continued telling Harry how Jo Ann described some of her episodes. "She claims that nothing hurts her, because she is paid for all of them."

44

MEETING OF SEXUAL ABNORMALITIES

When Mario saw Harry reading an advertisement about a meeting of the Association of Sexual Abnormalities, he was surprised when Harry said he decided to attend it. Fortunately, he found a group that meets once per week to discuss this very problem. He registered and attended his first meeting.

The speaker began by asking what are the causes of lesbianism? She began her answer by stating that there is no homosexual gene, so the answer must be environmental factors, such as upbringing, an absent mother, or affectionate father. Mothers typically have an advantage whereby they usually interact more with their children. However, homosexuals bring some mothers and sons even closer. This seemed truer for mothers.

When the lecture was over, Rubenstein interviewed many of the mothers. One mother recalled that her homosexual son, Jack, is definitely the closest of her three sons. She said that they always had a special bond.

The speaker told another view of mother and daughter. She told those present that the relationship between mother and daughter has always been the strongest and the best with anyone in her family, so it was always wonderful. One woman said she respected me very much for whom I was, and she gave me more respect than she gave to my brothers.

Nevertheless, this closeness could have a down side, at least temporarily, as many mothers initially blame themselves and these close relationships for their sons' homosexuality. It seems that feeling guilty is an inevitable component of mothering. Mothers take the blame when anything goes wrong with their children, even if it is not their fault. As a matter of fact, mothers often find themselves feeling guilty when nothing is wrong. It is not surprising that once they learned their sons are homosexual, they felt that they had done something to damage them, which was not true.

At this point, Rubenstein raised his hand.

"Yes, what is it?" she asked.

"Do you know if there is more or less crime among homosexuals?"

"First," the woman answered, "remember that murders with excessive violence are naturally associated with other forms of social pathology. Homosexuals, prostitutes, and alcoholics are more apt to be violent. Homosexual leaders claim that they are not pathological, rebellious, or sexually deviant. They contend that they are gentle, loving people. But homosexuals account for 3-4% of all gonorrhea cases and 60% of all syphilis cases. This is the result of unhealthy lifestyles and have historically accounted for the bulk of syphilis, gonorrhea, Hepatitis B, and the bowel syndrome, which may result from anal sex.

"Their lifestyle causes other problems: 25-33% of homosexuals and lesbians are alcoholics, and 43% admit to 500 or more partners in a lifetime, 28% admit to 1000 or more in a lifetime, and 79% say that half of those partners are total strangers. There are more ominous statistics. A Judge of the New York City Criminal Court said, "Homosexuals account for half the murders in large cities," and a captain of the Los Angeles Police was quoted as saying that, "30,000 sexually abused children in Los Angeles were victims of homosexuals. The median age of death of homosexuals is 42, the median age of death of a married heterosexual woman is 79. Homosexuals are 100 times more likely to be murdered (usually by another homosexual), and 50% of suicides can be attributed to homosexuals. What is worse is that there is a notable homosexual group, consisting of thousands of members, known as the North American Man and Boy Love Association (NAMBLA). This is a child-molesting homosexual group whose motto is "Sex Before 8 Before It's Too Late." This group can be seen marching in most major homosexual parades across the United States.

"The love between men and boys seems to be the very foundation of homosexuality. These homosexuals say that they are gay people, which is why they are called gay. But this skirts a major grammatical problem. Since the time of Shakespeare, the word gay meant joyous, merry, lively and happy. In recent times, we saw the titles of books reflect those conditions. For example, "Our Hearts Were Young and Gay" and "The Gay Divorcee." What can we tell our grandchildren now when they ask, 'What does gay mean?'

"Hollywood may have given homosexuals their name. In the 1938 movie *Bringing Up Baby*, when Cary Grant puts on a dress, Katherine Hepburn asks him, "Why are you wearing these clothes?" He answered, "Because I just went gay all of a sudden."

"So what can we tell our grandchildren now when they ask, 'What does gay mean?" Does it mean that they are queer? And how do we explain when men are loving men?"

45

THE SCIENCE OF HOMOSEXUALITY

After leaving the meeting, Harry Rubenstein felt that he was right about a link between homosexuals and crime. He thanked the speaker for the statistics, and he headed back to his office to share them with Mario Milano.

But Rubenstein needed more answers to the question: was Charles Eliot a bi-sexual? So, he visited a psychologist who told him, "It doesn't mean you date two persons at the same time. It just means that you are attracted to both men and women. Personally, if I find myself attracted to both sexes, I am completely faithful to the one I am in a relationship with. I would never cheat on anyone if I was attracted to someone else. Some people say they are just greedy and like the best of both worlds. I have known other bisexuals who have a boyfriend and a girlfriend at once. This is not a problem if all parties are accepting this arrangement."

Rubenstein was not happy with this definition, but it didn't seem to indicate that Eliot was bi-sexual. That left him with just one more question: is homosexuality inherited? He knew there were some scientists who are searching for a Gay Gene. They are watching fruit flies and other animals for the origin of homosexuality.

Dogs, cats, rabbits, rats, and other small animals all show some aspects of homosexual behavior. The male fruit fly touches a male partner, licking its genitalia, and curling its body to allow more genital contact. But some scientists believe that it is a dangerous leap to extrapolate observations from fruit flies to humans.

Scientists who study homosexuality believe that this subject is treated from prejudice, myth, and dishonest research. They offer examples of analysts who believe that homosexuals are perverts and neurotic, or that homosexuals produce other homosexuals in the same way that drug addicts produce other drug addicts. By calling homosexuals deviants, many analysts believe that they cannot be helped, thereby leaving the homosexuals to eschew treatment. Some physicians now believe that most homosexuals can be successfully treated by psychotherapy.

Researchers who seek answers by analyzing human sex chromosomes are convinced that genes that determine the sex of individuals can also tell which ones may be homosexuals. Men have both X and Y chromosomes, while women have two X chromosomes. Can a male sex-determining gene, which is found on the Y chromosome, predict the homosexuality of males? This leaves those who are researching females in a quandary. Since the female has no Y chromosome, she lacks this masculinizing gene. Rubenstein was very disappointed in the conclusions of all this research.

46

FINDING A NEW HOME

When Mario went home, he had other news that would delight his new bride. Because of the salary they offered him, he and Lucy could afford to live on Beacon Hill, the most historic neighborhood in Boston. Beacon Hill is a neighborhood of Federal-style row houses and is famous for its narrow, gas-lit streets and brick sidewalks. It is regarded as one of the most expensive neighborhoods in Boston because it is near the Massachusetts State House, and it is bound by Storrow Drive, and it is situated along the riverfront of the Charles River Esplanade, just north of Boston Common and the Boston Public Garden.

Lucy was so excited she threw herself on him and kissed him several times, before he stopped her.

"When do we move in?" she asked him.

"Wait a minute," he told her. "We haven't even picked out a place yet."

"Well," she responded," why can't we do it right now?"

"It's not so simple," he answered. "We have to make an appointment with the agent first. I will call her, and I will make arrangements for our visit. It may take a few days. They will probably want to check my credit history."

Lucy snapped him back to reality. 'What will I do with Ellen Bayard? I just can't leave her alone. She has done so much for me. David had an affair with a beautiful woman in the neighborhood. When the gossip flew around the area, he was about to marry her. All his friends told him she was not a good prospect, so he ditched her. They all said it was good riddance. Do you have any suggestions?"

Mario recited some common law, which applies because most wives do not have jobs. For this reason, the husband is obliged to provide his wife with "necessaries"—which includes food, clothing, and shelter. Criminal nonsupport statutes were created to prevent men and women from becoming public charges, which applies especially upon the dissolution of a marriage.

Mario continued, "Wives are at a disadvantage as property owners. Under common law, her personal possessions were considered to be the property of her husband. Women did not have the right to own property until the mid-nineteenth century. This "Married Women's Property Act" allowed women the right to enter contracts, sell land, write wills, sue and be sued, work and to work without their husband's permission, and they could keep their earnings.

"The situation is complicated by divorce, because some states have Community Property laws, which call for an equitable distribution of property. In all the other states, the rule is that each person owns whatever items are in his or her name. In this case, neither spouse can sell the property independently. But if the husband or wife dies, the remaining spouse has full survivorship rights. If a husband or wife dies intestate (without leaving a will), statutes provide for the surviving spouse to acquire a specified portion of the decedent's property.

"A statute might, for example, prescribe that the surviving spouse can acquire a one-half interest in the estate. The size of the portion depends on whether there are surviving children."

He tried to settle one issue quickly. "You wouldn't want Ellen to live with us, would you?"

Lucy felt obliged to help. "Why can't we take her into our house? She took me in."

Mario answered quickly. "We would have no spare bedroom, not on Beacon Hill."

Lucy accepted the notion that they could not help her financially, but she told Mario that Ellen can do the cooking, the house cleaning, and all the things she does now. "As you know, David claimed most of their assets."

Mario meditated for a minute, then he said, "This is why it is a disadvantage to have no children. Most parents rely on their children when they are old or when they have a financial problem."

"But Mario," Lucy said loudly, "this is not her fault. He had the barren seeds."

"That is true," Mario countered. "But we will not have any money left over if we move to Beacon Hill."

Lucy stopped his discussion. "She saved my life. She told me something that she has not disclosed until now. David has been abusing her for some time, and he has been using that hussy for sexual pleasures. He told Ellen constantly that she is of no use in bed. She showed me all of her bruises, and they were ugly."

Mario insisted that "Ellen must get a lawyer who can determine channels which assets must be shared."

Not too long after this discussion, there was good news about Ellen. Her loss of husband was debilitating, so she had to take medicine. When she felt better, she sought and obtained a job as secretary and copywriter for the World Publishing Company. It was clear quickly to her bosses that she was very intelligent, so she started her occupational rise. In a brief time, she was elected vice president.

In working closely with a man of approximately her age, they were physically attracted and started talking marriage. She is not sure she is able to marry yet, but Lucy is happy that she has found someone who loves her.

47

LUCY AS A SOPHOMORE

Lucy returned to campus in time to start choosing classes for her second year. She first selected American Literature (her specialty), and then she added American History, Political Science, European Art, and the required Algebra.

She was very pleased to read that the instructor in American Literature was Charles Eliot—a leader in the field, but then she realized that he was dead and lying in the morgue.

Lucy asked the secretary who would replace Eliot, and she said it was David Johnson. When she investigated his approach, she was happy to learn that he stressed the earliest American period, especially the poets of the New England group who dominated literary America. James Russell Lowell and Henry Wadsworth Longfellow were products of the New England colleges. They were the "Boston gentlemen of the early Renaissance." Later Robert Frost's "North of Boston" was evidence that he was a native from a lonely farmhouse, where he could gaze upon brooks and mountains. This sad poet became a poet of the people.

In dealing with modern poetry, Johnson praised Archibald MacLeish who wrote, "The poet, with the adjustment of a phrase, with the contrast of an image, with the rhythm of a line, has fixed a focus, which all the talk, and all the staring of the world, has been unable to fix before him. He applied this approach to the writings of E. E. Cummings, Stanley Kunitz and Robert T. S. Lowell, all Massachusetts natives."

David Johnson believed that the talent of success is nothing more than doing what you can do well, and he stressed Longfellow who was probably the best loved of American poets in his time, and his lines are still familiar today.

He told the class that we still remember Longfellow's poems because they have the felicity of easy rhymes, and they are imbued with a natural grace and song. Longfellow's approach to poetry was completely new. Van Wycks Brooks called Longfellow's time "the flowering of New England." Longfellow hobnobbed with Nathaniel Hawthorne, Ralph Waldo Emerson, Henry David Thoreau, and Oliver Wendell Holmes.

Longfellow wrote his first volumes of poetry, including "Voices of the Night" (1839) and "Evangeline: A Tale of Acadians" (1847), which depicts the expulsion of these French Acadians from their homes in Nova Scotia and New Brunswick.

In a later lecture, Professor Johnson turned to the 20th century, when he began speaking about Edward Estlin Cummings, (who always signed his works e. e. cummings). He is often linked with Walt Whitman and Robert Frost as the three most loved American poets; but Cummings was certainly the most difficult to understand. Johnson called Cummings "an American original," because his poetry is distinctly American and because he writes of his American experience in ways that show he is from American roots and American history.

48

LUCY GRADUATES

When Lucy graduated from Harvard University, it nearly corresponded with what might have been Helen and David's twenty-fifth wedding anniversary. Lucy was anxious to commemorate the occasion, but what could she do as they were about to break up?

She tried to learn as much as she could about the years before she joined the family. When she uncovered a scandal concerning David, their dating was not a passionate event. But they had more in common and as the years flew by, their love was smoother, but it did not offer more happiness.

When Lucy learned of the coming surprise anniversary dinner, she decided that she had to write a poem for the occasion. She knew Ellen would be overjoyed at the event. David was going to buy her something made of silver. Lucy decided it had to be a poem about the ocean, because they spent many days on one of Delaware's beaches.

It was a relatively quiet evening at the restaurant, with about a dozen persons in attendance. David was at his best as he spoke of his growing love for his wife. He enumerated all of her great qualities, and he delivered a sterling silver vanity set for her bedroom dresser.

Then he really shocked her, when the minister who had married them showed up to duplicate the wedding ceremony. Some eyes were foggy and wet.

When everyone had settled down, Lucy arose from her place to speak. "I cannot find adequate words to express my thanks to David and Ellen for adopting me when I was alone at twelve years of age in a country where I did not speak the language. I love them truly as if there are my real parents. I have composed a poem that I call "By the Ocean." I know how much they love the Delaware beaches. So here it is:

The ocean seethes under ominous skies
        The pounding surf enrapts
   The plaint of lover's eyes.
   Where the dipping wind flicks
   The rising tide; it is warm:
   Within my Ellen's salt-wet neck
   And involuting arms.
   Framed in my gaze like a saw-tooth gear
   Her breast dissects a lonely sail
   That tumbles, disappears
   In the ocean's veil.
   A gull with striding sways
   Compliments our unity.
   We are in passionate array,
   The wings, my Ellen and me.
   The tide has gone and sky is low,
   The ship is pointed to the vane,
   The gull has traveled where birds go
   Now only we remain."

Lucy could not contain her tears as her parents hugged and kissed her. "That was beautiful," they each said. "We will cherish it."

49

LUCY'S BIRTHDAY PRESENT

When Lucy's birthday approached, Ellen and David were at a stalemate as to what to buy her. Ellen found a perfect solution. "Why don't we take her back to where she was born?"

"Oh, that's a great idea," said David. "She must have some relatives who are still alive. I'll get the airline tickets, and we'll need a rental car, because as she told us, she was born on the eastern coast."

On May 4, 1942, he got three tickets for May 11th. When they told her on her birthday, she was flabbergasted.

"Wow," she said. "I'll be able to find my birthplace and maybe some cousins. I don't know if I can still speak Italian. It's been over ten years. But some of it might come back as I hear more of it."

When the given day arrived, they loaded the La Salle and headed for BWI Airport. The flight to Rome was excellent. They got free wine, a movie, and had turkey breast with peas. They arrived at Rome at 9:10 a.m. They got some Lira and picked up a rental FIAT and headed southeasterly through Molise, into Puglia and Bari. They saw that the Romans made most roads very straight.

Driving in Italy is not like driving in the USA, because the Italians use their lights and horns when they are coming toward you. They blink their lights when coming, and they use horns when passing.

Bari was much bigger than they thought. They got rooms at the Hotel Boston and did some sightseeing. There was a castle in the middle of town, and the cathedral was built in the 12th century. They were informed that Santa Claus originated there, because Saint Nicholas is the patron Saint of children and sailors.

Back on the road the following day, they headed for Santeramo en Colle (which means Saint Erasmus on a hill), about 26 miles from Bari. When they arrived, they went to the Comune (the city hall) to find Lucy's exact date and place of birth.

At Lucy's birthplace, the street was clean. But there was not much anyone could do, so it is easy to see why so many young people left. They could not find any relatives, so they left to go to Salerno. This drive would take them over the Amalfi Coast Road—one of the most spectacular rides of a lifetime. There were curves, hills, beaches and many trees. In some places the road was not wide enough for the automobile, so they rode on air on one side. There were no proper words to describe the beauty of the man-made and natural objects that melded along the coast.

They continued on to Gaeta on the Appian Way. They stopped at a very large stone beside the road that had CXX carved on it. This means it was built in the year 120.

Their final stop was Fiumicino Airport, where they confirmed the trip home. They had reservations at the Titziano Hotel, where they registered and cleaned up. Next, they walked the Via del Corso (the shopping street of Rome). After the long driving day, they were happy to walk for hours. They passed the Pantheon and continued on to the Via Vittorio Emanuello, where they stumbled into an amazing print shop. It had prints from the 1500s to the present. They bought two prints of the last century.

As the evening approached, they decided to eat at the Tre Scalini (three steps) restaurant in the Piazza Navone. It was closed for renovations, so they ate at the Quartro Fiume (four rivers) Restaurant. It is nearly impossible to find a bad restaurant in Italy. They all ordered the same: Tortelini in brodo (macaroni soup) and Melanzani alla Parmigiano (eggplant with parmesan cheese).

On the following day, they walked to Vatican City to see Saint Peter's Church and the Sistine Chapel. The Chapel ceiling has to be the most amazing painting man ever created, because Michelangelo painted it on a scaffold on his back.

When they prepared to leave Italy, they discussed what they had seen in these two weeks. It was more spectacular than they ever imagined. After landing in the United States, David calculated that they had flown almost 7,000 miles and drove 1500 miles. It would be difficult to plan a better trip.

50

LUCY FINDS EMPLOYMENT

After one of his presentations on poetry, Professor Johnson asked Lucy to stay after class for a minute. When the room was emptied, he said, "Miss Bayard." (He did not know she was married.) "You seem to have a very good command of what poetry really is, so do you think you could help me with grading papers and other clerical things?"

Lucy thought *This is the answer to my prayers. Now I can help Ellen with some of the costs of my education.*

"I'd love to," she answered him.

"Well, then," he said. "You take a taxi to my home. Here is the address on this card. You tell the driver I will pay the fare."

She went directly to his house, which was also along the Charles River, where she met the housekeeper. Lucy asked her if Mr. Johnson is difficult to work with. She did not hesitate. "Oh no, he is a very gentle person."

Lucy noticed that everything was in order, and she remembered her mother telling her that an orderly house depicts an orderly mind.

While Lucy often gloated over her new employment, MaryAnn sped through pre-school, kindergarten, and the early grades. She seemed able to grasp most concepts in mathematics, so she was well prepared for grades six, seven, and eight. She was using the living room couch as her bed, but now that she is on the edge of womanhood, Maria had to deal with this problem.

Lucy told Maria that the obvious answer is to move into a two- or three-bedroom apartment or house, and she volunteered to help her find a better job to pay for the extra rent.

Mario had a better solution. "If we are all going to pay more rent, we might as well buy a house with the same dollars."

Lucy showed her exuberance by jumping at him, "Do you really think we can buy a house?" she asked.

He replied, "I am sure there is a house somewhere in Boston that we can buy, but it won't be on Beacon Hill. There would be a big advantage in buying in East Boston. The prices would be lower, and Maria would have Aunt Rosina nearby. She could watch her niece for us if we both work."

Lucy said, "That would be fine with me. There would be good subway service anywhere in "Eastie.""

They began their search immediately. They told the real estate agent that they had to have at least three bedrooms.

She answered quickly. "I have just the thing for you. There is a three-story house on Sumner Street just two blocks from the Maverick subway stop. The price is right, and you will have several bedrooms so you can increase your family as you desire."

When she mentioned the price, Mario told her that it was in their neighborhood of prices. He signed the bill of sale and gave her a down payment. She told him that the paperwork would take a few days, and they could move right in because the house was empty.

When the Milanos brought their meager furniture to Sumner Street, they realized that they had much more space than they needed. As they grappled with the placement of things, a man approached them. He said, "Welcome to the neighborhood. My name is Rico Capriani. My wife's name is Rita, and we have two children."

"How old are they?" asked Mario.

"The boy is in high school, and the girl is in junior high."

"Does the boy go to East Boston High?"

"Sure," answered Rico. "It's free, and it's within walking distance. Rita wants to know if you could join us for coffee after dinner."

"That's very kind of you, but we have a lot to do this weekend because I have to be at work on Monday." he told Rico. "We would love to accept it some other time."

"We understand," he responded. "And what do you for a living?" he asked.

"I am an Assistant Prosecutor on a murder case."

"Wow," exclaimed Rico. "We'll have to be careful of what we say around here now."

Mario smiled as he exited. "We'll see you later."

As they placed most things on one floor, they realized that they would have one floor completely vacant.

They seemed to have got the same idea at the same time. "Why don't we rent it to Maria?" asked Lucy."

She was ecstatic about how things were working out, but she had a different problem. The 8th grade as all mothers know is the start of the worry period. Lucy wanted to help MaryAnn choose a good high school. Of course, she has Boston Latin in mind. Can she get in? Can she do the hard work? Can they afford the tuition?

She is buoyed by one statistic from a brochure: fifty-five percent of the students were girls. The Boston Latin students achieve a high proficiency in mathematics and English, so this might be a place for MaryAnn. It was a short distance on the subway from Maverick Square to Boston Latin.

Mario and Lucy visited Maria to discuss what school MaryAnn might attend. He told her of the one hundred percent proficiencies in mathematics and English, and that seventy-three percent of the students were free to join the social clubs.

MaryAnn responded, "The public schools are free, they have high ratings, and they are close by. You are paying for these schools with your high real estate taxes. There are three schools not too far from us that have good ratings: The Newman School on Marlborough Avenue, The Commonwealth School on Commonwealth Avenue, and MITed on Massachusetts Avenue."

Mario commended her for her good research and said, "Let's wait to see if you are accepted at Boston Latin."

Maria had other worries. How would she ever pay for the tuition? She decided that Mary Ann would attend East Boston High.

For a while Philip felt neglected as his parents seemed obsessed with his new sister. But whenever Phil's name came up at dinner, his proud father would say, "He has got to go to MIT."

But as the years flew by, it was clear that Philip Milano wanted first to attend Boston Latin School. He was a mathematical genius. When he completed every course with the highest grades, Philip was both glad and sad.

When Lucy read the list of famous alumni of Boston Latin, she was more than proud of her Philip. She could not believe the names as she read them: Benjamin Franklin, Samuel Adams, John Hancock, Ralph Waldo Emerson, George Santayana, Joseph P. Kennedy, and Leonard Bernstein. She knew her son was going to be someone famous.

51

SUNDAY TOURS

Mario knew that the Milanos needed to learn more about their new neighborhood, so he continued something that he called "Sunday Touring." After church and breakfast, they were to visit a new place each week.

Mario knew about the project to enlarge Logan Airport, and he could see the trucks going by day and night, so Tour Number Two was to the airport. When they got there, they were told that three years ago there was only one hangar and two airplanes. Now, several airlines were building new facilities, and commercial flights were multiplying almost daily. They all agreed it was an impressive project.

During the week, Lucy did housework and when MaryAnn returned from school, they took a stroll to learn the neighborhood. Getting to Maverick Square, they could walk in several directions. On this day, she chose to head up Meridian Street. When they passed the Columbia Trust Company, they knew that Joseph Kennedy was there running that bank. When he was not busy, he usually greeted school children on the sidewalk. They noticed that he wore a large rubber band around his sleeves because, at that time, manufacturers made all sleeves one size.

Continuing up Meridian they came to a very large area, which she learned later was the commercial center of East Boston. There was the Kennedy Coffee Company, the Chicken House, where customers could purchase live chickens, and just a few doors down was the Goodman Furniture store.

In the middle of this area was a large park with benches, and just to its left was the Central Square Community Center, where the dancing of teenagers lasted from seven to midnight every weekend.

Lucy was impressed with all the activities, but she did not know that the Central Square Library was just a half block away on Bremen Street. She did learn of its existence later, and she became a steady client with her children.

52

RICO DISCUSSES IMMIGRANTS

When Mario arrived home from work the next day, he found Rico on the sidewalk sitting on an old chair.

"Hey, Mario, how the hell are you?" he greeted him loudly.

Mario knew that Rico wanted a discussion. "Good. What are we talking about today?"

Rico was prepared. "I keep reading about all the bigwigs who want to limit the number of immigrants who can come to the United States. They seem to ignore that writing on the Statue of Liberty about greeting the "Huddled Masses." Do you know that Benjamin Franklin called the German immigrants "the most stupid of their nation? And do you know that the Immigration Act of 1924 was written to limit the number of Italians coming to this country. The Italian government was actually paying the poor Southern Italians to leave Italy. Those who left went to three places: one-third went to Argentina; one third went to Germany, and one-third came to the United States."

Mario had his doubts about the veracity of all these statements. He told Rico, "But we have been treated fairly well here."

"Oh sure," said Rico. "Eleven Italians were lynched when they arrived in New Orleans, and the Ku Klux Klan went after all Italians. The head of the Klan said that the Italians were worse than the blacks."

Mario had to respond. "These statements may be true, but spaghetti has been the number one food in the United States for years. It's now as American as a hot dog. I have to go now to see my beautiful wife."

"Hey, Rico," said Mario. "Do you know the joke about the woman who works in a meat market?"

"No," said Rico. What did she say?"

"She gave him the cold shoulder," he answered.

"Let's talk again later," Rico said as he went upstairs.

Mario told his family that they were visiting again on the Sabbath. The next morning, he said, "We are heading for Revere Beach."

After church and breakfast, they boarded a street car for Revere. It was not a long ride with stops at Orient Heights, Beachmont, and Revere. They got off at Revere Street, which was a short distance to the boardwalk.

Mario insisted on telling his family of the history of Revere Beach, which was the first public beach in the United States when it was established in 1896. This creation followed the establishment of the Boston & Lynn Railroad in 1875.

The beach is four and a half miles long, and it was built as a recreation for the working class. Especially for immigrants. The favorite attraction was the Cyclone, one of the largest roller coasters in the United States. On its final downward plunge, it travels at fifty miles per hour.

There were several places young children could enjoy. One was the Dodgem, which was a number of small automobiles that had bumpers on the front and back so that the children could bump each other. There were other places where the young contestants could aim a baseball at a target or put a large ball into a hole in the wall.

Mario wanted to get to an adult act, so he gave the children money so they could choose their kind of entertainment. Then he and Lucy went to observe the dance marathon. They were a huge hit, and the winners received a large payoff.

The rules were often called sadistic because the participants could not fall asleep. Some of them danced for twenty-four to twenty-eight hours. Later, one partner was allowed to sleep as long as they kept dancing. Spectators paid twenty-five cents to watch this torture.

The whole purpose was "Dance until you drop." Couples tried every device to stay awake. Some used kicking if a partner dozed off. Others used ice packs to the neck, and some used smelling salts. Although this torture was appealing to spectators, by 1935 most states banned these contests because of health factors.

On the return voyage to East Boston, most family members were pleased with Mario's choice of a family tour. The next Sunday, Mario chose a trip on the East Boston Ferry. He did his usual research on the origin of the ferries. East Boston was originally several islands.

The main island was Noddle Island. But in the 19th century, General W. H. Sumner Incorporated the East Boston Company, which joined five islands by landfilling. The Logan Airport was the largest landfill in East Boston history, but it was completed much later. Because of its water surroundings, Boston depended on its ferries. The East Boston ferry left from Lewis Street and landed at Atlantic Avenue in downtown Boston.

As the Milano's walked along Marginal Street, they saw the remnants of several manufacturing companies. There was the Metal Works and Foundry, the National Ice Cream Company (which was famous for its Fudgesicles and Eskimo Pies), and there was the Famous Goddess Bra Factory along the waterfront.

Mario told his family that, "There are two ferries, and they are used for different purposes. The North Ferry is for passengers only, while the South Ferry accommodates commercial traffic."

Mario paid his fares, and they boarded the ferry. It was not full. As the captain revved his engine, the water started swirling around the boat and it seemed to turn yellow. The roundtrip passage was cool and pleasant.

When they returned home, Lucy again started making her

famous meatballs and tomato sauce. The whole process took five hours, but it was worth the effort. The last two hours were simple. She just had to sit beside the pan that was slowly simmering to make sure that the meat did not stick to bottom.

While she cooked, Mario had a new hobby. When the Boston Red Sox purchased the contract of Ted Williams, Mario became a Red Sox fan. That evening the Milano's were invited to the Cipriani flat. They put on their church clothes to celebrate the occasion.

Rico Cipriani had recently retired from his job on the Boston subway. He had a bushy head of hair and a long black mustache. When he reached out to shake their hands, they could see that those fingers had labored long and hard in the fifty years he was employed.

Rita looked bigger than her husband, but he weighed much more. She was a very homely women with rough features, very dark hair along her upper lip and chin, and two dark brown warts on her upper cheek. It was apparent that the two children had received more from her than their father, who was actually handsome.

The Milano's were ushered into the parlor and given seats. The room had an eerie appearance because some chairs were covered with white sheets and the lighting was extremely dim. In the center of the room, just in front of the window, was a Zenith table radio. It was a deep mahogany and shaped like a cathedral window. Mrs. Cipriani turned one of the knobs to the right, and Franklin Roosevelt's voice came on in a loud, shrill blare.

"I am going to refer to some fundamentals that antedate parties and antedate republics and empires—fundamentals that are as old as mankind itself. They are fundamentals that have been expressed in philosophies, for I don't know how many thousands of years, in every part of the world.

"Today, in our boasted modern civilization, we are facing just exactly the same problem, just exactly the same conflict between two schools of philosophy that they faced in the earliest days of America, and indeed of the world. One of them—one of these old philosophies —is the philosophy of those who would 'Let things alone.'

"The other is the philosophy that strives for something new—

something that the human race has never attained yet, but something which I believe the human race can and will attain—social justice through social action."

None of the Milano's or Cipriani's really understood, but they marveled at the magnificent voice, and they knew Roosevelt was going to change things. He spoke of the "jungle law of the survival of the so-called fittest" and the number of good people who believed in this erroneous doctrine. When he spoke next of the public school children and their health problems, those in the room knew that what they had sensed was true. This was their man; this was the man to take the United States out of the jungle.

Roosevelt continued, "In the same way, there are two theories of prosperity and of well-being: the first theory is that if we make the rich people richer, somehow they will let a part of their prosperity trickle down to the rest of us. The second theory—and I suppose this goes back to the days of Noah—I won't say Adam and Eve, because they had a less complicated situation—but, at least, back in the flood there was the theory that if we make the average of mankind comfortable and secure, their prosperity will rise upward, just as yeast rises up, through the ranks."

Philip whispered to his mother that he had to go to the bathroom. She pointed in the general direction, and told him to be quiet. As he was about to enter the bathroom, he saw Mary Capriani standing in her bedroom doorway. He nodded, holding up the palm of his hand, then went into the toilet, and then joined her in her room. "Aren't you listening to Roosevelt?" he asked.

"No, I don't go for that stuff. Politics is for men."

"Well, what are women for?" asked Philip jokingly.

"You know. They marry, have children, cook, and take care of men."

As she spoke, she shut the door the rest of the way and leaned against it with her back. He did not notice because he was thinking he should try her out. He felt he should touch her breasts because the older boys had often spoken of getting the hots from feeling tits. He moved up close to her and kissed her. The next time he kissed her, he carefully placed his right hand on her left breast and awaited the reaction. She only squeezed him a little more tightly. He was not sure of his next move; he felt no emotion. But he went on kissing her.

"You'd better stop, Philip," she urged him "You can't do it here. My father would beat me up if he found me with another boy."

He returned quickly to his chair, and Roosevelt was still lecturing. "This concentration of power has led to a three-fold struggle for domination. First, there is the struggle for dictatorship in the economic sphere itself; then the fierce battle to acquire control of the Government, so that its resources and authority may be abused in the economic struggle, and, finally, the clash between the Governments themselves."

"Vuole lei una tazza di caffe?" (Do you want coffee,) asked Mrs. Capriani as the speech ended.

"No grazie e troppo tarde. Mario lavore domani." Lucy told her it was too late, and Mario had to work tomorrow.

Everybody hugged and kissed, which was the Italian custom, as they said their goodbyes. But Mario could not forget the screams that emanated from the Cipriani house next door when all the windows were open. It seemed to be a Boston custom that husbands beat their wives, especially when they were drunk. It was a time when women were not sacred. Life was sacred but not women.

PART IV THE KILLER

THE RAPE OF CHARLENE

As Mario studied the murder, he needed to know more about Charlene Eliot. What he learned surprised him. Charles Eliot's sister, Charlene, had a very unusual life. Her parents must have expected another boy, but when it was obvious that she was a girl, they raised her as a boy and called her Charlene.

She went to all the best schools, and when she finished high school, they made her take the grand tour of Europe: London to Paris to Rome. When she returned, Charles asked her to visit him. She drove to his place along the Charles River.

He may have had a vitamin deficiency, because he was of bad temper, vain and insecure. A Harvard cardiologist believed he was deficient in B-12, and this can cause anemia. He wrote that it can begin in the stomach, which causes ulcers, headaches, fatigue, and irritability.

On this particular day, Charles was nice to her until he asked her to sit beside him. He seemed very interested in her travels until he began to put his hands in places she did not expect.

"What are you doing Charles?" she asked him.

His answer did not satisfy. "We are brother and sister, so we can be together closely."

"Charles," she said fiercely, "you cannot touch me there."

Her response enraged him. He tore her blouse and started to strip her. She was unable to prevent what he did next. He raped her violently until he had emptied his seed into her. She ran out of the house crying and drove home where her parents had already retired.

The rape changed her completely, especially as the baby grew in her womb. She despised all men, so she was much warmer when she was with women. She decided that she would be bi-sexual, but that she might prefer being a lesbian. Her new lover was Molly Flanagan, who had been serving as a maid in her parent's home.

Whenever her parents retired early, Charlene and Molly would have time to show their love for each other. Charlene became aware quickly that making love with a woman was different from doing it with a man. Molly told her that they could get a dildo.

"What is that?" asked Charlene.

Molly answered, "It's an object shaped like a penis that can be used for masturbation or lesbian love. It is really a sex toy, and they come in all shapes and sizes."

"It sounds gross," said Charlene.

"Well," retorted Molly, "if that is gross, then we will have to rely on lesbian love which is purely oral sex."

Charlene was still puzzled. 'What do you mean by oral sex?" she asked.

"It means using your tongue."

Charlene seemed to grasp the essence of the answer. "You mean putting your tongue where the dildo or penis would go?"

"Now you have it," said Molly. "Now come and kiss me."

As she did that, Molly unclipped her bra and kissed her there and at other places.

After a while they were satisfied, and Charlene told her about the rape, and when she was finished she went to an end table for a cigarette. She reached in and found Charles' gun. As she picked it up, she wondered why he had a gun.

Molly was mortified. "You mean to tell me that your own brother raped you. If that is true, then you should get rid of him," she added.

"What do you mean?" Charlene asked.

"You can draft a plan. It's easy because he lives near the Charles River. You can begin by visiting him and chatting to relax him. Then you can invite someone who can bring a gun."

Charlene interrupted her. "He already has a gun. You mean you are going to kill him?"

"You can call it self-defense," Molly explained, "because he was raping you. This whole operation will be easy, because no one will hear the shots and no one will see you putting him in the river."

"How soon do I carry out our plan?" Charlene asked.

"It's up to you to choose the date," Molly declared.

"Wednesday seems to be his quietist evening," Charlene said.

"But I will need to wait until someone else can help me."

During the next week, Charlene went to Charles' house again. They sat on separate sofas, and they began a social visit. When they were settled, Charlene knew how to excite her brother. He hated Roosevelt and the Democrats, so she began there.

"What did you think of the Supreme Court killing Roosevelt's plan to expand the size of the court from nine to as much as fifteen?"

"That was a wonderful thing they did, and do you know why?"

"Why?" asked Charlene.

"Because," Charles was very happy to answer her query, "he should really be a Republican since his family has great wealth and they live in Hyde Park."

"I have a bigger question," Charlene told him.

"Okay, spill it," he said excitedly.

"When the Germans invaded Poland in 1939, we passed a Neutrality Act. Are you in favor of this act that allows us to sell arms to all belligerent powers?"

"Well,' he said as he looked at Charlene. "You picked a good one there."

"So, what is your answer?"

"I must be in favor," he began, "because the United States still has millions of unemployed, and this law will open up many of the closed factories."

By the end of the second question, Charles Eliot was falling asleep.

Charlene told Molly to go home, and she sat on the couch to rest a while. As she dozed, the front doorbell rang. She was puzzled, because she was not expecting anyone. She opened the door carefully and she saw a woman she did not know.

"What is it?" she asked.

"Mr. Eliot invited me to his home when he visited my business," she answered.

"He is asleep," she told her, "but he will awaken soon. What is your business?" she asked Jo Ann.

Jo Ann had to lie. "I am employed at a beauty parlor," she said softly.

Charlene was puzzled because she was not aware that her brother was utilizing such an establishment.

At this very moment, Charles awoke. "Oh, hello," he said looking at Jo Ann in a state of puzzlement. "I was not aware that that you were coming tonight," he told her.

Jo Ann had to respond. "You invited me last week," she said curtly.

"Well, then," he said loudly, "let us have a drink. Charlene take out some of that French brandy we bought in Paris."

Charlene reacted robotically as she brought in and poured the liquor.

When Charles had consumed two glasses, he asked his sister to sit next to him. She was very hesitant because of the rape that had occurred last year. He sensed her alarm. "Come on over. I won't hurt you," he advised her.

But as she sat beside him, he began to repeat his violent act. He tried to tear her blouse as he gripped her arm. She struggled to get free, but he reached down to rip open her pants, and when she screamed and resisted, he punched her in the face causing her to bleed.

Jo Ann Kelly went to Charlene, and when she saw her plight she asked, "Where is his gun?"

"It's still in that same place," she shouted as she pointed. Then she gave Jo Ann the go sign. Jo Ann, wearing gloves, walked over to Charles and pumped two bullets into his chest. They waited a few minutes to make sure he was dead, and they dragged him to the bank of the river and rolled him over into the water. It was not a long way.

They looked at each other and smiled. Charlene said, "Good riddance to bad rubbish."

Jo Ann Kelly looked at Charlene and asked, "What shall we do with this gun?"

Charlene told her, "Take it to the river. They will never find it there in all the muck."

The next day, the murder was all over the morning newspapers. *The Boston Globe* and the *Boston Herald* had the biggest coverage of this crime of Saturday, September 30, 1942. Lucy read every line, and then she turned to other events of that day.

The front page highlighted the news that the Allies had sunk 41 U-Boats in September. The Style Section told her that the Zodiac sign was Libra. The Sports fans were elated because NBC broadcast the first televised football game in history.

But consumers were delighted that the average automobile cost only $700, and gasoline could be bought for ten cents per gallon. Those earning small salaries were happy to read that bread was only eight cents per loaf, and a pound of hamburger could be obtained for fourteen cents. Persons of means were jubilant when the papers published that an average house could be bought for $3,800.

53

LUCY IS PREGNANT

Not long after they bought the house on Sumner Street, Lucy got what she wanted: she was pregnant. She survived those first three months of agony, and soon she was doing housework as if she was working as a longshoreman. She even tried to whistle.

When Mario saw her working, he was concerned. "You should not be working so diligently," he warned.

"Oh, you just don't understand the whole process," she answered. "The womb is a cradle that protects the baby. It is a fascinating part of the body, and it must be kept healthy. Any irregular flows will create problems for the mother. When the baby is born, all the parts of the body—the bones and muscles—are in perfect sync. They are all in harmony. It is holistic with mind and body.

As the ninth month approached, she slowed down as she pondered the miracle that was to happen at any hour of her day or night. Her contractions began at 5:00 a.m. on June 30th. As they worsened, Mario called an ambulance. When they wheeled her into the operating room, Mario asked the medical doctor if he could witness the coming miracle.

Dr. Colangello was very concise. "Mr. Milano, you know that it is not allowed. Why don't you go walking for an hour or two, then we will see how things go?"

As soon as Mario was gone, the doctor told a nurse to prepare for any kind of delivery. "It should be normal, but we must be ready for any complications."

He told the nurse that the uterus was already dilated and the fetus seems ready to join the world. When it gradually made itself known, he said, "It's a boy, and it is very normal."

Mario took the doctor's advice, and he headed toward Harvard Square. He stopped at a coffee shop, where he bought a croissant to go with his coffee. He also bought a *Boston Globe* to take his mind off what was happening at the Massachusetts General Hospital.

The entire front page was covered with stories about the German victories in Europe. He worried about his draft status, but he knew that with a child he would go into a special category of exemptions.

As he read, he completely ignored the clock on the wall, and he lost the sense of time. When he got rid of his reverie and glanced at the clock, he jumped out of his seat and came close to running toward the hospital. Inside he caught Dr. Colangello in the hallway. "How did it go?" he asked while almost out of breath.

"You have a beautiful, healthy boy," he said and added, "They are both inside," as he pointed. But he wasn't finished. He pointed at Mario and said, "If men were to deliver babies, the population of the world would decline because men have a very low tolerance for pain."

Mario gave him a quick "Thank you" and headed into the room that was full of new babies. He found Lucy in the center of things, and then he saw his new offspring. When he reached for him, she yelled, "No, No. You can't touch him yet."

"Okay," he snapped. He leaned over to inspect his son. The thought of being a father of a man warmed his heart. He was puzzled by the blue eyes and fairly light hair, although there was not much of it.

Lucy was semi-conscious, and when she awoke, she said she was dizzy. "What should we name him? We each have a male grandfather," she reminded him. "Which one do we select?"

"Do you want to stick to the Italian custom, or do you want to break away?" he proposed.

Lucy responded, "Let's just call him son for now."

When they all headed home, they put son in the crib that they had assembled earlier. Mario leaned over the edge and said proudly, "He looks alright to me." Then he told her, "Now you have what you prayed for."

The way he uttered those words made her edgy. Were all fathers like that, she wondered. He seemed a stranger at times. "Did she do something wrong? Was this her fault? Before the child was born, they were as cuddly as possible.

Dr. Colangello dropped in to inspect his patient. He was there to give her advice: "You must have the same dedication as any athlete. No drugs, no alcohol for days."

When Mario kissed Lucy the next morning, he told her she was as beautiful as ever, and he emphasized that she was still very young. At the same time, he wondered what his boy would become. Would he become strong and handsome, and would he treat women in a chivalrous manner?

Lucy also pondered the future. As the delicate baby rested in her arms, she noted first the blue eyes. She felt it pulling on her heart, and a wave of strong love seemed to fly over her to the infant baby. She was happy that she had brought it into this sad world with much love.

As Mario gazed at their miracle, he thought of a current popular song:

Y ou must have been a beautiful baby
  You must have been a wonderful child
And when it comes to winning blue ribbons

You must have shown the other kids how
You must have been a beautiful baby
'Cause baby look at you now.

PART V IT'S A BOY PLUS GIRL

THEY NAME HIM PHILIP

After many hours of disagreement, Lucy and Mario agreed to call their son Philip, after Maria's mother's father Filippo (Philip in English). By the time young Phil was three years old, it was clear he would be either a mechanic or an engineer.

His play toys were his father's tools in the basement, many of which were out of his reach. But it did not stop young Philip from reaching many that were in difficult places.

Whenever Phil's name came up at dinner, his proud father would say, "He has got to go to MIT." However, when Philip was ten years old, he tried to be the man of the house when his daddy was away. He was tall, handsome, and quiet. He had characteristics that women would easily fall in love with, but he had a shy demeanor.

As the years flew by, it was not clear what Philip Milano wanted to be or do. When he was very young, he dreamed of being another Michelangelo. A local neighbor who was a commercial artist gave him lessons, and Philip became very good at drawing. His friend urged him to apply for a scholarship at the Museum of Fine Arts.

Philip obeyed by sending in some sketches, and he did win a summer scholarship. When he reported to the museum, he was very disappointed to learn that the subject was charcoal drawing of Greek and Roman statues. He did attend every day, and he was pleased that he learned much about the human form.

By the end of summer, Philip had to choose a middle school. He favored Boston Latin School, of which both parents approved, because even at his early age they knew that he was a mathematical genius. When he completed every course with the highest grades, Philip was both glad and sad.

Philip confused both his parents when he told them that he wanted to learn how to play a guitar. They acquiesced to his demand as they always did later. In short time he was strumming popular songs. But they were totally confused when he began to strum country music with a twang. His favorite was "Red River Valley," which was brought to the American West by a Canadian. Philip kept singing the second stanza:

S o come sit by my side if you love me
    Do not hasten to bid me adieu.
Just remember the Red River Valley
And the one who has loved you so true.

N ot only did Philip prove that he was superior in mathematics, but one day one of his instructors was confronted with a very profound question. Philip surmised that the one asking the question was Jewish. He asked, "How can top scientists tell us that the universe was created in 13.7 billion years, while the Bible tells us that God created earth over 5,000 years ago.?"

"What did the Professor say?" asked Mario, who was eager for a response to this ponderous question.

Philip paused for a moment and then stated that Professor Goldberg was dumbfounded. He went around the question until he found an answer. He spoke loudly, so everyone in the class would get his answer. "Scientists depend on experiments for answers, while Christians and Jews depend on faith. He recommended that the class read a book by Rachel Carson, *The Sea Around Us*. He told us that, "Carson was not a minister, and that she did not want to debate about religion."

Philip told his dad, "I found the book in the library, and it is very well marked with authority. It offers a great achievement as a work of science. And she stated that this book was not meant to challenge faith, but it was a summary of the beginning and growth of the oceans. She provides an enthralling story about how the oceans were formed. Then she explains how life began in the primeval seas.

The exhibit in the biology building in Washington told us a good deal about the family who are the Denisovans. They left Africa about 60,000 years ago, and they settled in Europe and West Asia. There are few skeletons, but we learned later that they are relatives of the Neanderthals. The Denisovans were found in Siberia, Australia, and New Guineau.

"The exhibit was fascinating. It covered all the rooms, and it began with just dirt. The guide told us that each room that followed was two or three million year later. In room two the earth was bubbling, and in room three a small snake-like creature entered the scene. In each room later, the animal took on a human feature. This exhibit seemed to verify that the Earth was over thirteen billion years old."

When Philip finished speaking, his dad approached him. "You have been smoking. Why are doing that?"

Philip answered, "All the Hollywood actors smoke."

Mario did not like his response. "They get paid for it; all you will get is bad health."

What Philip said next disgusted Mario. "Everyone I know smokes. And all the ads for cigarettes say that they are healthy for you. I rejected Camels and chose Chesterfields, because as the ads say they are "Milder and Better Taste." All my friends kid me, because they claim that Chesterfields are a girl's cigarette."

Mario stopped him. "If everyone you knew jumped off the top deck of the Empire State building, would you follow them?"

The next day, the science class got into a second dispute concerning the origin of man. The teacher asked, "Are we all homo sapiens?"

The dispute centered around whether we are mainly Neanderthals, as DNA suggests. The disagreement resulted from research that tells us that as much as ten percent of our DNA was inherited from hominids that are not homo sapiens.

"This small percentage was crucial for us by adding such things as perspiration and liver functions. The scientists called it "adaptive introgression," which means that in the millions of years we were developing we were adding necessary components. Our human traits depended on a continuous addition of genes.

"It seems that the Denisovans, who were very different from the Neanderthals, are part of our DNA. But we don't have many of their full skeletons and fossils. They made all types of tools, but all we know is that they seem to have lived in the eastern parts of Eurasia and we don't have a well-defined group of their skeletons or archaeology that we know must have been left behind by the groups."

Goldberg surprised the class by telling them, "Your assignment for tomorrow is to report on Denisovans." Not many grasped the essence of the controversy, so on the next day, he wanted to test his students' knowledge of current events. But when this failed, he asked the class, "What does Kristallnacht mean?"

There was total silence again. He stammered as he began to answer his own question. "It took place On November 9th and November 10th, 1938, when the Nazis in Germany torched synagogues, vandalized Jewish homes, schools and businesses, and killed close to one hundred Jews. But that was just the beginning. What was called the 'Night of Broken Glass' saw some 30,000 Jewish men arrested and sent to Nazi concentration camps. Before Kristallnacht, Nazi policies were usually nonviolent, but later conditions for German Jews grew increasingly worse. During the last four years, the Nazis worked to reach their goal of what they called the "Final Solution" to the "Jewish problem." Hundreds of Jews escaped this inhuman torture by leaving Germany through Switzerland, and in 1939 a kindertransport (a children's train) was created to rescue Jewish children from the Nazis.

When he finished his explanation of Kristallnacht, Goldberg's eyes were damp, so the class left in total silence.

54

THE GALLOS GET TOGETHER

Once they settled in their new house, Lucy told Mario that they had to visit her Aunt Rosina, who lived not far away, at the corner of Brooks and Bennington Streets. It was about five or six blocks from where they lived on Sumner Street.

The four Milano's stood by as Lucy pressed the doorbell. Rosina screamed and hugged each of them as she said, "According to me, you are all Gallos."

Lucy wanted to change the subject. 'When did Giovani die?"

"He has been dead for two years, and he is buried in the Malden cemetery."

"How old are you now?" Lucy asked.

She answered in Italian. "Io sono tanti vecchio." (I am very old).

"How many years?" asked Lucy again.

This time she spoke English. "I am eighty-seven years."

Lucy gave her the old Italian response. "Per cent anni." (May you live to be 100).

When they got settled in the apartment, Rosina wanted to know everything about the two children. Lucy was very proud to brag about the school record of her niece and nephew.

Rosina offered the adults coffee and pizza dolce (sweet pie) and the children gelato (Italian ice cream.) While they were consuming these delicious sweet things, they reminisced about their years in Italy, and they all agreed it was better in the United States. They were especially enamored of the toilets in this country.

When Mario told her that he was an Assistant Prosecutor, Rosina was very proud and very impressed. She said, "Lucia, you have a good man, so you better keep him."

She was more than proud as she told her aunt, "He's not going anywhere except to our house." She kissed him on the cheek as if to say that she was a satisfied wife.

When Rosina got together with her family, they always involved her singing in Italian. In each case, she broke into her full voice which probably was heard by her neighbors. In this case, she favored the song that was titled in her name. This is what she sang, which is translated into English:

O j Marri (O Marie)
  Quanta suonno ca perdo per te (I have lost much sleep)
Famma durmi (Let me sleep)
Abbracciata nu poco cu te (In your arms with yours about me)
Oj Mari oj Marie (O Marie, O Marie)

E veryone cheered, but Lucy told her aunt that she must go home to prepare her Sunday dinner. As they exited, Lucy gave her their home address and phone number. "Come see us anytime. Don't spend your life being alone. It's not healthy. And we are only a few blocks apart."

When Lucy was preparing the Sunday dinner, Mario decided to read some of his mail. He found a report on civil rights violations of Italians. Several Congressmen submitted a resolution which calls on the federal government to investigate the civil liberties violations of Italians during the ongoing war.

The resolution calls for the U.S. Justice Department to investigate and prepare a report on government policies affecting 600,000 Italian Americans.

These wartime violations began on December 11th, 1941, when FBI agents shipped hundreds of Italians to internment camps in Montana, Oklahoma, Tennessee, and Texas. In so doing, the government classified all Italian residents in the U.S. as "enemy aliens."

Italian American parents were particularly perturbed because their sons, who were American citizens, were being drafted and hundreds more volunteered to fight for their country.

When the Milano's moved to Sumner Street, their favorite place to visit was Wood Island. It provided all kinds of recreation, and it was all free. It was a long walk up Bremen Street and on to Bennington Street to Neptune Road. As they entered the park, they passed the baseball field and the handball court. On the right was the hot dog and cola stand, and just to its left was the bathhouse where persons could change into a swim suit or shower. Boston Harbor, with its sandy beach, was straight ahead. And from that venue visitors could see the clock on the tallest building in Boston—the Customs House.

One Sunday after the war began, they made the trek to Wood Island, and to their surprise, they were greeted by soldiers who were carrying rifles. Mario Milano asked the guards, "What is the reason for your being here?"

He told him, "We are guarding enemy aliens."

Mario had investigated the conditions for enemy aliens, and what he learned was very troubling and unfair. "Do you know," he asked the soldier, "that German prisoners are given a broad range of educational and leisure activities. Some are taking classes, some are playing sports, usually soccer. Most camps have libraries. Can you explain any of this irregularity?"

The guard hesitated for a short while, then he responded. "I was told that there is a shortage of workers, especially in the farms, so German prisoners are filling that void."

"Okay, but why aren't Italians given these same privileges?"

When there was no answer, Mario turned around and told his family, "We can enter by another road."

When they got to the alternate road, they encountered a wire fence with a large number of Italian soldiers imprisoned there. Mario used his crude Italian to ask them where they were from. Most answered names from southern Italy. When he returned home, he called Aunt Rosina and he asked her if she knew about the prisoners.

Her answer surprised Mario. "Oh sure. I talk to them all the time. And I do what many of the other women do. I bring them a nice big plate of pasta." She hesitated as if she did not know whether to tell him more. "You know, not all women are nice. Some give their pasta and their bodies. It is a sinful disgrazia."

Mario was not surprised, but he was sorry to learn of this sinful practice.

55

PHILIP VISITS BEACHMONT

When they were about to leave Aunt Rosina, she mentioned that they have a great grandfather in Beachmont. She told them, "He is your father's grandfather. His name is Domenico Pintoriello. He was involved in the bootlegging business during the 1930s. When Prohibition was repealed, he suffered a great loss, but the people he worked for got him another good job. When Suffolk Downs Race Track opened, they gave the jobs to the loyal Democrats."

Philip asked, "How did this Amendment pass? All those dry states said they would never okay it."

Domenico was ready with his answer. "The big money must have put on the pressure. States like Indiana, Alabama, and Utah even joined in the fight. All those Baptist ministers could not keep the public from drinking, and the country needs the liquor taxes and the farmers need the jobs and the income from the grain. It seems that the farmers are farmers first and Baptists second."

Philip marveled at this knowledge of current affairs, and he was anxious to get his grandfather's opinion about all the social problems that had caused him to make the trip to Beachmont in the first place.

Philip asked him first how he became a citizen.

He puffed up his chest and said, "I am citizen Pintoriello." Then he pointed to the large American flag in the living room, and he spoke vociferously that, "I am from the same country as George Washington and Abraham Lincoln. I love the United States of America."

Philip wanted to stop his boisterous speech. "What you think of Roosevelt now?" he asked.

Domenico was never out of words. He had a ready response. "He is doing everything possible now. He closed the bad banks, and he created a lot of new relief programs. He is feeding the hungry people and giving jobs to the states. They say he is going to use the people who are out of work to build a lot of things the country needs, like roads, parks, bridges and airports."

Domenico left for a minute, and soon he returned to the living room with glasses on a tray with a pitcher of wine, some cheese, and some hard Italian bread. Philip Milano left in a happy condition.

The next week, Philip went back to visit his great grandfather. He wanted a chance to explore the rich neighborhood. As he circled the house, he perused the landscape. He noticed the beautiful garden with flowers of all colors. He did not know their names. The lawn was beautifully green, and in the center was a wooden bench where the old man would sit in the sun.

When his great grandfather came out to greet him, he asked, "How did you know how to grow these?"

"I just follow the instructions on the packages," he responded.

Looking about, Philip enjoyed the freshness of the ocean air on this bright day. At that moment, he hated his house in East Boston, and he felt the same every time he saw the house in Beachmont. *There's Revere Beach over there to the left*, he said to himself. And in front of him was the ocean. It looked so different from this distance, sort of a deep blue. Why was it green when you got closer?

Below him a narrow-gauge train was heading for Lynn. It clipped along at about forty miles per hour. He had never ridden one, but he imagined that it would be very exciting.

As they were discussing flowers, a young lady came out to greet him.

"Hi."

Philip's head snapped around in the direction of the greeting. He had a distinct reaction on seeing her, much like a dog might have on smelling freshly-cut meat. Man, what a babe!

"Hi," he answered. "Do you live there?" He pointed to the white frame home next door.

"Ya. I was born there."

Why hadn't he seen her before? he asked himself. He had been to grandpa's house several times. *It ain't fair*, he thought. *Gees, I gotta make time with her. But how can I do it? I just can't ask her to go out with me right away.*

"Why haven't I seen you before?" he asked.

"I don't know. I guess I was away every time you came. You're Mr. Pintoriello's grandson, aren't you? I've heard all about you. He says you are a smart boy."

"It isn't fair," he said "You know my name, but I don't know yours."

"You could have looked on the mailbox," she teased. "I'm Janet O'Brien."

Just as I thought, said Philip to himself. *No good-looking blonde dame like that could be Italian. Cripes, I'll never marry a dago girl. They all look the same with their dark oily skin, their long noses, and their large ankles.*

He walked around the hedges and stood next to her. "Do you go to Beachmont High?"

She nodded yes.

He wasn't ashamed to say, "I go to Boston Latin."

He watched her face as she seemed totally surprised. She told him she was fifteen, to which he answered, "I am sixteen."

When Philip was finished admiring the flowers, Janet told him, "I love to sit here when the sun is high to eat my lunch. The nearby bees never bother me, so we share the beauty of nature."

When Janet began to brag about all the Irish who controlled the politics of Boston and Massachusetts, Philip had to retort. "It was Christopher Columbus and Amerigo Vespucci who found and named America." He started to name other important Italian Americans, but she stopped him.

"I know about the contributions of Italians, so let's call it a draw."

She had to go inside, so he said, "We can talk more next time."

As he walked back into the house, he recalled what the older boys on the street used to say: that it wasn't just to piss out of. He remembered the excitement of those first pubic hairs. Gees, and all those commitments he had made for himself. Maybe all his thoughts were crude, but this is what little boys are made of. Why in hell do those girls keep their legs crossed all the time when all the guys are on the make? He remembered what a high school friend had said, that if all the women were laid end to end, it would just describe the situation in East Boston.

After Philip had met Janet O'Brien, he found every pretense to visit his great-grandfather Domenico. Each visit he would say his perfunctory hellos and immediately go out to wait for Janet to make an appearance. He tried to act nonchalant, but she teased him by not coming out at all on some occasions and by making a very brief visit on others. It infuriated him that he could get nowhere with her. Every other girl he ever met he could at least get a date with, but Janet was hopeless. Still, he did not give up.

He was not aware that she was playing with him. Her every action was a camouflage, every word was an evasion. *I can't get anywhere with this friggin' bitch*, he kept saying to himself. To his high school friends, he gave a different story. For them it was real progress, although he was very careful to avoid any implication. He did not want them to think that she was just another piece of cheap tail. This one is different, he kept insisting, but they tried to tell him that if you tip dames upside down, they all look alike.

Philip marveled at how cool Janet was in his presence. He wanted to hold her, but he had no idea of how to approach her. With Mary Bianca and the other broads, he just kissed and held their boobs. But what avenue could he take this one down? He must get a date with her as a beginning.

He stood on the lawn longing for Janet. *Why in hell doesn't she* come out? he wondered. *I should stop wasting my friggin' time on this dame. Why can't I be happy with Mary Bianca or Josie Cipriani?*

"Hello, Phil."

Cripes, she's a beauty. Why should I take that dumb East Boston stuff when I can get something like this? Well, I don't have her yet, but dammit I will.

"Hi Jan. "What are you doing today?"

"Nothing. Do you want to come inside for a while?"

He was so conflicted; he did not know what to say. It was the first time she had ever invited him inside.

When he had recovered from his shock, he said. "Let's go."

She led him into the entry and then into the large living room. It was the best looking home he had ever been in. He did not know the types of colonial furniture, but he did know that it cost a lot of money. The accessories fascinated him. Everything had a nautical theme. The drapes were lined with fishing net; the clock was a ship wheel; an old compass sat on the round maple table. They even had a telescope facing the ocean.

What shocked him completely was the east wall. It was all mahogany and covered with shelves full of books. As he walked to get closer, he noticed all the gold bindings. He thought this was for him —he had to marry someone with money.

"Where does your father work?" he asked, as the curiosity got the best of him.

"Oh, he's a foreman in a coat factory in Lynn. What does your dad do?"

"He's the Assistant Prosecutor in that case involving the murder of the Harvard Professor."

She was obviously impressed, because she said nothing.

Philip edged closer to her on the sofa and calculated his chances. He wanted to feel her, but he reasoned that he must play it cagey on the first time. She would surely not notice if he put his hand from the back of the chair to her shoulder. Boy, maybe she had the hots, too. Even society girls get hot pants. And with this rationalization to embolden him, he started to lean over to kiss her on the mouth.

Instantly, her hand was over his mouth and his head was being pushed to one side.

"You'd better go, Phil. I'm not like the East Boston girls you know. I thought you were a nice boy. You'd better not see me again. Goodbye."

Philip pondered his next words. He thought first that he would tell her to go frig herself, but he was not going to accept defeat so easily.

"I'm sorry, Jan. I only wanted to kiss you. I know you are not like other girls. If you were, I would not be here. You are special, and I have wanted to kiss you since the first time I saw you."

It was a flawless performance, and Janet O'Brien took the bait. "Do you ever go to the Youth Center in Lynn? There are dances there every Saturday night."

"Ya, I'll drop in some time."

As he attempted to leave, she said, "Oh, don't go. We can have lunch outside. I always sit here in the sunshine near the pine tree. Sit here; I'll bring a tray out."

In just a few minutes, she bought two sandwiches, some cookies, and some hot tea. He didn't tell her that he did not drink tea, and he did not tell her that this noontime special would probably be his last one.

When Philip got home, he decided he needed some hot love, so he contacted Mary Bianca. He was tired of that snotty Janet. It was the right time to meet Mary, because some of the gang were going to swim in the old reservoir ballicky.

He did not have to explain to her the meaning of the word. The boys brought a bottle of gin and passed it around. Everyone, girls included, began swilling the alcohol, and it wasn't long before all the couples were in intimate positions.

Philip had no problem with Mary. She was ready long ago. He did not have to struggle. They got in the back seat of the car, and he began with gentle kisses, but she wanted more as she reached for his private parts. He did not have to be told what was next. It would have been a comic situation if someone had brought a camera and photographed all the naked bodies.

When he got home, Philip decided it was time to visit the Old Howard Burlesque Theatre, because he read in the morning paper that Zorita was back after several months. Her act began with a middle aged man telling a bunch of dirty jokes, then she came onto the stage from the right side.

As she headed toward the center of the stage, everyone saw that the snake was coiled around her body from breast to knees. When the music got louder, the snake uncoiled itself until it was lying on the stage. Zorita did her bumps and wiggles to keep up with the beat of the music, and when she was ready, she picked up the tail and simulated the sex act. As she moved in passionate array, all the men in the audience yelled, "Put it in."

When she ignored their cries, they screamed louder. "Put the f---king thing in."

But Zorita knew that there were policemen in the last row making sure that she did not violate any city laws pertaining to an act such as hers. She bowed and headed off the stage, carrying her pet with her.

PART VI MARYANN

MARYANN MATURES

MaryAnn knew a lot more about entertainment than about education. She knew all the lyrics of Sinatra's songs and most of the Glenn Miller songs and she loved the movies of Clark Gable, Errol Flynn, and Henry Fonda. The new decade offered so many promises of prosperity, but she seemed to ignore the news of Germany's capture of most of Western Europe.

She totally ignored everything that was happening all around her, but she cared for the families that waited in the soup lines without shoes, who were served some thin, watery soup. Somehow, she disregarded the dark significance of life at that time. She was not aware that a popular song offered lyrics of "Gonna take a Sentimental Journey." For her it was all a romantic dream. When the "March of Times" offered nothing but weary war news, MaryAnn was thinking of Sinatra's "I'll be seeing you in all the old familiar places."

She loved some of the odd lyrics of her time. One of her favorites was "How about doing Hey Hey, Tweet, Tweet, Tweet, Tweet Twa." She also loved some of the jazz tunes, especially those of Jimmy Rushing of the Count Basie band. Her favorite song was:

. . .

"If you don't like my peaches
        Why do you shake my tree?
Get out of my orchard
And let my peaches be."

Her favorite vocalist was Kay Starr, who was known as a Jukebox Queen. She excelled as a swing, country and pop star. She was most happy when she sang with Count Basie. She was born in Oklahoma, so it was natural for her to begin as a country and western vocalist, but in the 1930s she switched to swing bands including Glenn Miller, Coleman Hawkins, Lester Young, Bob Crosby, and Count Basie. Although she was three-fourths Indian, she was thought to be white. She was considered a master of the blues, just as Peggy Lee was. Being a country girl she never learned to read music, so she was often unable to respond to such questions as "What key do you prefer?" and "What is your range?"

When MaryAnn reached puberty she had to deal with her monthly duties. Maria tried to explain what would occur, but MaryAnn demanded independence in dealing with this procedure. She decided to investigate how women dealt with this condition now and in the past.

At the library, she learned that the first pads were produced in 1896, but that the more recent products dated to 1920 and 1936. The most recent innovation was to attach a string to a piece of absorbent cotton. She had no interest in these improvements, but all she knew was that she was now a woman.

This inability to acknowledge product improvements showed up in everything she did. No matter what Lucy tried, she could not make a student out of her child. MaryAnn had no marketable skills, but she did admire all of the Rosie the Riveters.

When MaryAnn was very tired of all the criticisms about her, she shocked her mother when she said, "I think I am a boy or I should be one. You treat Phil a lot better than you treat me."

This upset Lucy. "You don't understand. He works hard. He does things well. He gets top grades.

MaryAnn stopped her. "A lot of mothers fall for their young sons. We discussed this in our Marriage Class in high school. Our teacher said that the young boys take the place of their husbands. I want to be a boy. A lot of people are changing sex. I never really felt like a girl. There are several cases at Massachusetts General Hospital where the doctors are adding male parts to girls to complete the task."

Lucy was totally flustered. "MaryAnn you are a girl and a pretty one at that. Some day you will fall for a handsome man."

"No," she screamed. "I want a name like Tony or Ed or Jim. I will not marry a boy; I will be one. I went to the library, and the librarian showed me a whole shelf of books on "Becoming Transgender."

Lucy hugged her and told her that things for women are improving everywhere. "You have many skills you can use, and you are very kind when confronting those in need of help."

56

MARYANN JOINS THE NAVY

M ary Ann chose all the easy courses such as How to Cook and Current History, which she could read in the daily newspapers. But she had to take algebra. It was at this point that her education took a surprising turn. When her teacher told her that she was very clever with numbers, she guessed that she must have acquired some of Philip's genes. But she also remembered that they did many games of numbers.

Her teacher told her that there was a new program offered by the U. S. Navy for women who could translate messages using numbers. At that moment, MaryAnn thought of all the crossword puzzles she and Philip worked on daily.

"Is it open to everyone?" she asked her teacher.

"Yes," she answered, "but you will be up against women who have college degrees."

MaryAnn was all excited. "Where can I go to enquire?" she asked.

"They have built some Nissen Huts on the Mall in Washington, D. C."

When she got there, she was amazed at the number of girls and women who were waiting in line. When they called her name, the chief executive explained the program. "It was created on May 25,

1942. Mrs. Roosevelt was working hard to have the Congress accept women and blacks for military service. Now, if you are accepted, you will be sworn in as a WAVE. (Women Accepted for Voluntry Emergency Service). You must have at least a high school diploma and you must be from twenty to thirty-five years old."

After this initiating speech, MaryAnn was taken inside a building for a number of tests. When they were completed, the Naval inspectors told her that she had some hidden skills about numbers. She kept thinking about Philip's numerical skills, and she was certain that he must have passed on some to her.

There was at least one bad element: she had to complete high school before qualifying for the program, which was three months ahead. As time marched on, she checked her mail every day. Then it came—a solemn looking envelope that she almost tore her nails opening.

When she opened it she screamed, "Mom, I'm in the Navy now."

Lucy hugged her and asked, "Where will you report? You will have some place to go that will help the war effort."

"I am ordered to report to a dormitory on the mall in Washington D. C. It says to not bring a lot of clothes because we will wear clothes that are issued."

She quickly packed a small bag with mainly toilet articles. Philip drove her downtown, and when he left her, he did something he seldom did. He hugged and kissed her.

When she entered her new living quarters, she was surprised at how meager things were. Before she could survey the area, several women approached and they welcomed her to the barracks. MaryAnn learned that they were from Maine, New York, Maryland, and Massachusetts.

The next day, they got down to work: they had to learn how to use computers, how to translate foreign messages, and how to juggle numbers. This was more difficult, because they worked in teams. She was surprised to learn that her mate was a New York Jew, whose name was Sarah Heiman. MaryAnn pulled that standard joke on Sarah by saying, "Some of my best friends are Jews."

She laughed and answered, "Yes, and some of my best New York friends are Christians."

The applicants came from several female colleges, so MaryAnn felt out of place, but before long the non-college women out-numbered the graduates. By the time the Navy closed the applications, they numbered almost 4,000 code-breakers who worked three shifts per day.

The one fact that troubled most of them was the rigid sexual punishment for any woman caught as a lesbian or if anyone was found to be pregnant. This especially bothered the married women —all of whom were immediately discharged from service.

57

SHE CALLED HIM "HANDY ANDY"

He was standing behind her in the lunch line. He was tall and seemed taller with his cowboy hat on. "How are you'all?" he asked.

"I'm okay," she answered.

"If you are okay," he told her, "You must be from Oklahoma."

"No," she answered, "I am from Massachusetts."

"Well," he announced proudly, "I am an Okie from Muskogee."

She had to ask him, "Are you allowed to wear that hat?"

"Well, you are partly right. I can only wear it at lunch. My name is Andrew Cosgrove, but everyone calls me Andy."

Each day he waited for her, and they became friends. He wanted to teach her the Texas Two-Step, but she preferred the swing or jitterbug. She did agree, however, to go dancing with him. On the dance floor, he told her, "I know this variation of the two step, which is an essential dance."

MaryAnn was surprised at how quickly she learned the quick, quick and slow, slow steps. But Andy was thinking more of love than dance.

As he did every evening, he walked her home to her barracks. On this particular night, it was very late and everyone was asleep. Before she could stop him, he was in her room. He got beside her as she lay on the bed. She could feel his tongue on her face, and while she whispered "No" to him, he put that tongue in her mouth.

She was helpless because she could not scream, and soon he pulled her pants down and entered her. She kept saying "No" in his ear, but he was determined to complete what he had started.

"Don't you feel the longing?" he asked her.

But her body was frozen as he pounded her. "You must go now," she begged.

After he was gone, she laid in bed asking herself, *Should I tell the Administration? Or Should I tell my mother? Or Should I remain silent?* She did not want to tell anyone what he had done to her. If she told the Navy, she would be evicted immediately. She did not share this episode with anyone, and she never spoke to Andrew again.

58

MARYANN COMES HOME ON LEAVE

When MaryAnn Milano retuned to East Boston, she paraded all over the place with a posture that seemed to say, "Hey, look at me." She learned that there existed a poor socio-economic status for women in the 1940s. Most of them lacked higher education. And those who were educated did hit a glass ceiling.

As MaryAnn returned home, Lucy greeted her warmly with a question. "Just what are you doing in your job?"

"Mother," MaryAnn answered loudly, "I have told you before. I cannot divulge what my job is. I can tell you one sad episode. A friend of mine, Bernice Long, was discharged because she was caught in an embrace with one of her friends. They were kissing mouths and other parts of the female bodies. When they were tried, the naval judge said that they were in *flagrante delicto*."

Lucy interrupted her. "What does that mean?"

MaryAnn was embarrassed to answer. "This is a Latin phrase that indicates that the two women were imitating copulation. The two Latin words mean that "the crime is blazing." But it really means that they were caught red-handed in a perverse sexual activity."

"So, they were lesbians," said Lucy.

"Yes, Mother. It is really a shame, because these two persons gave up a thrilling chance to do war work that was needed by those who were risking their lives at sea. Some of these women were virgins. In one case, a woman who tried out a sexual experience told her roommates that it was fun, but she didn't even know that she had a clitoris."

The next day, MaryAnn returned to her dormitory, and each week the work got harder. They had to memorize the Japanese codes and the passwords of the merchant ships that were delivering men and goods to the American forces. These girls who were studying codes learned that hundreds of American ships were being sunk by Japanese submarines and other war vessels.

MaryAnn was so excited about her new skills that she went around telling other code breakers that her group was translating over eighty codes per day. She was still perplexed about the numerical skills that were hiding in her brain. It had to be connected to all the number games that she and Philip played while growing up.

When she was in the eighth grade, Philip had taught her the basic equation for obtaining trend lines:

Y= a + bx, with b being the rate of growth.

She knew now why he insisted that she understand this fundamental equation. She was better now at remembering numbers.

59

MARYANN SEEKS NEW EMPLOYMENT

At the end of World War II, MaryAnn was one of the many code workers who were sent home. Philip was really happy to see her.

The first thing he said to her as he hugged her was, "Well, you really did your part. I am proud of you."

"How did we win the war so quickly?" she asked him.

He was very happy to give her an answer. "The Eighth Air Force won the war in Europe. It had the most casualties and the most deaths, but it completely destroyed what Hitler called his 1000-year Reich."

MaryAnn was still perplexed.

As a former member of the Eighth Air Force, he wanted to brag. "We bombed all of Germany to reduce her effort to carry on a war. First, we destroyed all of their submarines, then we went to their oil refineries. Later, we went to the factories along the Rhine, and finally we pulverized all of their railroad depots, so that they could not send replacements to any battle. They quit on May 8, 1945."

MaryAnn said, "You must be proud."

He did not respond. He just hugged her again.

MaryAnn did not know what she would do next. Nothing that she did for the Navy applied to civilian employment. As she struggled with unemployment, she felt that she would do better if she learned a new skill, so she enrolled at the Emerson Dictation School. It was not difficult for her, so she completed the program early. What she had to do next was to find employment using her new skills. She was not successful until she went to an agency that offered to find her a job if they kept her first paycheck. MaryAnn Milano agreed, and she was assigned to the Bay State Financial Corporation, which was located on Commercial Street, just off Devonshire Street.

The first thing she had to do was to improve her wardrobe, so she headed to Filene's basement, which was all she really could afford until she got her second paycheck at Bay State.

The second thing she learned was that it was not a bank. It was a large group of stock brokers who dealt almost exclusively with Wall Street. She still had much to learn about shorts and longs, puts and calls, high-yield bonds, and conservative-safe ones. She made friends with the women, but she had to depend on the men when she needed help. She was most happy that the men did not make overtures concerning after-hour activities.

PART VII THE CHILDREN LEAVE HOME

PHILIP LEAVES FIRST

.

As the Milanos expected, soon their children created their own households. When World War II began in 1939, the effects of the Great Depression began to recede, and the U.S. economy began to grow again. After the attack on Pearl Harbor, on Dec. 7, 1941, the United States immediately turned the nation into an industrial war-production machine, which put thousands of Americans back to work, many in munitions factories, and many worked longer workweeks, which meant higher earnings. Because of war needs, the electrical industry found itself in need of electrical engineers. The industry was transformed from a narrow specialty into a nation-wide supplier of pervasive technologies of the 20th Century.

When Philip graduated from MIT, he found work immediately with the Electric Light Co., headquartered in Springfield, Massachusetts. Because he graduated from MIT, he was offered a high-level job at that defense firm. His parents were amazed at his beginning salary.

That evening, Philip celebrated by going to a local night club in Boston with a group of his MIT buddies. They chose a place in the Combat Zone—a name given to a stretch of Washington Street that featured adult movies and high crime. But it was also an area of strip clubs. It was near Scollay Square—the red light district.

Philip danced a few numbers, and soon he met a cute young lady who seemed to grasp him where ever he was. Since she was inebriated, he told her that he would pick her up tomorrow.

When he met her the next afternoon, she suggested that they go to a quiet beach nearby. It was a warm, sunny day, so she wore a light dress.

She chose a place that was not very populated. As they walked, she stopped and climbed up a slight hill, sat down, and pulled her dress up to her knees. She put her arms behind her and leaned back. As Philip approached her, he noted that her legs were wide open. When he got close to her, he could not believe what he saw. She had no pants on. He was totally excited by the view.

She sensed his anxiety as she pointed to some tall grass nearby. She was ready to do what he longed for. But he had never before witnessed such an intensity of desire. They had a few wet kisses, and her legs spread open wider. He felt it was like a storm in the sky, and in a few moments it was over. He patted her belly and covered her private part. They were mostly quiet as he drove her home, never to see her again.

As he was driving home to East Boston, he reflected on what had just transpired, and he remembered a popular ditty from his Air Force days:

I n the shade of the old apple tree
    Way up her dress I could see
A little brown spot with hair on the top
And it looked like a p---y to me

B ut then his thoughts shifted to when he advised his kid sister about sex and to "save it for your husband." He turned morose because of his contradictory action. He swore that he would never again engage in such a vile episode.

But not long after, he found a beautiful young lady from Salem, Patricia Endecott, who graduated from Smith College. She was descended from John Endecott, who was a governor of Massachusetts before John Winthrop.

Philip met her at a dance at the Salem Community Center with one of his MIT buddies. Later, he had to take long drives from East Boston to Salem to see her, but love conquered all.

When Philip learned that Patricia loved poetry, he asked his mother which poet he should read so that he could talk to her about poetry. She suggested John Donne, Elizabeth Browning and William Blake.

As he did with all topics, Philip plunged into poetry. When he was ready, he met her on her own territory. He learned a good deal about that subject. He was particularly impressed with a brief poem that he found without an author that spelled out his feeling for this woman. He recited it to her:

"I long for the fullness of your pointing breasts,
    I would delight to lie near the warmth of your waist.
I would kiss your eyes and the curve of your chin.
Your kindness and your sensitivity they comfort me."

She responded with a stanza from the Song of Songs:

"My lover is handsome and strong;
    His eyes are as beautiful as doves by a flying brook,
His lips are like lilies wet with liquid myrrh.
His body is like smooth ivory, with sapphires on it."

. . .

As their romance deepened, Philip's letters to her became more intense. His last paragraph of one affected her the most: "Oh, if I may now suck fully of the milk of your kindness and comfort. Your milk shall spread prosperity over me like a torrent. I delight in the fullness of your pointing breasts and your dreamy small eyes."

After several days of discussing poetry, Philip questioned her. "If God inspired poets to write the Song of Songs, did he not also inspire daVinci to create those sinewy muscles that athlete's carried into athletic contests?"

Patricia agreed that all creation resulted from the hand of God. She had one more statement to make. "Philip, you should know that a woman is interested in everything about her man even before she knew him." Then, she pursued the topic of writing. "Philip," she began, "You are very intelligent and informed, so why don't you write books?"

Philip was not prepared for that question. "I don't know," he answered slowly. "I have studied a lot of English writers, but I did not see myself as one of them. I am a scientist. But I have thought often of leaving a legacy to my children and writing would be one way. I'll give it more thought, but I must teach to put bread on our table."

Soon after they were married in Salem, and they honeymooned in Europe, after which they settled in their small mansion in Marblehead.

When Lucy thought about what happened, all that she could do was to remember where she came from in Italy. She kept thinking that she and they were on different planets.

60

MARYANN'S BARRIERS

aryAnn's situation was radically different. She wanted to be involved in elementary education, like her mother, but because she always disliked school at all levels, she was confined to jobs requiring manual dexterity.

MaryAnn agreed to apply for one of the factory job openings in Lynn, which became the leading shoe manufacturer in the United States. As an amateur historian, Philip investigated how Lynn became a leading industrial city. It began with a small-scale setting of the shoe industry in the early 19th century. As transportation improved, its manufacturing moved from small shops engaged in custom work to larger-scale production, which meant that it could employ less skilled workers, including women and children, who replaced journeymen.

The next innovation occurred when Lynn shoe manufacturers, Charles A. Coffin and Silas Abbott Barton, became interested in the early electric industry. Its electric company merged with Edison Electric Company of Schenectady, New York, which became General Electric in 1892. It had two original GE plants in Lynn and Schenectady.

Initially the General Electric plant specialized in arc lights, electric motors, and meters. Later it specialized in aircraft electrical systems and components, and aircraft engines, which evolved into the jet engine plant during World War II—the result of research contacts at MIT in Cambridge.

During the late 19th and early 20th centuries, Lynn's immigrant population rose to 29,500, mostly Polish and Russian born Jews, who were the largest single group. At the same time, some of the Catholic churches conducted services in Italian. By the beginning of the 20th century, Lynn was the world leader in the production of shoes. Its 234 factories produced more than a million pairs of shoes each day, due mainly to the mechanization of the process by an African-American immigrant named Jan Matzeliger.

MaryAnn was happy to see that the shoe companies were hiring black men. She saw one, and she became friendly with a tall good-looking black man who said his name was Jackson. He looked like an athlete whenever he raised the sleeves on his shirt.

One day they struck up a conversation about the plight of Negroes. MaryAnn tried to convince him that blacks were better off in Boston than in most places in the United States.

"Tell me," he responded, "how many black lawyers and medical doctors are there in Boston? We have to defend our sexuality all the time, and we are treated like we are nothing but ignorant studs."

But she told him, "In Boston blacks were free, and they could go to schools."

"You are right there," he told her, "but how are black women are going to develop nursing skills for raising children when the children were taken from them in the slave states?"

"But don't forget," interrupted MaryAnn, "that Boston was the center of the anti-slavery movement, and it has supported a culture of invention. It is commonly known as Yankee know-how."

"You got me there," he exclaimed as he walked back to his job bench.

Because of a faulty reputation for high crime and vice, a popular rhyme about Lynn became popular throughout Massachusetts: "Lynn, Lynn, the city of sin, you'll never come out the way you went in. What looks like gold is really tin, the girls say 'no' but they'll give in. Lynn, Lynn, the city of sin." Another variation was "Lynn, Lynn the city of sin: if you ain't bad, you can't get in!"

MaryAnn decided that she would apply for employment at the Lynn GE plant. When she was interviewed, the man in charge of employment asked here, "What can you contribute to GE that would make us hire you?"

MaryAnn paused, and she remembered a quotation that applied now: "You never get a second chance to make a first impression." Then she spoke, "Well, I can write very well, so I can help you to turn out brochures and other documents to emphasize the importance of GE to the community and the United States. Communication is important to GE and any corporation."

The man seated near him said, "My name is William McKee, and I agree with you that good writing is necessary for any organization. When can you start?"

MaryAnn answered quickly. "Thank you, Mr. McKee. I can start anytime."

McKee replied, "Let's begin by calling me Bill, and you can report to the Employment Office tomorrow. It's on the first floor. When you have completed all the documents, come back here and we can discuss what functions you can deal with."

MaryAnn said her good byes and she hurried home to Tom Collins. When she kissed him, he knew she had some information to give her.

"Okay, tell me what happened."

"I got a job at GE. I don't know what I will do yet, but it will require some writing."

"Well, they are smart because you are good at that."

"How about if we celebrate? Let's go to Javelli's in Day Square."

"I have dinner already prepared, but I will serve it for tomorrow. Let's go," she informed him.

Day Square was one of the busiest places in East Boston because a number of streets joined at the square. It was on the road to Chelsea, the North Shore, and the tunnel to Boston. There were a number of handicraft shops, which included the upholstery shop, Quality Bakery, the auto repair shop, and a gasoline station. In addition there was a diner, a drug store and a fish market.

It took a while to find a parking place, but they knew it was worth the effort because Javelli's was a fine place to dine. They had a complete dinner, and when they got home, they continued their celebration with more wine. They both sensed that their party would finish with lovemaking, but they were not aware that they made a connection earlier, something she would learn after three or four months.

When she missed her monthly for three straight months, she knew she was carrying a child. He was born six months later, and he looked like his grandfather. They quickly chose the name Dylan, who was an uncle in the Collins family.

Young Dylan was a large baby, and he grew up even bigger. By the time he was a teenager, he was over six feet tall. He was really a good athlete at any sport he tried, but he favored baseball. When he was a senior in high school, he was the best hitter on the baseball team and he was an excellent center fielder. He was surprised to receive four-year scholarships to both Boston College and Boston University.

MaryAnn asked him if he could expect any more scholarships.

He smiled before he answered. "No, Mother. MIT does not provide scholarships, and I don't think I have the grades for Harvard."

When his father learned of these awards, he was a little embarrassed because he had told Dylan many times that sports were a waste of time. His usual statement was, "You need to study more."

Tom Collins was delighted about the awards because he knew that his parents did not have enough money to cover four years of college. He hugged his son and said, "Well Dylan, I guess you were right to spend all that time on sports. This will really help the family financial condition."

61

PHILIP JOINS THE FRAY

As several of Phil's buddies volunteered for military service, Phil asked Patricia to hear him out about joining the Army Air Corps. She told him, "You have a good position with a good salary, and your prospects are very positive."

"You are correct," he said, "but you are forgetting about the draft. I don't want to walk across Germany in the mud."

She had no response, so she told him, "Go ahead, sign up. I'll be here when you return."

"If I return," he added.

He easily passed the written examination, and after signing applications at the Commonwealth Avenue recruiting center, he reported to the Armory for his physical. It was all routine, except for those injections. When he saw the size of the needles, he decided to close his eyes when it was his turn. His arm was swollen for only a day or two.

Because there was a shortage of training planes, he waited four months until he was called to active duty at the Southeast Army Air Corps Training Center at Montgomery, Alabama. Basic Training was at Randolph Field, Texas. He was assigned a slate-blue uniform as a flying cadet. Flight training lasted seven months, for which he was paid $75 per month. Pre-flight training involved the mechanics and physics of flight. After completion of this segment, they were given ten hours at the flight simulators.

Primary training was sixty to sixty-five hours in a two-seater Stearman, Ryan, or Fairchild airplane. Advanced training was flying in formation and by instruments and either in a single or a multi-engine plane. A recruit needed seventy-five to eighty hours to receive his wings.

Philip became a great pilot, so he was assigned to a P-51 squadron in England. The P-51 had Rolls Royce Merlin Engines. At altitudes above 20,000 feet, Philip was sure that his Mustang was superior to the ME 109 (Messerschmitt).

When Philip went to his barracks, he met an older British man who was cleaning the area for the new arrivals. Philip knew that he was picking up the personal belongings of the pilots who did not return from today's mission. Philip knew also that they would examine all the objects to make sure that nothing returned to the states that was embarrassing, particularly for married men.

They shook hands, and Philip was anxious to ask him about all the burnt buildings over London.

He did not respond quickly, but when he did, he told his new Yank friend, "We are sure happy to see you Americans here. We need your help. The Blitzkrieg (the lightning War) took place in 1940 and 1941. In 1940, the Germans bombed London for fifty-six out of fifty-seven days and nights. Liverpool, the largest seaport, was a main target, but Birmingham and Manchester were also bombed."

Then he seemed to become happier when he stated, "But by 1941 the German offensive failed its major objective of invading London. It could not develop a strategy for halting British production (which was aided by American help). Boy, we are sure glad to see you Yanks here."

When the Americans were assembled for an orientation, the major told them, "For the first year and one-half the bombers that we escorted were in serious jeopardy because the fighter planes did not have a sufficient amount of gasoline to escort the bombers into

Germany. The result was very high losses for bombers. A very innovative mechanic at one bomber base asked his colonel, "Why can't we attach fuel tanks under the wings of fighters?" This simple declaration will probably save hundreds of American airmen for the rest of the war."

The major had one more bit of advice to offer the new pilots. "There is no such thing as bravery, only degrees of fear." When the major finished giving the recruits all of his advice, Philip went to the mailroom, and he was surprised to receive a letter from his love.

She wrote: "My Darling, my heart beats faster for you. I cannot wait until you return. Leave those British women alone. I'll provide plenty of love later. Don't forget that those teenage girls, who thought they would soon be victory girls, could not deny any serviceman what they craved."

During the briefing for his next mission, the major told all he pilots, "You will be like Pistol-packing mamas as you bomb Berlin." The cheer was very loud.

From that day, the American fighters patrolled the skies looking for German planes that were about to attack a B-17 Bomber Group. When they met, they did their dog-fights at about 30,000 feet. Most of the pilots believed that they would rather die in the air than in the German mud.

When these pilots were not fighting in the skies, they usually went on a two-day leave each month, usually to downtown London. Philip prepared for his first leave by putting on his smartest uniform. His hair was perfectly parted and in place with the help of a commercial chemical.

He first entered a pub where he downed a Half-and-Half beer. Getting back in the street, he was approached by a prostitute.

"How about it, Yank. Five pounds and breakfast in bed."

He was kind in answering her. "I have a wife at home, so I thank you for the offer, but I must be true to her."

As he continued walking, he thought married men had to use all of their wiles to not succumb to the offerings of the prostitutes who were everywhere in downtown streets and pubs.

Philip asked one of the Brits why there were so many young women serving as street walkers, and the answer satisfied him. "Many of these women have lost a husband in the war which for them has been going on for four years. Many are hungry because the farmers have gone to war, and food is very scarce," He added, "You can see it in their faces and their teeth."

Philip felt sorry for them, and he pledged to himself to give a prostitute a one pound note each time he was visiting London, but he would not accept their service.

Philip got more bad news. His best friend, John Carlton, was killed while they were protecting the bombers as they crossed the German line. There were many more 109s than there were P-51 Mustangs. A few days later, he received a copy of the letter that was sent by President Roosevelt to his sister. She told him that John died doing what he really wanted to do, but he did not believe her. How could he be happy dying at twenty two years old? Philip thought that life was unfair.

Back at the base, Philip was involved in several dog fights, but he survived them all. And after he had flown fifty missions and had three kills, he was sent home. He hopped a ride in Scotland on a transport plane and landed at Dallas, Texas.

He was ordered to Denver for R & R—the closest Army base to relieve warriors of their PTSD. In a few weeks he was considered normal by the medics and was ordered to report to the Classification Center at Santa Ana, California.

When he was checked in, he made his first trip to Hollywood. It was fortunate that there was an electric train going from Santa Ana to Hollywood, where all the young women were gorgeous—all waiting to receive a contract to make a film.

He got a table at a restaurant and bar, where he ordered a bourbon and water, and he was surprised when the waitress told him, "There is no charge for our servicemen." He was more surprised when one of the gorgeous babes asked if she could join him. He nodded with his head, and he pointed with his finger to the chair beside him. She was stunning and very talkative. "Where are you from?" she asked.

"I am from Massachusetts," he responded. "And where are you from?"

"I'm an Okie," she told him. "I was born in Tulsa. Oklahoma was all farms and oil until recently. I was the Oklahoma Beauty Queen, so I thought I could get into films."

"How big is Tulsa?"

"Oh, it's about 150,000. Do you know that the oil money in Tulsa provided the means for it to become an aviation depot? Douglas Aircraft just completed its plant to build bombers, and at the same time Spartan Aircraft trained hundreds of pilots for the war needs."

She asked Phil, "Can you dance?"

He assumed she meant swing or fox trot, but she began by doing the Texas Two Step. When he did not join in, she offered help. "Watch me, now," she said as she positioned him. "This is a partner's dance, with a leader and a follower. The leader chooses the steps as they walk around the floor in a counter clockwise direction. The leader puts his right hand on the follower's left shoulder."

Philip stopped her lesson. "Let's sit down. You never told me your name."

"My name is Theresa. But they call me Tessie."

"Hello, Tessie. Tell me how you are doing in Hollywood."

Her eyes got misty as she began to speak. "It comes down to one thing. If a woman agrees to be on her back she gets hired immediately, and those who protect their privacy and their virginity wander throughout the city seeking employment."

"You are doing the right thing," he told her, "So be happy that you are saving yourself for your husband. I know because I have a much better marriage because my woman waited also."

There was only a moment of silence until he continued speaking. "Women are stronger than men, even their sex drive is stronger. Women come in all sizes. Some are literate, some cannot even carry on a conversation. Some would even agree to an open marriage in which both can roam outside of their own bedrooms. You will be much happier being part of a traditional marriage."

Tessie seemed to perk up when he finished speaking. She went around the table and kissed him on the cheek.

"You are lucky my wife is not here," he told her as he smiled.

"I am glad I met you," Tessie said. "I am bolstered by your good advice. Good night and best of luck."

62

GO EAST, YOUNG MAN

P hilip returned to his base thinking that he had enough of Hollywood bimbos. The next day, he asked the C.O. for a meeting. When they met, his first question was, "Is there any way I could get closer to Massachusetts?"

The Colonel told him, "There is a Northeast Division in Maine."

"That would be great." Philip responded.

"There would be some flying over the ocean," he was told.

Philip had a ready answer, "I flew over the North Sea on some missions. It could not be very different."

"Okay," said Colonel Rodgers. "I will draw up your transfer papers right away. We should favor those who have survived combat. Fifty missions is enough." Then he quoted Kipling, "Remember, 'if you can keep your head when all about you are losing theirs, you'll be a man my friend.'"

In two days, Phil was packed and on his way to Presque Isle Army Air Field. He had investigated its history. It was built by the Civilian Conservation Corps in 1930, and in 1941 it was appropriated by the U. S. Government. It is used as a stopping point for planes that are going to and from the United Kingdom. This unit was activated in 1942, when our planes were ferried to England by way of Greenland and Iceland—the very route he had taken on his way to combat.

For the next year or two, Philip Milano just waited for the war to end, and when it did, he returned home to Marblehead to his wife, Patricia, and his son Dylan, who was now two years old.

When he completed his going-out physical. The medical doctor told him that he might not be able to sleep for a while until he could forget all those B-17s going down and those that disappeared when the bombs in the Bomb Bay exploded. He stressed that it will keep coming back until he could totally forget. Philip was not sure what he should do next.

When Patricia learned that Philip was coming home, she did something she had never done before. She cleaned the entire house from bottom to top. She began by cleaning all the windows. Then she completed the dining and living rooms, leaving the kitchen for last. After she cleaned the plates, glasses and bowls, she was dead tired, but she was quite proud of her accomplishment.

When he entered his front door, the two embraced with a long kiss. This was a prelude to what would transpire in the evening. But he learned about fatherhood immediately. As he and his wife were sleeping, he heard his son crying. He told Patricia, "I'll take care of this." He picked up Dylan and he began to sing a tune that he learned from a friend:

"**G**o to sleep little peep
   "Go to sleep little peeper
   "Go to sleep little peep
   "Be a great little sleeper.

His dad told him to "stop fussing." He must have heard him, because he switched to a soft whimper and he fell fright to sleep. Philip then did something he had never done before. He changed his diaper, wrapped his son in a blanket, and put him back in his small bed. The next thing he was sure of was that soon his son would be sixteen years old.

In the morning, Patricia came down to the breakfast table with a small black book in her hand. She asked herself, "Was he pliant? Did he lust over other women?

"What is this book?" she asked. "What do the circles, squares and diamonds mean with names beside them." Then she really shocked him. She pointed a finger in his face and asked, "Did you fuck any of them?"

And she started throwing dishes, glasses, and cups at him. He watched for a while, and he became very upset and spoke loudly. "You have it all wrong. This booklet is ten years old. It's been in my luggage all that time. The circle means that girl would allow you to kiss her on the lips. The square means she won't allow it. The diamond tells you that she will let you put your hand on her breast."

"Now, when I went to London, I did not go to find women. I went to find relief from combat. They have been in a war for five years, and they are very tired, hungry and show the pangs of war. You see it on their skin and on their teeth."

She interrupted him. "I think I am pregnant. Do you want me to abort it?"

He screamed at her. "We are Christians. We do not destroy life."

After she stopped throwing things at him, she apologized. Then they embraced. She surprised him by saying, "I know that the way to a man's heart is through his stomach. I've been practicing for weeks."

Both the breakfast and dinner she served him were very edible.

63

IT'S A GIRL

Their second baby seemed easier for her than the first one. She was in the hospital for only five days. When they reached their home, they repeated the problem of the first child. What shall we name our beautiful daughter?

She threw him a curve ball. "Don't you think we should stop using family names?" she enquired.

"You are right again," he said. "So, what do we name her? Do you have a favorite name for a girl?" he asked.

There was no response.

She cast the question back at him. "How about one of your old girl friends? Did you have a favorite before you married me?"

He hesitated to answer her question. Then he spoke softly and more quietly. "I did date one girl for an entire year, and she just walked away from me without saying a word. I would not name my daughter after her."

"That's okay," Patricia said. "Is there another girl you have dated?"

"There is one who lived in Marblehead, but she has the name of one of my aunts—Anna. I don't think I want that."

Patricia tried a new approach. "How about Hollywood? Did you have a real crush on any star there?"

"Now you have hit a home run," he said. "When I was fifteen years old, I fell madly in love with the dancer, Eleanor Powell. I saw all of her pictures, and I did not lose that crush until I graduated from high school."

"Well, Philip. How does Eleanor Milano sound?"

"It is okay by me. Maybe I could have a crush on my daughter."

"Cut that out," she said pointing a finger at him. "We will name her Eleanor."

64

PHILIP TRIES FOR A PH.D

Patricia knew that Philip was in a quandary, so she suggested that they sit and discuss his options. The choices were three: go back to a job in industry, teach at the high school level, or get a doctorate. Philip never made quick decisions, so it took several discussions.

Patricia knew why he was meditating, so she told him, "Phil. You went to MIT. Your grades were superior, so you have the answer to your perplexity. God gave you brilliance, so don't waste it."

Philip interrupted her, 'So. you are saying that I should continue my education. Am I right?"

She agreed. "I know it's what you really want."

"Okay," he said jubilantly. "I will contact MIT right away. But how will you be able to work with a two-year old son?"

"I talked to my dad," she told him, "And he assured me that he would help us if you continued your education."

"Patricia," he said loudly to get her attention, "I have never told you this, but I wrote a book when I was in the sixth grade. It was about a flyer in the First World War. I named him Thaddeus, and he was in a continuous dog fights with the Red Baron von Richtoven. Thad eventually won those battles."

"What happened to your book?" she asked.

"Well, I loaned it to one of the older guys on the street, and when he moved away he took my book with him."

"That was mean of him," she said as she hugged him.

And so Philip Milano began his Ph.D program. He thought it would take years, so they discussed finances. He would need some sort of employment at MIT and free tuition. One other problem interrupted his mental process.

"You realize that this means that we will have to postpone adding to our family," he said sorrowfully.

"Well," she responded, "I still have at least ten years of childbearing. So, let's get on with this lengthy process."

It sure was long. He first had to pass the graduate Record Examination in Physics. It was mostly quantitative and analytical problems. Then he had to pass the qualifying exam, and then there was the ultimate barrier: the thesis. He knew of the category everybody called ABD, which meant "All but the dissertation." A large percentage of students wound up there. But in the beginning it all went well. He did get free tuition.

It was more difficult to get five professors to serve on his thesis committee. The Physics Department was at the forefront of many areas where new aspects of physics can be found. Philip learned that several MIT professors were studying the largest things in the universe, and they also studied the smallest things: elementary particles or even the strings that may be the substructure of these particles. But before he started working on a topic for his dissertation, he had a question for his Committee, "Can I minor in English?"

They each seemed stunned by his query, and the Chairman was irritated by the question. "As you probably know, the minor must be in a cognate field such as political science or sociology."

Philip was prepared to answer. "Since I was in the sixth grade, I dreamed of writing a book, and since then, I have chosen only English courses for electives. So far, I have taken classes in Shakespeare, Milton, Browning, American Novel, and British Criticism. Because I am the child of Italian immigrants, I was always behind in my English courses, but I am making up for my disadvantage. I like the quotation by Benjamin Jowett, "One man is as good as another until he has written a book."

The Committee asked Philip to leave the room for a minute, and ten minutes later they recalled him. "We considered your request, and we are breaking custom by approving your request. Your grades are excellent, and we believe you can be an excellent physics professor and creative writer."

Philip was elated and he chose "String Theory" for his topic. This is a theory in which pointed particles are replaced by one-dimensional objects called strings. Some physicists call it a part of quantum mechanics.

Although other students often worked in groups, Philip preferred to work alone. Two years later he was defending his thesis, which he passed easily. So in June he had a new title, "Doctor," and what he needed was a job.

Long before he got his doctorate, he had decided that he wanted to teach. There were seven major universities in the Boston area, and he assumed he could get a job at one of them.

For reasons that he could not fully understand, he favored the Jesuit Boston College. He knew from one of his MIT friends, who became a Jesuit priest, what the procedure was at the Jesuit Campion Center: two years of Novitiate, three years of graduate studies, four years of theology and three to five years of ministry. The entire process took twelve to fourteen years.

But before he could go out job seeking, MIT offered him a contract as Assistant Professor, which he did not turn down.

65

PROFESSOR MILANO MEETS HIS STUDENTS

Philip learned early that MIT students were first rate. During any lecture, he was peppered with questions. Before he could answer any of the questions, he remembered a quotation by General George Patton, "Never tell people how to do things. Tell them what to do, and they will surprise you."

Usually he could deal with them, but one question stymied him. It came from an American Indian, who asked, "Why is the Government taking most of the best Indian lands?"

Philip wondered what this question had to do with physics. He was aware that during the nineteenth century the monies that were allocated for Indians were often stolen, but he did not comprehend the gist of the question.

"Tell me the situation," he asked his student.

He was quick to respond. "It all began when the Army Corps of Engineers was given the duty of controlling floods. They accomplished this by building dams over the most fertile lands. My people used them to grow medicinal plants, and the animals that roamed the areas were our food and the timber was used for fuel. In one case the Government took over ninety percent of our lands by condemning them, and they paid us very little. Where can we go, and how can we survive if the dam floods all of our best land?"

Philip meditated for a moment, then he remembered that his father is a lawyer. "This is not a question of science," he told his student. "It is one for the law. I will take it up with the dean of the Law School."

When he got home, he brought up the issue with his father, who was very slow to answer. Then he remembered that in the late nineteenth century, the Congress passed a law that allowed the Army Corps of Engineers to control water boundaries in the Western United States. He was not very hopeful that this could be changed soon, so the plight of the Indians could not easily be improved.

Philip informed his student of this situation on the following day, which left him in a quandary, but he recalled another quotation from a high school teacher who told him that, "To teach is to learn twice."

66

PHILIP MEETS A POET

As Professor Milano was walking across campus one afternoon, he was surprised to hear someone calling his name.

"Professor Milano," she said loudly as she walked toward him.

When he turned to see who was calling, he was amazed at her loveliness. She was stunningly beautiful.

He stopped. "Did you call me?"

"Yes, I did. My boyfriend is in your class, and he raves about your lectures. I am an English major, and he tells me that your lectures are like poetry. Have you studied poetry?"

He did not want to discuss his life's history to a stranger, so he brushed her off by lying, "I did take a few English classes."

"Have you ever written poems?" she asked.

Again he was stymied, and again he lied. "I did write poems in England on days when I was not flying. It would not have any meaning for you, because it is about a bombing mission."

"Can you recite any of it for me. I hope to teach poetry when I graduate."

"It is eighteen pages long, and I have a copy in my office. I have tomorrow afternoon off, so if you want to read it drop by."

He hoped she would not come to his office, but she was there after lunch. She pulled a chair next to his and she sat on its edge, so she could be closer to him.

Reaching for his poem, he told her, "This won't interest you because it is all about a bombing mission to Berlin."

"Oh no. You are wrong. I have relatives who served, some of them in Germany. Please read me a few lines."

He began:

T akeoff

T he plane stretched in the sky
        Between the sun and Moon;
    Morning stretched to the first step of nature's tribune,
    Sneered at evening
    That rested on the back of day.

M y watch tells time.
        What does eternity tell?
    That limitless space of vapor and gel
    The spires of the white-washed church
    Was like a cathedral
    On the greening college grounds,
    The blind held their seeing hounds,

B ombs Away
        The Junkers left us at the IP
    To Wait;
    Our bombsight zeroed on the autobahn
    And Brandenburg Gate

Evasive action ceased on the run
The plane responded to the bombsight
Above unter den Linden
Crazily they seemed to say
Nach dem bahnhof
Running all the way
With a barren simper and a laugh

She effused over his reading as she moved her voluptuous breast against him. He moved slightly away from her and said, "You know, I do not even know your name."

She responded quickly. "Oh yes, my name is Corinne Geistner, and I am a German. They call me Corrie."

He then did what he had promised that he would never do again, except to his wife. He reached down to the juncture of her legs, and soon they were one.

When they had completed their sexual activity, he was fearful of being caught in *flagrante delicto*. Walking home, he was morose, and when he entered his house, Patricia saw the wrinkles in his trousers.

"Where have you been?" she asked loudly.

He had to lie. "I was at the library doing research on some aspects of string theory that troubles me."

She was not satisfied with that response. She recalled a statement of Mark Twain, "Figures don't lie, but liar's figure." Have you been seeing one of your young bitches?"

"You have it all wrong. The one I met today is just one of my students who had a legitimate question."

67

PATRICIA LEAVES

They ate in silence that evening, and the next day Patricia and the children were gone. He searched for her for days without luck. He went to her mother, who told him, "She does not want to see you ever again."

He remembered Milton's *Paradise Lost.* "What tho the field be lost. All is not lost."

When he returned to the empty house, he decided that he could not live there anymore because it had too many memories of Patricia and the children, so he went to the church to ask a priest where he could find shelter.

Father Sullivan suggested Saint Michael's Shelter. Philip thanked him and drove there. Another priest met him at the front door. "Welcome," he said. "Are you unemployed?" he asked.

Philip answered, "Yes, I am right now."

"Well, we have room for you now. Let me show you where you can sleep. Follow me."

They walked silently down a corridor until he stopped and said, "This is it. It is meager, but we have women who come in daily to keep all rooms clean."

Philip walked in and perused his new dwelling. He agreed it was meager. There was only a chair, a bed, and a small dresser. "This is fine," he told the priest, who informed him of the meal hours.

Father lectured him about the shelter. "Sometimes people fall on hard times, and they have nowhere else to go. When this happens, they often turn to homeless shelters so that they have a place to live temporarily. Most stay at these homeless shelters for a short amount of time, until they can get their lives back. Sadly, the number of homeless shelters in the country is growing, and the Department of Housing and Urban Development has indicated that millions of Americans qualify to take advantage of them.

Philip had only one question, "Father, is there a library here?"

The priest answered, "Well, we do have a small number of books, but you would do better if you went to the public library which is within walking distance."

Philip thanked him, and he sat down to establish a daily routine: take a long walk in the morning, and after lunch go to the library to work on his poetry. He could not make friends, because he did not want to waste time, which he considered precious.

He thought about his family and being alone. Who would bury him? He had buried his parents, so he visited his mother's grave and he wept profusely. She had been his whole life, and now he had sacrificed it for one romantic episode. Now he would carry this burden for his remaining years.

He thought of the poem "For want of a nail," which tells us that "For want of a nail the shoe is lost, and for want of a shoe the horse is lost, and for want of a horse the rider is lost."

When John Kennedy won the presidency in 1960, Philip was especially pleased, both because he favored most of Kennedy's programs and he was just a few years younger than the President. Philip thought that like him, Kennedy was really a poet. He read and re-read a part the inaugural address:

"Let the word go forth from this time and place, to friend and foe alike, that the torch has been passed to a new generation of Americans—born in this century, tempered by war, disciplined by a hard and bitter peace, proud of our ancient heritage."

Although he was tough and charming, Philip was convinced that only a poet could produce words like those. It re-charged his writing skills. But as the days rolled by and then the years, he became more distracted and partly insane. He gave up on string theory and returned to his second love—poetry.

He wrote a new poem to ease his sorrow:

M y Love's a Falling Rain

M y love's a falling rain
        And I an arid land;
No part of her domain
Can I command.

H ow strange to lie here—
        My sky overcast
Only to whither and sere
When love has passed.

H e decided to return to the poem he had worked on for many months after he completed his bombing missions. He loudly read the first stanzas:

O pitiful sleep—eyelids dragging eyeball to the grave
        Fingers groping for release from the dream's hold.
Dogs gouging landscapes into open graves,
Sheep plucked from soft fields
Snakes lying passively at the water's rim.

·   ·   ·

Washed in a brown basin;
      White blood splashed on red eyes,
Dripped into eddies,
Then scurried to oblivion
When hands swish into faces
As shells would from those terrible places.

Acres of rivers running down our flak
      Mountains of trombones at our backs.

Level off at the coast, they had said
      Over Beachy Head
Get the Group in tight
Before Dunkirk comes in sight.

Through the Ruhr
      Down flack alley.
Who'd be sure what the tally?
Only Haw Haw and Axis Sally.

We climbed on course
      Watching strategy shake from its nap
And spread on the ground
In the shape of a map.

The miles of vapors
      Streaked along the astrodome
Like a speeding train
Taking its people home.

. . .

W here sky?
        And how high?
The earth and sky caress the sunrise
O dazzling sun O limpid air O cool daybreak.

S ir, do you have a standard operating credo
        To move us on our way?

W hen Patricia left Philip, she decided to change her name. She was told to go to the Social Security Office, where she presented her driver's license. The official there refused her request because she was still married, and she could not find Philip to obtain his approval.

During the next month, he did not go to the library, because he was rewriting his poem-- "Mission to Big B." *Would it ever be published?* he asked himself. It was his masterpiece, he thought, although others might not describe it as such.

68

PATRICIA FINDS PHILIP

She walked into his room. She wanted to cry, but she hugged him and kissed him ferociously. "So, this is where you have been hiding. I searched for you every day. Your children kept asking for you. You poor thing."

He had to interrupt her. "I searched for you every day also, but I did not have resources to locate you, so I just settled in at the shelter and I worked on my World War II poem."

Patricia was confused. "What happened to your job at MIT?"

He hesitated. "Well, I was let go, because several students complained to the Dean about my incoherent lectures."

She stopped him. "We are going back to our home to become a family again."

This time, he stopped her. "Where have you been hiding?"

She did not answer quickly. "I took our children to one of our houses on a Caribbean Island, where they both attended school. You will be happy to know that Dylan is as smart as you were, and he won a scholarship to Harvard University."

Philip was totally confused. "Who paid for all this?" he demanded.

She asked her brain for help in answering. "Well," she began, "while you were away, both of my parents died, and I inherited all of their assets, which included three island homes, and their large home in Cambridge."

"And what about our home?"

"Well, we did not need it any longer, so I rented it. Tell me Philip, what have you been doing all these years?'

"Well, I usually walked in the morning and I revised my poem in the afternoon."

"Oh, you poor thing," she exclaimed. "Can you not forget that war?"

"I have tried to forget it, but I keep dreaming of all the Flying Fortress's going down. I want to honor my buddies who died in the air. You know that the 8th Air Force had more deaths than all the other World War II Groups. I cannot stop honoring them."

Then she asked him a peculiar question. "Do we want any more children?"

He was silent for a while, then he answered slowly, "Well I am thirty nine years old, so the answer is up to you."

There was nothing but silence.

69

THEY MOVE AGAIN

They moved into the Endicott's mansion in Salem. As they got out of their Cadillac, Philip saw the two very large columns surrounding the front door and the half angel and half demon above it. He could not believe what he was seeing. It was a three-story dwelling with a long-screened section on the first floor. The living room was gigantic with a huge fireplace and an eighteenth century painting above it. There were several long-legged tables in each room, and each had a walk-in closet and a bathroom.

As we went into the dining room, he saw the very large oak table with eight chairs, and it had two fireplaces. There was a keeping room with all antique furnishing. In the corner was a 19th century tall case clock of butternut, which was made in Massachusetts. As they walked around, they saw an oil painting of a horse, which made Philip believe that they were excellent horse riders.

Continuing their tour, they went downstairs to the cooling room, which was used to store perishable foods. It was a dugout stone cellar. They decided to replace some of the old things, but they kept the original woodwork, which they cleaned with linseed oil.

Patricia spoke few words as they wandered throughout this immense structure that Philip thought could be a museum. Then his mind drifted back to the shelter, from which he walked each morning and wrote beautiful lines as revisions to his poem, that one English teacher had told him was good enough to work on throughout his life. But now he was no longer alone. They are a family again, so he must alter his daily schedule.

As he day-dreamed about the house and the poem, Patricia invaded his thoughts. "Well, what do you think, honey?" she exclaimed happily. "Isn't this wonderful for our family?"

He snapped her back to reality. "And what are we going to do with this relic when our children are married and gone?"

"That is a long time from now," she told him.

"Are you really going to cook in this museum?" he asked.

"Well, my parents employed a cook, and we can afford one now."

There was a long silence, and then she was ready to ask the question she wanted to ask throughout their marriage. "When are you going to let me read this poem of yours that seems to consume you?"

"I did not think you had any interest," he told her.

This stirred her up as she spoke more loudly. "Philip, we are married and in marriage the two become one in many ways. Any thing you do I have an interest, and any thing I do you should care about."

He walked slowly toward her, reached his arms around her, pulled her toward him, and gave her a long, deep kiss. "You are right. You are always right. I apologize. I have not been my real self for some time. When I unpack my things, I will give you the entire poem. It is fifteen pages long, and I would appreciate your editing it, which you are good at."

70

THE PRIZE

When she had finished reading and editing the poem, she approached Philip, and she spoke slowly. "I am sorry I ridiculed your poetic work. That teacher of yours was right. You could work on it all your life, and you did. It is a work of art. If you publish this novel, you should put the poem as an appendix so that your readers will understand why you spent a large party of your life improving it."

Patricia did not tell Philip that she had submitted his poem to The Academy of American Poets. When the judges announced the winners of the 2017 prizes, most poets did not know Philip Milano, who was not listed among the most valuable poets in the United States. He was given a prize but was not awarded one of the monetary prizes. He was named a poet in the early stage of his career.

In announcing Philip's prize, the Academy noted that he taught physics at MIT for several years, and it stressed that it is very unusual for a scientist to win such a prize. When summarizing his long poem, it wrote. "We always think of the ground soldier as the most important of the war, but Philip's "Mission to Big B" (Berlin) explains why the 8th Air Force had the highest casualties of World War II, and according to General Rand, it won the European War. This is why our committee was unanimous in granting him this prize. So Philip Milano, come up to the stage to receive your award."

When they got home, Patricia kissed him and told him how proud she was of his love of poetry.

"I should not have criticized you for all the times you were working at something that was important to you."

PART VIII ABOUT THE MURDER

A VICTIM SHOWS UP

On the third day of the trial, Rubenstein was shocked to learn that a woman was outside of his office who was willing to testify that Eliot raped her. He told his secretary to send her right in.

She was a plain looking woman who gave the appearance of a person who worked in an office. He interviewed her, and on day four of the trial, Rubenstein asked the clerk to call his new witness to the stand.

"Would Miss Dean come to the witness box? Please state your name."

"My name is Doreen Dean."

"And what is your occupation?" the prosecutor asked.

"I do clerical work, including dictation,' she told him.

"Now please tell the court how you met Charles Eliot," he asked.

"Well, I guess he got my name from the Yellow Pages of the telephone book."

"And what did he want you to do?" Rubenstein asked.

"He said he was working on a new book, and he wanted to dictate some parts rather than type them himself."

"And did that job go well?" he asked her.

"It began well, but after an hour or two he tried to get friendly."

"What exactly do you mean by that, Miss Dean?"

"He started groping me, and I thought he was going to rip my clothes from my body. He was like a mad man. He dragged me to the couch and started to undress me. I fought him as best as I could, but he was much bigger than I was."

"So," asked the prosecutor, "did you get away? What was the final result?"

"He tried to rape me."

"Did he complete the task?"

"I don't think so. He appeared to be dysfunctional."

Rubenstein wanted to ask her about that word, but he was sympathetic about the embarrassment he put her through so he demurred. "Thank you, Miss Dean."

Stephen Stepinski raised his hand, and Judge O'Connor asked him, "Is there a problem?"

Stepinski said, "I have a problem with the last witness."

"What is it?" asked O'Connor.

Stepinski took time to phrase his question. "I do not understand what relevance the last witness's statement has to the case at hand. Eliot is dead, so she cannot prosecute him for any crime."

"Perhaps the prosecutor can answer your question," said O'Connor.

Rubenstein began slowly. "I was simply trying to tell the Eliot family that he had committed many crimes, and that his family cannot attempt to paint him as a positive figure in their family history."

O'Connor rebuked Rubenstein. "We are here to find a murderer, not to improve the Eliot family history." He continued, "Now Mr. Rubenstein, do you have any other persons who can help us find the criminal?"

"Yes, I do," he answered. "My assistant, Mr. Milano, has gone through Eliot's biographical material, and we have a list of persons, mostly homosexual, who had numerous contacts with him."

"Would the clerk call Joseph Malmo."

The man who stood up was very tall and had very light hair. When he was seated, Rubenstein asked him a number of personal questions: name, address, occupation, and most importantly, "How did you get to know Mr. Eliot?"

"I met him at the 'Just for Men' bar. It was a typical homo place. All the men were holding hands or kissing when they were not dancing."

"Did he ever mention his family when you talked to him?"

There was a moment of hesitation. "I believe he said he only had one sister."

This was just what Rubenstein wanted. "Did he ever mention what happened to her?" he asked Malmo.

The witness seemed to be frozen in place, so Rubenstein repeated his question. "Did he ever talk about his sister?"

This time he answered. "Charles did not seem to love his family."

Rubenstein pressed on. "Please explain that last sentence."

"Charles gave me the impression that his sister was a slut because he said she was ready to fuck anyone who came by."

Rubenstein was very anxious to get more about the sister. "Did he ever mention that he had assaulted her sexually?"

"No, he did not."

"Let me change the subject a bit. There is some evidence that he raped, or tried to rape, more than one woman. Did he ever even hint of that possibility?"

Malmo looked confused. "I know that he did not like women, but I saw him as a gentle person. He even made love gently."

"Now, one person has already testified that Charles Eliot raped his sister. Are you saying that you do not believe that's possible?"

Malmo answered quickly this time. "That is impossible. I know he was a very gentle person."

"One last question. Did he tell you that his sister moved to Louisiana?"

"No, he did not."

"Would Mr. Johnson come to the witness box?"

The man who walked by was another Scandinavian. He was certainly over six feet tall.

"Now, Mr. Johnson, what is your full name?"

"My name is David Thinglar Johansen," he began. "It used to be Johansen, but we Americanized it to Johnson."

"And what do you do for a living?" Rubenstein asked.

"I am an assistant professor at the Harvard Business School."

Rubenstein faced him and said, "So, you knew Professor Eliot."

"Yes. I was his assistant."

"Then you knew him well," Rubenstein spoke loudly. "Just how well did you know him? Did you socialize with him?"

Johnson knew where these questions were heading. "We did go out for drinks occasionally."

"Did you go to that homosexual bar where everyone congregated?"

Johnson wanted to get to the end of the questions. "We went there only twice, but we spent more time in his house."

Rubenstein was preparing a trap. "So. Are you a homosexual also?"

Johnson was riled by the directness of the question. "I don't believe that my personal life should be made public," he said.

Rubenstein silenced him immediately. "We are trying to find a killer, so all questions are germane. Let me continue my probe. Did you perform homosexual acts in his private home?"

"I refuse to answer," said the witness, "because it would ruin my career."

"I'll take your response as a positive answer," Rubenstein told him. "I want an answer to another question. Did he ever talk to you about his sister?"

"I think the only time he mentioned her was when he told me he only had one sibling, and she was it," Johnson told him.

Rubenstein knew he was getting nowhere, but he was still convinced that the murder had something to do with homosexuality.

When the trial was adjourned, all of the participants filed out of the courthouse. As Jo Ann got close to Johnson, there was something about him that interested her. She boldly approached him and began a conversation.

"You teach at the Harvard Business School?" she asked.

"Yes. I teach English Lit," he answered.

"That was one of my favorite courses as a student," she said.

"Really? Who was your favorite author?"

"I liked modern poetry."

He said, "Really?" again. "And what was your favorite book?"

She began slowly. "The instructor, John Holland, gave high praise to Ted Roethke. We used his first book, *Open House*, completed in 1941, for the classroom analysis. W. H. Auden praised it profusely, and it was reviewed favorably in *The New Yorker* and the *Atlantic*. Holland told us that these poems showed Roethke's love for William Blake and John Donne."

When she met Johnson again on the following day, she commenced her analysis. "In 1942, Roethke gave the Morris Gray lecture at Harvard."

"I know," said Johnson, "because I was there. His presentation was phenomenal."

Johnson looked at Jo Ann in an admiring way. "I think it is wonderful that you favor Roethke as I do. But you have to be aware that his poetic pleasure stems from his intellectual confusion. He breaks away from tradition, and he presents sounds, rhythms, and even erotic phrases. As Ted himself said, 'You have to approach his poems as if you were a child.' But some of his poems actually explode."

Johnson told her that he favored lecturing by quoting some of Roethke's famous lines. Such as "We need more people who specialize in the impossible." And, "One of the virtues of good poetry is that it irritates the mediocre." After he said this, he thought of a line from Carl Sandberg about using slang in poems. He wrote that "Slang is like taking off your coat, spitting on your hands, and going to work."

At that point, JoAnn believed that Johnson was a perfectionist. As they got deeper into poetry, Jo Ann became more attracted to

Professor Johnson, so she was more than surprised when he asked her, "Don't you think we should continue this discussion sometime soon?"

"Oh, that would be nice," she replied.

"How about if we make it dinner?" he inquired.

"That would be nicer," was all she could answer.

That dinner was just the beginning. She knew he was a bi-sexual, and she remembered she too was one, so they would have to be just friends. She remembered that bi-sexualism is a romantic attraction towards both males and females. But it does not mean having an equal sexual attraction to both sexes. And she learned that most bi-sexuals eventually became sexually liberated, and they would fall for a person of the opposite sex.

Each night that they were together, they argued reasonably about a modern poet, but their physical attraction grew. When they tired of poetry, he fixed cocktails for two, and soon they were bound to each other. Despite his large size, he was very gentle with her. It did not trouble him that other men had used her on demand for any sexual desire. He kissed her softly on the mouth, and when he did, she reached down to fondle his erection.

He very gently removed her outer garments, and then he carefully slid her pants from her body. It was the first time in many months that she was not paid for sex. When they reached their climax, she realized that intimacy without payment was very different, but because she had never been in love before, she was not certain that she really was in love. Despite her uncertainty, she and John met regularly for poetry and pure love.

Going home in an ecstatic state, she had to explain to Rose what she was doing all these evenings with David Johnson.

"We both love poetry, she began, "so we enjoy our evenings together."

Rose interrupted her. "You are not letting him kiss you on the lips, are you?"

Jo Ann had to fabricate a response. "No, we just sit together and hold hands occasionally."

Rose wasn't buying the fib. "Come on. You are not the same person. You are not falling for that guy, are you? He is a bi-sexual. What could you two do to please each other?"

JoAnn tried to walk away, but Rose was insistent. "You cannot lie to me. We have been lovers for a long time."

Jo Ann again tried to walk away, but Rose grabbed her arm. "I want the truth now."

"Okay" said Jo Ann. "I have fallen for David Johnson. He is smart, he is handsome, and he is very gentle. He's like a big cuddly bear. And we have both given up our bi-sexuality. We are doing it the old fashion way, and it is really pleasurable. He wants me to give up being a prostitute. I guess he is proposing marriage, because he wants to take care of me. Rose. It's a wonderful feeling to have someone love you."

Rose Bianco was stunned at what Jo Ann had told her. "I guess then we are through. I'll have to find another roommate."

Jo Ann hugged and kissed her and said, "I wish you all the best."

Then, they separated for good.

71

THEY SETTLE IN CAMBRIDGE

When JoAnn Kelly left Rose Bianco, she accepted David Johnson's offer of marriage. They were married by a Justice of the Peace, and as soon as word got around that he had married a prostitute, the dean called him into his office to tell him that he could no longer teach at the business school.

But their first big problem was to find an apartment. The best they could find at Johnson's lower salary was a two-bedroom apartment for $879. This included gas, water, heat, and trash collection. The surrounding area is beautifully landscaped and was near shopping centers and entertainment spots.

As soon as they were settled, David told Jo Ann that he had to find employment, so he headed to Rindge Tech. It began in 1888 as the Cambridge Manual Training School, which was open only for boys. It got its name from Frederick Rindge, who provided funds for its library. David had researched its history. He learned that Cambridge had a 350-year history of public education, Johnson headed for 459 Broadway. He was very surprised to see crowds in the street discussing what should be the role of the United States in the European war. He wanted to join one of the groups, but he had to find employment. When he got to the main building, he asked for an interview with the principal, Grant Whitcomb. They began with basic questions, then Whitcomb asked him, "Why did you leave the Harvard Business School?"

Johnson hesitated, then he responded. "I had a basic disagreement with the dean concerning a very private matter."

Whitcomb seemed to ignore his answer as he asked, "What do you teach?"

Johnson was happy to change the subject. "I teach English Literature, especially modern poets."

The principal seemed quite happy with his specialty, as he told Johnson, "Of course we cannot pay you as much as you have been receiving, but our salaries are on the higher end of the high schools in the area."

They reached an immediate agreement, and Johnson was asked to begin at the start of the next month, which was just days away. He rushed home to his apartment, found his wife scrubbing the kitchen floor, picked her up, and gave her a long, sensuous kiss.

"I got the job at Rindge Tech," he told her.

While David was awaiting his new assignment, Jo Ann was wondering what she would do next. As a wife, she had to leave her life as a prostitute. She got her answer on the evening news. It told of the hundreds of women who were replacing men in the factories. When she learned that it was only 8.5 miles to Waltham, she decided to apply at the Waltham Watch Company.

She was hired immediately, but she had no mechanical skills, so they told her to walk up and down the aisles and pick up all the boxes that were filled with clock parts and take them to the next department for completing the process.

Jo Ann was quite happy to have a job, and she was happier to learn that the subway went from downtown Boston to Waltham. She was not shocked at the language in the factory, but she was surprised at how many of the guys were making her offers of a prurient nature.

While talking with some of the women at Waltham, Jo Ann learned about Norembego Park, which was not far away. David was eager to satisfy any of her wishes. They took the subway to the Totem

Pole Ballroom, which *Variety Magazine* called "the most beautiful ballroom in America." It featured big band music and cozy two-person seated areas.

The young teens always tried to douse the only light by the side of the chair, but it was a fairly strict place that discouraged many young couples from attending. Men had to have a jacket and tie, and women could not wear bobby sox. A dress was required. As they entered the main ballroom, they realized that they had not danced for many weekends. They spent the evening watching young couples displaying their skills at twisting and twirling in the jitterbug.

72

A WITNESS TO THE CRIME

W hile Rubenstein was trying to put all the pieces of the crime together, Mario Milano entered the court room totally out of breath.

"Why are you huffing?" Harry asked him.

"I was tending the phone while you were away, and a man called asking for you. I told him you were tied up with the trial, and he answered, "That is why I am calling." I told him I was your assistant, and he hesitated to tell me why he wanted to speak to you only. He said, "I think I know about the killing, but I will only tell Mr. Rubenstein. I reminded him that according to *Black's Law Dictionary,* failing to give evidence that needs to be given or not disclosing some piece of information when asked to do so is a crime, and that he must tell me about it. When that seemed to work, I said, "I will get my pen and paper, and I will take down your information, and I will deliver it to Mr. Rubenstein in the court room."

Mario sat down and continued. "So, he began his story. He was out on the river all day in his small motor boat, and when it started to get dark, he decided to go home. His house is along the Charles River, so he put the engine in a low speed and headed from the Boston Harbor up the river. As he went along the right bank, he saw two women dragging something from their house toward the river. He could not see what it was because it was wrapped in a large piece of cloth. When they got to the bank, they rolled what they carried into the river." Mario paused. "I asked him his name, but he would not give it until I told him that I would not deliver this information until he identified himself. He relented and said his name was James Conway, and he lives up the river a short distance."

Rubenstein explained to Mario, "This information may not be worth anything unless we can identify what it is that they dumped into the Charles River. And we need to know the names of the two women also."

Mario had an idea. Talking to his boss, he explained, "Can we not go to all the houses along the river to learn the names of all the persons living there. In this way, we might be able to identify the two women, and we can ask them what it was that they dumped into the Charles River."

Rubenstein thought it was a great idea, and he told Mario, "Start working on it tomorrow."

73

QUESTIONS FROM THE POLICE

When the court was adjourned, Rubenstein went to the police files. There had to be something here that could give him a clue. It was a very big file, but he went through it page by page. The autopsy told him nothing he did not know, but the scientists gave him one clue. There was one female blood stain on Charles Eliot. How did it get there, and how did it survive in the Charles River?

Rubenstein headed immediately to the science lab. He stopped when he read Robert McKenna, Director. He knocked on the door.

"Come in," was the response.

He opened the door, walked in, and looked around. It was definitely a place for scientists. There were all kinds of blood photos on the walls, and a few skeletons on top of file cabinets.

"My name is Rubenstein," he told the director. "Is this your photo?" he asked.

McKenna picked it up, perused it, and said, 'Yes that's mine."

"Can you tell me anything about it?" Rubenstein asked and then added, "How can a woman's blood get inside a man and survive under water?"

McKenna paused for a short time while he thought about the

questions. "The only possibility is that they had a struggle, during which he hit her hard enough for her to bleed, and some blood got inside him before he wound up in the river."

Rubenstein took time to analyze the answer. He began, "Now if the blood got inside of him and was not contained in some organ, would it not wash away?"

McKenna appeared to be stumped, so he remained silent.

Rubenstein began again. "Would sister and brother have the same kind of blood?" he asked.

The scientist was ready with an answer. "They can have similar DNA but different kinds of blood."

"So, we cannot tell if they are brother and sister," said the prosecutor.

McKenna finally grasped what Rubenstein had in mind. "You think the sister killed her brother or vice versa. It might be more difficult for her, because if she shot him, she would have to get his body in the river. If she is smaller, that would be nearly impossible, unless she had an accomplice."

Harry Rubenstein thanked the scientist, and he left with several questions in his mind. Where could he get answers? After much soul searching, he had one good thought: the Style Section of the newspapers. He went first to the *Boston American*, where he asked for the head of the Style Section.

"You'll find him in the second office down the hall. His name is Dennis Conrad."

Rubenstein knocked on the door and entered when someone answered.

"Hello, Mr. Conrad," he said as he offered his hand. "I'm Harry Rubenstein, the prosecutor in the Eliot murder case."

Conrad said, "Call me Dennis, and how can I help you?"

"Well, you can call me Harry. I need to know if you have any style columns on the sister of the murdered man, Charles Eliot."

Dennis Conrad walked over to a file cabinet and started to seek the topic alphabetically. "Here is the entire file," he said as he handed it to Rubenstein.

"Can I take these with me or must I use them here?" he asked Dennis.

"The company rule is no file leaves the building, but since this is a murder case, you can take them for two days. Please bring them back on time."

Rubenstein appreciated his generosity. "I promise I shall return them on time." He left quickly.

He went first to his apartment, and he started reading the file. It was very full of social events. He was surprised that the sister's name was Charlene Eliot. The parents, who made the grand tour of Europe —London, Paris and Rome—must of thought that Charlene is as close to Charles as they christened her.

As he went through the thick file, one name seemed to dominate the events. It was Robert Lowell, a descendent of many famous Lowell's. Lawrence Lowell was a President of Harvard, Percival Lowell discovered the planet Pluto, and James Russell Lowell was a famous anti-slavery advocate and editor of the *Atlantic Monthly*. It was such a paramount name in Massachusetts that a city was named after it.

For a long time, Robert and Charlene were a famous couple in Boston. They went to the Polo Club; they attended the Boston Pops and Boston Symphony concerts, and they were invited to most of the gatherings at Beacon Hill, the North Shore, and Newton.

74

BACK TO THE TRIAL

Rubenstein called Thomas O'Connell to the stand. "You are the Chief of Police, is that correct?"

"Yes, it is."

"Can you tell us how you found the gun that was used to kill Charles Eliot?"

"We called in The Army Corps of Engineers to remove all the sediment that was beneath the surface of the Charles River. Then we used a dredge on a long boat that had a dredging ladder capable of digging about twenty-five feet down into the river. Another boat checked the bottom of the river for sediment buildup. This is required because the buildup disconnects the deep water and leaves shallow pockets that deep boats cannot pass through. If the dredge does its job, the bottom of the river will remain deep enough for large ships and barges to pass through without any problems. The dredge took about twenty to thirty days of dredging to find the gun."

"Thank you, Mr. O'Connell."

Rubenstein told the judge that he ordered his clerk to take the gun to the lab to trace it to find the owner. It was a simple task because the numbers were not obliterated. The lab sent its finding, and the owner was Charles Eliot, the murdered man.

He called Mario to his office, and he asked him, "Now, is there any way we can find out how many persons visited him in the weeks before he was murdered?"

Mario was stumped for a minute, then he offered one suggestion. "Eliot did have a housekeeper. She should know who came and went into the house."

Harry was elated over the idea. "Get on it right away," he told Mario.

Mario had a difficult time finding the Eliot house because it was hidden in the woods behind all the trees. He kept traveling along the river until he found a sign that read "Home of Charles Eliot."

When he knocked on the door, Molly Flanagan answered. She opened the door and asked if he had an appointment.

"No," he told her, "but I am from the office of the prosecutor in connection with Mr. Eliot's murder."

"Yes," she told him. "Come right in."

She pointed at the couch and told him to be seated. When he was comfortable, he asked her, "Were you working the night he was killed?"

She thought for a moment, then she said "I worked all day, and then his sister told me to go home."

"So, you were not present when he was killed?"

"No, I was not."

Mario continued his questioning. "Was anyone else in the house besides Charlene?"

"I cannot answer your question because I was told to leave."

"Let me try another approach," Mario told her. "Do you not keep his appointment book?"

She was upset with the question. "I am a housekeeper, not a personal secretary."

"Well then," he responded, "who keeps his appointments?"

By this time she was totally upset with his questions. "He keeps all his records himself. He would never allow anyone else to go through his desk."

By this time, Mario had to apply pressure. "As an assistant prosecutor, I have the right to examine this entire house. I thank you for your help. You may leave. Now I will start my investigation."

He headed first to the desk, where he found the appointment book on top and opened it. The only name for the day of the murder was his sister, Charlene.

He recalled Molly. "Wasn't there another woman in the house? What was her purpose? Do you know anything about her?"

"It was not my business to make enquiries about her. I left each day at the same hour, so I do not know what went on after I left."

"Do you know her name?" Mario asked.

"It was strange. He never called her by a given name. He used sugary names like honey or sweetheart."

"So," Mario asked her. "There is no way we can identify her?"

"Not that I know of," Molly verified his statement.

"Did this unknown woman live in this house?" he asked.

"I do not know for sure, but I think she lived upstairs."

Mario returned to his office, and he was confronted by Harry Rubenstein. "How did it go?" he asked.

"I didn't get very far. The professor kept his own records, so there are no schedules of visitors or appointments. The maid knows nothing, and she was sent home early on the night of the murder." Mario changed the subject. "Since we have the gun, can we ask the research group to look for fingerprints?"

Harry looked perplexed. "I don't know if a print can survive under water. We can ask the scientists."

"I'll go down to the lab," Mario told him as he headed in that direction. He knocked on the door, and Bob McKenna shouted, "Come in."

Mario shook his hand. 'Do you remember me?" he asked.

McKenna nodded, saying, "You are with the prosecution, aren't you? How can I help you?"

"Yes. My name is Milano, and I have a simple question again."

"Okay, let me have it, said McKenna.

"I think I misled you," Mario said. "It's not simple. Here it is. Can a fingerprint survive underwater for several days?"

McKenna had a puzzled look. "That's one I never encountered before. Let me ask our water expert, Ted Phillips."

He picked up the telephone. "Is that you Ted? I have a strange question from a prosecutor. He wants to know if a fingerprint can survive under water for several days. You have never had such a question before? I'll tell him. Thanks for trying."

Before hanging up, McKenna said, "Wait a minute. How about an experiment? Can you put a fingerprint on a gun and drop it in the river for several days? I will tell the prosecutor. Thanks for the help."

Facing Mario, McKenna told him, "Phillips says to come back in a month."

The time escaped Mario as he realized that it has been more than two months since he asked the question about fingerprints on a gun that have been under water for a long time. He opened the written report, and he started reading:

Fingerprints are perhaps the most common physical evidence used to identify victims and offenders and are considered one of the most valuable types of evidence to be recovered during a criminal investigation. With few exceptions, everyone has fingerprints and not one print has ever been known to duplicate another fingerprint.

The three fingerprint class types are arches, loops, and whorls. Arches are the least common type of fingerprint, occurring only about 5% of the time. This pattern is characterized by ridges that enter on one side of the print, go up, and exit on the opposite side.

Prints come from the surface of each friction ridge of our fingers, palms, toes, and feet, which have minute pores that exude perspiration. The composition of our perspiration is approximately 98.5 to 99.5% water and approximately .5 to 1.5% solids like chlorides (salts), urea and amino acids. When these print-bearing areas come in contact with certain foreign surfaces, they leave a detailed outline of the ridge impression called a "latent print."

It is essential to use someone qualified and capable of photographing such prints before they are destroyed. Studies have shown that fingerprints can be recovered from certain surfaces (metal, glass, and plastics) after being submerged for days.

Here is a suggestion to help you: if the evidence was used in a serious crime, such as murder, assault, or robbery, and the item is a gun or knife, it would be best to have a laboratory technician conduct the examination.

Remember that the longer the item is submerged, the less chance you have of recovering any prints. However, if the print is protected in some way from direct water exposure, the print will maintain its structure longer than one exposed to the ambient water.

S igned,
       Robert McKenna

W hen Mario returned to his office, he found a report from the Fingerprint Division. He read that the prints on the gun are definitely female, so he went directly to see Rubenstein.

"We have the good news. The print on the gun is female. How should we approach this now?"

Rubenstein pondered the question, then he responded, "We have no choice but to recall all the women who have testified in this case to have them leave their prints for our analysis. If any print matches the one on the gun then we can grille her until she confesses."

Mario stopped him speaking as a lawyer. "Can we under law require that any persons be forced to deliver their prints? Can they object?"

Rubenstein replied, "You are the lawyer, so you will have to research the question. Tell me what you find out as soon as you can."

Mario decided that he should return to the Harvard Law School for an answer. As he walked on to campus heading to Jackson Hall, all the memories of his student days were illuminated.

Entering the building, he told the secretary that he is a former student and an assistant prosecutor on a murder case. He asked her, "Are any professors in their office now?"

She looked up the faculty schedule and said, "Right now only Professor Jones has office hours. Do you want me to ring him up?"

"Please do."

"Professor Jones, there is a former student and current prosecutor in my office. Can you answer a question of his now?" She said, "Go right in. It's the third door on the left."

Milano knocked on his door and heard a robust "Please enter."

He was very surprised to see a very large black man, because when he was a student there, were no colored persons on the faculty. He put out his hand and said, "I am a former student, and I am investigating a murder case."

The professor shook his hand and spoke as if he was in a hurry. "What is your question?" he asked.

"Our murder case is winding down because we have a fingerprint that was on the gun that killed a Harvard professor. We know now that it is a female print. Our question is: can we require all the women who have testified in the case to give us their fingerprints? Is this a violation of their civil rights?"

Professor Jones did not respond quickly. It is obvious that he was trying to think of an answer to the question. He seemed to be thinking as he spoke. "Ultimately, the court decides what evidence will be admitted into the trial. The basic function of a prosecutor is to seek the truth about criminal actions, so that if a prosecutor discovers evidence that would put the defendant's innocence in doubt, he must turn that evidence over to the defendant, who has a right to challenge the evidence. I repeat that decision is made by the judge."

Mario was not happy with the answer, but he thanked the professor and headed back to his office where Harry met him.

"Any good news?" he asked in an excited manner.

Mario was not jubilant about Jones' response. He told Harry the exact words he was given. The prosecutor was not totally discouraged. "I think," he began, "we can get to this judge. He seems to be flexible about many issues. We must not irritate him with our comments. We need to feed him sugar, not salt. We will tread lightly concerning items that are disputable. And when we have softened him, we will ask our question about fingerprinting."

76

A DETERMINATION ON FINGERPRINTS

On the following day, the case resumed, but before the prosecutor could question the witness, attorney Stepinsky's assistant, Debra Boland, had a legal question for the judge.

"Your honor, this whole line of questions is immaterial, because Miss Kelly was arrested for prostitution, not murder."

O'Connor thought for a moment, then he told the attorney that some answers are germane to the case before the court. "So let us proceed."

At this point, Harry wanted to summarize the case. "Your Honor, we are getting closer to a decision in this case. We now know that Professor Eliot was killed in his own home with his gun. We also know that the fingerprints on the gun were from a female. This tells us that he knew the person who killed him. We are unable to find a document of any kind that would tell us who visited him on the day of his demise, because his housekeeper told us that he would not allow anyone to see his desk or the things upon it. He required absolute privacy concerning all activities and affairs. Now this effort for absolute privacy makes it more difficult for us to find the killer. There is one action we could take that might give us a solution to this horrendous crime."

Judge O'Connor leaned forward after that last sentence. "What exactly do you have in mind, Mr. Rubenstein?"

The prosecutor arose and walked slowly toward Judge O'Connor. "Your honor, we have interviewed several women in trying to find the killer. If we could recall all of them to obtain their fingerprints, we might find the guilty one. I know that this is up to you, but we are trying to find a murderer. If none of the fingerprints match the one on the gun, then we will continue our search. You remember the old expression 'Leave no stone unturned.'"

O'Connor was momentarily stumped. He surely knew of the issue before him, but he could not ignore a possible solution to a murder.

"Mr. Rubenstein, the court rules that you can proceed with your attempt to obtain fingerprints from the women involved in this case. We must seek justice. That is why we have courts."

Rubenstein left the courtroom, and he phoned McKenna to thank him for the report. McKenna offered a suggestion. "You may want to go back to the house where the murder took place to investigate if gloves were worn by any visitors or if any woman left gloves behind her."

Rubenstein then telephoned Mario of the unexpected result, and he told him of the scientist's suggestion. Mario immediately offered to investigate the possibilities, and his boss approved. He drove back to the Eliot home, this time finding it quickly. When he knocked, he was glad that Molly Flanagan answered.

"Why are you back?" she asked.

"I need to know if anyone left gloves here in the last few days."

Molly surprised him. "There was one pair left."

Mario lurched toward her. "Do you know the owner?"

Molly pondered the question, then she answered. "There were three or four women here at various times, but I cannot recall if any wore gloves or just brought them."

"Can you give me their names?" Mario enquired.

She reflected on his question, then responded. "As I told you the last time you were here, Mr. Eliot told me nothing about his lady friends. All I know is that there were several."

"Well then," Mario weighed her answer, "if you think of any names, please tell me right away."

Mario spoke to Harry Rubenstein after his visit. His boss said, "We have no option but to wait until all the experiments are completed, so go on home to your wife and kids."

When Mario got to the top of the Sumner Street hill, he noticed Rico Cipriani sitting on his chair on the sidewalk. He greeted Mario, saying "Let's talk."

"What's the topic today?" Mario asked.

"I want your opinion about one of my son's teachers."

"What's the problem?"

"Mr. Stein says that Hitler has some pre-conceived notions about the Third Reich, which makes him more dangerous than Mussolini. He wrote all these views in a book, which says Mussolini makes more noise, but Hitler is more dangerous." Then Rico switched to Italian. "*Questo insegnante e Giudeo.* (This teacher is a Jew) But my son says, "Yes, he is a Jew but he is a good teacher and all the students like him."

Mario broke in, "What's the question?"

Rico was prepared to answer. "Everyone is mad about Hitler, because he takes the land and money from the Jews. Stein says that because there are few Jews in the United States, they could never control our country. But if they have most of the money, they can give all new jobs to their own kind. They will not hire Christians."

As they were debating these Jewish problems, Tony Bonito came by with his ice wagon. The area was soon crowded with children asking for small pieces of ice they could lick to keep cool.

"What size today?" he asked Mario.

"It's pretty hot. We better have a seventy-five cent piece."

Tony took a knife and cut off a large piece, which he grabbed with some thongs, and he carried it upstairs and put it in the icebox.

When he got back downstairs, he asked Rico, "What are the great democrats doing in Washington, D. C. these days? When are they going to reduce unemployment?"

Tony was convinced that the Russian system was the only feasible answer, because the employers will never recognize the unions.

Mario had to silence him. "Tony, you are forgetting the National Recovery Administration, which was established by President Franklin D. Roosevelt in 1933. The goal was to eliminate 'cut-throat competition' by bringing industry, labor, and government together to create codes of 'fair practices' and set prices."

Tony was game for argument: "That slogan, 'We do our part' is a big lie."

Mario had to answer. "The NRA makes the workweek shorter. There are no more children in the factories and no more sweatshops. So things are much better. And Tony, you must know that the Russians are having serious problems producing goods and farm products. There is starvation there now, and we are sending food as people are dying in the streets. That system is a complete failure."

"Let's finish this discussion later. I must talk to my woman."

"Wait a minute," said Rico, "I want to ask you one final question."

"Okay. What is it?"

"Do you believe priests when they lecture?"

Mario spoke firmly. "I believe them when they are quoting scriptures."

"Did you read the Globe today about Father Coughlin?" Rico asked him.

"No, I did not. What did it say?"

"I'll read you some of it," Rico told him. "Charles Coughlin is pastor of the Shrine of the Little Flower in Royal Oak, Michigan. Shortly after launching this parish in 1926, Coughlin pioneered religious broadcasting that was rivaled only by Huey Long's. Coughlin was probably the first to build political power almost entirely from a radio show. How a young priest beginning with homilies based on papal messages could quickly gain such mass-media clout is a fascinating story. But Coughlin was always an anti-Semite with strong sympathies for European fascism. Coughlin's rhetoric, and even his political and psychological motivations earned him the title of "the father of hate radio." Today reporters are rapidly consolidating a profit-minded media industry, and entertainers, politicians, and activists infringe on or try to take over journalists' jobs. What do you think Mario?"

"Remember Rico," he answered, "that Christ said, 'Upon this rock I will build my church.' He did not say priest. We have had problems with priests for 500 years. Read the poems of Robert Browning. We are all sinful people, priests and laity."

Rico caved in. "Alright, this time you win. Go kiss your woman."

"Thanks for your kindness," Mario answered in a smart-alec way. He went upstairs, and he did greet Lucy with a kiss.

"Anything new?" she asked.

"No. We are still waiting for the fingerprints."

"Well, I heard something new from Philip. I was upstairs, but I heard the whole story."

"What was the subject?"

"It was about dancing, but it was more than that. Phil went to the Raymor Ballroom with Henry Saverino, Al Huskins, and Paul Grey, and they were downstairs speaking loudly, so I could hear all of it. At the intermission, they all met to discuss their progress. They were all talking about how they could get laid. When it was Phil's turn, he related his experience with a beauty he had met. She had dark hair and was very attractive. He told his buddies that she couldn't be Italian. He asked her to dance to the music of Count Basie that was full of sex. Just as they headed for the dance floor, the band played a waltz. He told her he did not know how to waltz, so she told him she would teach him. They got more friendly as the night went on. She said her name was Shirley Goldstein, and that she was a German Jew. He told her his name and offered to take her home. When they got there, they stopped inside the outer door to kiss and to start other things, but she stopped his forwardness telling him he wasn't kosher. When he asked her what that meant, she told him, 'You are not circumcised.' When he asked her what he had to do, she said, 'You better ask your father.' So I guess this is in your bailiwick, Mario. Should we do anything about this?"

"I guess we will have to have a father to son talk."

The following day, Mario told his son, "We have to have a talk."

Philip said, "I'm ready. What's the topic?"

Mario began, "As you know, there are many Jews around the Franklin Zoo, so you need to know at least the fundamentals of that religion. Every Jew learns that there are three groups that make up the twelve tribes, and more important there are five books of Moses. Judaism is monotheistic, and God promised Abraham that he would make a great nation of Jews. A Jew must be born of a Jewish mother, and a male baby must be circumcised, which means removing the foreskin of the penis, so when a woman says to you that you are not kosher, she means that you are not circumcised. You have a foreskin which is difficult to clean because it folds over the penis. Another important element of Judaism is food. They cannot eat meat and dairy together. Do you understand, Philip, what I have just said?"

"Yes, Dad."

77

ANOTHER SUNDAY TOUR

When they had finished breakfast on the next Sunday, Mario reminded them that they had not been on a tour for a long time. "It is time for another tour of East Boston. Do you know," he continued "that the best Clipper Ships were made just a few blocks from here. In the heyday of the clippers, Donald McKay was a giant among shipbuilders. He was born on a farm on the east side of the Jordan River in Shelburne County, Nova Scotia. He attended a common-school, then he immigrated in 1827 to New York where he worked as an indentured servant as a ship carpenter. When his indenture was completed, he became a freelance shipwright. Soon his skill made him a leading New York shipbuilder."

When they had changed into their walking clothes, they headed down Sumner Street to Border Street.

"This is where he built a number of packet ships. As his skills in design and construction became known, McKay received many other assignments, and in 1844 he was chosen to build a ship for transatlantic traffic by Enoch Train, founder of the White Diamond Line. Train convinced him to set up a shipyard in East Boston. Soon after, McKay had his shipyard, and in 1841 he formed a partnership with

William Currier as master shipbuilder. Then he was chosen in 1844 to design and build the *Joshua Bates* for the Boston-Liverpool line. In 1849, the White Diamond Line asked him to build the Boston packet *Parliament*, which crossed the Atlantic Ocean from East Boston to Liverpool, in direct competition with the Cunard line, which started that service in 1839. McKay personally supervised every step in the construction, and his ships set speed records. His *Flying Cloud*, launched in 1851 in East Boston, was the fastest ship ever to sail. She made it from New York to San Francisco in eighty-nine days."

Mario continued his historical story. "But During the Civil War, Confederate raiders sank one hundred fifty Yankee vessels, including fourteen clipper ships. After the war, McKay built and sold several ships, some designed as grain carriers, but he ran into financial trouble when he proposed to build a new, magnificent ship, the *Glory of the Seas*, at his East Boston shipyard. He commissioned a Greek goddess for his prow and adorned the ship with ornate carvings and flowing Grecian draperies. The *Boston Traveler* described the 101-ton ship as having three decks and suitable cargo space to make it ideal for the California freight business. It was McKay's perfect ship, but he couldn't sell her. He took the ship around the horn to the Golden Gate, but he could not meet mortgage payments, He was left with only his house on White Street, in East Boston, which is still standing." Mario stopped. "This is where they built all those magnificent ships."

78

CONFIRMATION

They headed back home, and the next morning, Lucy told Philip that he was to prepare for Confirmation. It was this preparation which gave Philip his first opportunity to get to know his pastor, Father Gallagher. This squat, bald, funny-looking man with the big belly had a very loud voice that he used to keep parishioners from dozing during the service. Philip hated the thought of spending several afternoons with the priest, but he knew it was his Catholic duty to join St Michael's army of warriors against the devil.

Because Father Gallagher came from Ireland only a decade ago, he still had a brogue, but he continued to give the Sunday sermons. He still offered instructions to many children who were in his Sunday school classes.

During his weekly visits with Philip, Father Gallagher appeared to lack compassion, but in reality he was a very warm person. Their conversations ran a very wide gamut. One day in particular, they were discussing the true church and why the Catholic church was the best road to heaven. Philip remembered that his friend Jim Black was a Lutheran. "What is the difference?" asked Philip.

The priest spoke slowly. "A long time ago, Martin Luther was an Augustinian priest who lived in Germany. He was a very religious but sensitive man who worked always to bring about the perfection on earth which God desires us to work for. He saw sin all around him and sensuous living, and he decided that something had to be done. He found out that priests were bringing about these conditions because they were accepting money as satisfaction for delinquencies. But they were also using women for their purposes. In analyzing them, he confused immorality with original sin. He said that man is hopelessly corrupt and that he lacks the moral free will to be saved. He tried to have the Pope change the rules concerning indulgences, but the final result was that he was excommunicated. So he set up his own church with only three sacraments—baptism, Eucharist, and penance—and ruled that the bible was the only proper rule of faith."

Philip interrupted him. "Why didn't the Pope change things?"

"Of course he did, my boy, but Luther failed to see that it was the priests who were wrong, not the church. There were conditions and limitations pertaining to the use of the indulgences. No one could buy eternal forgiveness, but only the temporal punishment could be forgiven."

"But why did they excommunicate Father Luther?" asked Philip.

"You must understand," said Father Gallagher, "that this man was a victim of what we call melancholia. He was easily depressed and stayed depressed for days. Everything he did he did with a passion, and he was therefore an excessive man. He himself said that he was subject to diabolical obsessions. That means he thought the devil was in him.

"You can see Martin Luther's legacy in the history of East Boston. Since his revolt all the Christians have not accepted one another. I must tell you a story to show how hate can spread among the people. Today the Catholics are calling Protestants names in East Boston, but yesterday, it was just the opposite. When I first came to this parish, I studied the roots of the Catholic Church here.

"At first there was much friendship between the Catholic priests and the Protestant clergy, but then some secret groups were formed whose only purpose was to get rid of the Catholics. They all had very patriotic names, but they were sinister groups. The worst of all was the one called the American Protective Association. They were a bunch of over-patriotic bigots who appointed themselves defenders of America. This was a very strange self-appointment because most had only recently come to this country from Canada. But they decided that the Catholics had no right to take part in any civic cere-monies in East Boston because they were members of a secret, sectarian organization, meaning, of course, the Pope. Now, Philip, it is true that the Italians and Irish brought some organizations from their old countries to these shores but so did the English and Scots. The Ancient Order of Hibernians and the Sons of Italy have as much right to exist as the Rosicrucian's or the Masons.

"Because these groups had not learned to live together in a peaceful way, there was a riot in East Boston in 1895. We still suffer from the hate and intolerance that came with that riot. The trouble really began when Irish and Italian groups would march with priests leading the processions and carrying foreign flags alongside the American flag, but the actual explosion resulted from a plan to have a large Fourth of July celebration. The Catholics seemed to be in the wrong, because they protested having a float of a little red school-house as it was the symbol of the Protective Association. It was their intention to eliminate all Catholic schools."

79

THE CASE GETS HOT

The fingerprinting took more than a single day, because it was a messy operation. Each woman had to be sworn in and then her fingerprints were taken. Each had to put ink on her fingers and press them onto a special piece of paper. Then each had to clean up, which was not an easy task. The court had to provide towels and cleaning materials to remove the ink.

It was done alphabetically, so Jo Ann was in the middle of the group. She did not appear to be nervous, which puzzled Mario. When it came her time, she proceeded jauntily to the front of the room and put her fingers forward with a smile. Then she cleaned up and headed home, where her husband was waiting for her.

When the lab was ready, McKenna called Rubenstein to give him the results.

"Okay. What did you find?"

"The answer is not what you expected."

"What do you mean?" asked Harry.

"Well, only one of the prints matched."

Harry was baffled. "Whose prints are they?"

"That is the surprise. They belong to his sister."

80

A SOLUTION

When the trial resumed, Harry Rubenstein was buoyant. He was sure he had captured the killer. He reviewed the last few days for the judge. Facing O'Connor, he told him, "We have accomplished the impossible. We must thank the dredging company for finding the gun, and we cannot thank our laboratory enough for uncovering the prints on the gun that had been underwater for many days. It was scientific genius."

"Now let us solve this crime," he told the bailiff. "Please call Charlene Eliot to the stand."

When she sat down, she was all decked out in expensive clothes. Rubenstein got closer to her when he asked, "Tell us about your life with your brother, Charles."

As she began to tell the court her family history, Rubenstein stopped her.

"Miss Eliot, I want you to tell us about your experiences with your brother."

Her face showed her agony. "My problems began two years ago when I had just returned from a tour of Europe. He wanted to know all about it, so he invited me to his house for dinner. It was all very pleasant until he gave me a glass of wine and then a second one. It all seemed very proper until he asked me to sit next to him. He then put his hands under my dress and started to undress me. I tried to stop him, but he just ripped my pants off and proceeded to rape me. I did not know if I was pregnant until the third month. Our baby was born six months later. He did not want to have anything to do with the child, so I stayed away from him.

"About a year later, he invited me to his house again, and he promised to behave, so I accepted his invitation. I was surprised to see that he had also invited Miss Jo Ann Kelly, who was a prostitute that he admired, but not for sex.

"We had a fine dinner, and then we started to discuss current events—mostly anti-Roosevelt affairs. It was all quite proper until he had his servant, Molly, serve us two large glasses of brandy. Then he started groping me again. I shouted for his to stop, but he continued trying to rape me a second time. Again, he ripped my blouse and tore my pants, and Jo Ann yelled, "Where is the gun?" I pointed to the same place. Jo Ann shot him two times in the chest."

Rubenstein halted her story. "If she shot him, how did your prints get on the gun? You are lying, are you not? You are the killer. Why are you blaming Miss Kelly?"

Charlene was weeping as she screamed, "I did not kill my brother."

The crowd in the courtroom was buzzing over this quandary, when Jo Ann Kelly stood up and yelled, "Stop this. I cannot watch this travesty of justice any longer. She is innocent. Her prints are on the gun because she picked it up when we were first together last year. My prints are not on it because I wore gloves on the evening of the murder. She has suffered enough with her brother who was a polished rat. What normal man would try to rape his sister twice? As I said when we dropped his body into the Charles River, 'Good riddance to bad rubbish.'"

She then reached into her purse and pulled out a .45 pistol. When David Johnson saw it, he yelled, "JoAnn, no!"

She turned to him and answered, "David, I love you," and placed the gun just above her left ear and pulled the trigger. Parts of her flew in all directions, and her husband, who felt part of her skull land on him, screamed the loudest and wept the most.

Harry Rubenstein shouted to the clerk of the court, "Clean this mess up!" as he and Mario Milano trudged out of the courtroom. With their heads low, Harry said, "Just another day and another dollar."

The End

EPILOGUE

As the years passed, Lucy acquired several commendations. First, she was voted "Teacher of the Year." As her fame spread, more and more white children enrolled at Whittier Elementary School until the black/ white ratio reached 50 percent. The Executive Board noticed this improvement, and they appointed her Assistant Superintendent. Mario was proud of her, but he might have been more proud of the big raise she got from her new position.

They discussed often how to allocate this new prosperity. The children offered them a choice that they found hard to reject. "Why don't you buy a summer home by the ocean?" they suggested.

Because the children were now adults, Lucy and Mario called a family meeting to discuss this option. It was a well thought out debate, but they wound up with four different choices, so Lucy took charge. She told them, "Your mother and father will make this important decision."

Lucy and Mario got back to the original choice of whether to buy a home near the ocean. Mario suggested a place where he and his buddies used to go when they were teens. "I know that there is a ballroom nearby, because we went there to hear Peggy Lee when we were high school students."

"Where is it?" asked Lucy.

"It's at the very bottom of New Hampshire, just over the Massachusetts line. It is called Hampton, and it's very close to the ocean. We would need to drive up to Lawrence and just over the line."

"It sounds very interesting, but can we afford a place near water?"

"The best buy I found is a three-bedroom place with just one bath and a garage. The price is $70,000. There is a Salt Marsh Walk with a marine biologist each year. It keeps the balance of land and water during the walk. Rubbish is picked up on Labor Day each year, and all elections are held at the Winnacunnet High School."

Lucy wanted to verify what she had asked earlier. 'You are sure we can afford this?" she asked.

"Yes, I know we can."

"Then let's do it," she told him firmly. "We can use it as a family gathering place."

Mario contacted the real estate agent, made the down payment, and got the keys to the place. As Friday approached, the entire family kept urging Mario to take them to see their new house. He gave in. He ordered each of them to pack a bag for the weekend. Their cheers were very loud.

On Friday afternoon, they headed north on Route 1, past Saugus, Danvers, Newburyport, Salisbury, and into Hampton, New Hampshire. They found 301 Royal Street easily, and everyone jumped out to walk around the property. It was small, but neat.

When they entered, they were all happy to see a fireplace in the middle of the living room. There were acres of trees for burning. Lucy and Mario took the master bedroom, and MaryAnn and Philip had their own private rooms.

Philip brought his portable record player with several swing records. MaryAnn was elated. "Oh good," she exclaimed, "we can practice our dancing."

Philip silenced her. "Nobody dances with his sister."

MaryAnn stopped him. "I guess you forgot that I taught you how to do the fox trot and the swing."

Lucy joined the discussion, "You are lucky to have a sister," she said firmly. "So be thankful for your good fortune."

After dinner, Lucy suggested that they play whist. "You remember whist, don't you? It is a descendant of a 16th century game of Trump. It became very fashionable throughout Europe in the 18th and 19th centuries. It was brought to the colonies by the British soldiers."

When she saw their blank faces, she went over the rules for them. "The game is played by two pairs on each side. Each person is dealt thirteen cards and then they bid for trumps. The dealer gets to accept the highest bid or he passes. Then we play the cards, each person follows the lead unless that person does not have any card of that suit, then that person can trump the card."

At the end of the evening MaryAnn, who loved to play cards, had the most points.

As the years flew by, the Milano's spent most of their weekends at Hampton. Each day they read the daily newspaper and some paperback books they brought with them. One article caught Mario's attention. It was copied from a San Francisco newspaper that quoted from one of Eleanor Roosevelt's daily columns. It was a letter to the First Lady:

"I feel that you have done much good. If some people would cooperate and take some of the suggestions you offer, it would do a great deal of good to help living conditions and to promote interracial good will which would make an incalculable stride toward the victory we all look forward to. Evil has such a grip on the weak and the selfish that it is difficult to separate the roots, to isolate and destroy them."

After her children were married and gone, Lucy turned to something she dreamed about all her life. She wanted to write books. When she approached the subject with Mario, he asked, "Why do you want to write?"

It took her a while to answer. "I did win the literature prize in high school."

"But that was a long time ago," he responded.

"You are right about that," she agreed, "but I have another reason."

"And what is that?" he asked.

"Well, everyone wants to leave some item of immortality when they leave Earth. Some leave just their children. Others leave antiques. That is not enough for me. I want people to read my books in years to come."

"So, you want to be another Jane Austen, who wrote six novels."

She ignored his comical approach to criticism as she began writing books. She wrote using a pen name—Lucile Gallon. Her first book was auto-biographical about a young Italian girl who left Italy under unusual conditions. It was a best seller.

This allowed her to switch to novels about crimes, which subjects Mario helped to provide from his daily experiences as assistant prosecutor. Everything she wrote got published immediately and was on the best seller lists. She thought she had died and gone to Writer's Heaven.

In 1980, Lucy began to have urinary problems, which her primary physician determined was cancerous. When she died, she was buried next to her father in Malden, Massachusetts.

ABOUT THE AUTHOR

August C. Bolino joined the U.S. Army Air Corps in 1942 and completed his navigation school flight training at Selman Field in Monroe, LA in October 1943. He was assigned as a member of a Boeing B-17 "Flying Fortress" combat crew at the 388th Bomber Group at Knettishall, East Anglia, England, where he flew 30 combat missions including two on D-Day, June 6, 1944. He received the Distinguished Flying Cross and the Air Medal.

After being discharged from the military, Bolino enrolled at the University of Michigan under the GI Bill, where he obtained an MBA degree in finance. In 1957, he finished his Ph.D. in economics at Saint Louis University. He began his teaching career at the University of Washington in Seattle and moved to Idaho State College (now University) and Saint Louis University.

In 1963, he was appointed chief of the division of economic analysis of automation in the office of Manpower Automation and Training to the U.S. Department of Labor in Washington, D.C. In 1964, he served as assistant to the U.S. Commissioner of Education in the Department of Health, Education, and Welfare. In 1978, he was elected Vice President for Research of the Ellis Island Restoration Commission while teaching full-time at the Catholic University of America in Washington, D.C.

When Ellis Island closed, the US government tried to rent or sell it without luck. After hiring a leading architect, they decided to tear down all thirteen buildings to make a picnic area. When Bolino was asked his opinion, he said, "Look up. There is a second floor to the

Great Hall that was never used. Make it into a Family History Center."

This is now the most popular place on the Island. Bolino received a commendation from the US House of Representatives, along with a plaque installed near the center bearing his name and the year.

OTHER TITLES BY AUGUST C. BOLINO

The 8th Air Force Won the War in Europe (2018)

My Life (2016)

An 1872 Case of Murder in Utah Territory (2014)

Men of Massachusetts (2012)

The Kid and the Clipper (2006)

Brother Brigham's Trial (2002)

Thomas Angel, American (2001)

From Depression to War (1998)

The Ellis Island Source Book (1990)

A Century of Human Capital by Education and Training (1989)

The Watchmakers of Massachusetts (1987)

The Ellis Island Source Book (1985)

Career Education: Contributions to Economic Growth (1973)

Manpower and the City (1969)

The Development of the American Economy (1966)

The Development of the American Economy (1961)

www.ingramcontent.com/pod-product-compliance
Lightning Source LLC
Chambersburg PA
CBHW020230260626
47156CB00002B/622